Corkscrew

Corkscrew

A REID BENNETT MYSTERY

Ted Wood

CHARLES
SCRIBNER'S
SONS

NEW YORK

Charles Scribner's Sons
Macmillan Publishing Company
866 Third Avenue, New York, NY 10022
Collier Macmillan Canada, Inc.

This is a work of fiction. Names, characters, places, and incidents either are the product of the author's imagination or are used fictitiously. Any resemblance to actual events or persons, living or dead, is entirely coincidental.

Library of Congress Cataloging-in-Publication Data

Wood, Ted.
  Corkscrew: A Reid Bennett mystery.

  I. Title.
PR9199.3.W57C6   1987   813'.54   87-13036
ISBN 0-684-18853-8

10 9 8 7 6 5 4 3 2 1

Printed in the United States of America

To my daughter Anne,
who trained Sam

Corkscrew

ONE

♦

There were more than a dozen motorcycles in front of the motel. Most of them were parked diagonally in a row, like military machines lined up for inspection. The remaining four were still in motion, circling and crossing chaotically, making the whole area as frightening as the touchdown point of a cyclone. The riders were shouting and whooping and laughing, standard motorcycle-gang uglies, all of them, in leather jackets and chains. One even had a polished Wehrmacht helmet. In the middle of the lot an injured dog was squirming. Jack Wales, the motel owner, was crouching over it, glancing around fearfully at the bikers.

I stopped the police car and hissed at Sam, my German shepherd, to stay where he was. He's trained enough that he could have fought any one of the riders and won, but if all four of them tried to run him down, he wouldn't stand a chance.

I left the car window open so he would be only two seconds from me if I needed help, and got out. Wales looked up at me. "Look what these bastards've done, Chief. He's dying."

The guy in the German helmet swung his bike around and gunned it between us, nearly hitting Jack. He was roaring with laughter.

I asked Wales, "You see who hit him?"

1

"No," he said miserably. "I was inside and they all pulled in to the coffee shop." He jumped with alarm as the four riders re-formed and zoomed by again, trying to make us run. They weren't scared. They had fourteen men against the whole Murphy's Harbour Police Department, me.

I crouched by the dog. He rolled his eyes up to me and whimpered. "I think his back's broken, Jack. He's finished," I said. One of the bikers came close enough to reach out and almost tip my hat off. I ignored him. "Is he your dog?"

"No, he's a stray," Wales said. "He comes around to get fed. I don't think anybody owns him. He'll just die in pain unless—" He stopped and looked at me. There were tears in his eyes.

The bikers had reached the end of the lot again and were lining up to come back. I pulled my .38 and cocked it. The bikers saw me and diverged, all going separate ways now, wondering what was next. I patted the dog's muzzle and put the gun about six inches from the killing spot in the center of the skull, just behind the eyes. "Good-bye, old son," I said, and pulled the trigger.

I stood up now, looking around at the bikers. They had surrounded me, back about thirty yards, quartering me so I couldn't cover them all. Then the one with the German helmet gave a roar and came straight at me.

I've seen guys like that before. I'd canceled out his fun with the dog. Now he was going to play with me instead, making me jump out of his way, run if possible. But I knew if it started they would all do it and I could never get free of them. Even if I got back in the car they would zoom around me like mosquitoes. They would own me and my whole little town. My only comeback would be legal action, summonsing them for dangerous driving. They thought.

I let him accelerate for a half second, locking eyes with him until I could see he meant to run right over me if I didn't move. Then I raised the Colt and put a bullet through his front tire.

The tire turned into a streamer, flapping black and flat for a moment until the wheel jammed. His bike jinked sideways, tossing him over the handlebars to land on his back in front of me. His helmet had come off, and his long hair spread out over the dirt. I moved ahead and stepped on the hair, close enough to his scalp that he couldn't even bring his hands back to hurt my leg. Any movement would have torn his hair out.

"Hold it right there," I told him. Then I took out my pouch of six spare shells, broke the gun and tipped out the spent cartridges, keeping my thumb over the good ones, and pushed two replacements into the chamber. I didn't intend to do any more firing. Legally I had already overstepped the guidelines laid down for use of the gun. It's supposed to be used in defense of your life. He hadn't meant to kill me, just break me up a little.

Behind me the door of the motel coffee shop burst open, and the rest of them tumbled out, all shouting and swearing, heading for their bikes. All but one, who walked up to me.

"You're Reid Bennett," he said. I glanced up, pushing the gun back into the holster but not fastening the flap. The guy on the ground suddenly got his breath back in a great howling whoop.

"Yes," I said, and smiled at him as if he were a tourist asking directions. He was the standard biker, five nine at most, but meaty, squarely built from his barrel chest down to the beer belly that strained at the wide belt he was wearing. He was about thirty, I judged, dark haired and carrying a full set of whiskers that were turning gray on him. He was wearing a leather jacket with the sleeves torn off over a T-shirt and had crude jailhouse tattoos up both arms.

"I heard about you," he said, and grinned, showing a space where two front teeth had been in his good old days.

I said nothing. Behind him the other bikers had all started their machines and were moving out to circle us. He lifted one hand, and they all stopped, as disciplined as a bunch of marines responding to a drill instructor. "Yeah," he said, and showed me his gap again. "You worked in T'rannah one time, right?" I said nothing, glancing down at the guy on the deck. He was trying to pull his hair free from under my boot. I prodded him with my other toe. He looked at the leader, then relaxed again, trying to make it look like his own preference.

"Yeah," the leader said again. "You was the cop who killed two Black Diamond Riders one time. No gun, nothin', just your hands."

I still said nothing. Behind me Jack Wales swallowed nervously. He was afraid. He knew my record; the whole town did. He was wondering if it made me a marked man, if he was in danger now for having called me. He could be. I wasn't sure yet.

The leader laughed. He turned around, and I caught sight of the back of his jacket. His insignia said Devil's Brigade, done in brass studs. Natty. "Hey," he called, then made a cutting motion with one hand, and all the noise died as the whole pack of them cut their motors. He looked back at me and smirked, like an uncle who's just done a clever card trick. I waited, and he spoke up in a growl that sounded like too many cigarettes or a lot of practice. "This cop's a brother," he said. "He done them two Diamonds in T'rannah that time."

I stood still, looking at him and waiting. That Toronto incident had cost me my marriage and my job as a Metro Toronto detective. I'd lost the first and quit the second when the media branded me a murderer. Now it looked as if it might be paying a bonus. The biker stuck out his hand. "They call me Russ."

I didn't hesitate. Bikers and police are oil and water, but I'm alone in Murphy's Harbour. If I stoked up a feud, they could tear down half the town before I could call in reinforcements from the Ontario Provincial Police. So far the honors were even. One dog down, one biker humiliated. I shook his hand. It was softer than I had expected. Maybe he wore gloves while he was running over dogs.

"Hi," I said. I didn't want friendship, just respect.

He didn't try to crush my hand, and none of his guys started their bikes or moved any closer. He just smiled at me, showing that ugly gap. "Now we're even," he said calmly. "If you hadn't greased them other guys, we'd take you apart, gun or no gun. Unnerstan'?"

I didn't nod or make any acknowledgment. Like stags in rutting season, we were establishing turf here. Maybe he had me figured for a mad dog, a guy who would have put bullets into six of his riders before they killed me. Or maybe he was genuinely glad I'd killed two of his rivals. I just stood my ground, like Gromyko at an arms conference.

He pointed to the man on the deck. "He can come with us. We'll send a wheel back for the bike."

"Okay," I said, and we let go of one another's hands, our eyes still locked. I took a step back, away from the biker's hair. He swore and sat up, rolling on one elbow and reaching for his helmet. Russ was cool, I thought. It must have looked to his crowd as if I were backing down. Cheap at the price.

He walked away, and one of the other riders started his bike and came over to pick up the Goering look-alike. He got on the pillion and spat, missing me. Then they all started their bikes and waited while Russ started his, a big Yamaha with upswept handlebars, and led them out of the parking lot and north onto the highway.

Jack Wales came out from behind me, as if I were a tree he'd been sheltering under. "Christ, Chief, they're evil."

I nodded. "That's the first time I've come across that crowd," I told him, "but bikers are all bad news." I didn't bother spelling it out for him, but motorcycle

5

gangs are the biggest menace in the whole spectrum of organized crime. They run all the amphetamines and most of the cocaine in Canada. They also control the pornography business and most of the illegal guns. And they live by and for terror. If I was lucky, this would be my last look at this bunch. They would take their problems farther up the road, somewhere that had more policemen to deal with them.

"Come on, let's move this chopper out of the way." Wales helped me push the bike up on the patch of thin grass at the north end of the lot. Then I picked up the dead dog and carried it over to the garbage dumpster that stood beside the first motel unit. Wales held up his hand. "Hold on, Chief. I'll get a garbage bag."

He came back with the bag, slipped it over the dog and knotted it, then dropped it into the dumpster and we walked back to the coffee shop. Wales looked around at the litter of cups and spilled coffee the bikers had left as they ran out.

"Pigs," he said passionately. He reached under the counter and came out with a bottle of the Jamaica rum that's bottled by the Liquor Control Board, no-name rum, solid booze value. "I need a snort," he said. I could see his hands were trembling. "How about you, Chief?"

"I'll pass, thanks, Jack. Can I use your phone?"

Without speaking, he reached under the counter and brought out his telephone. I picked it up and dialed the Ontario Provincial Police. They answered, first ring, and I reported the name of the group and the way they were headed. "They're coming back later to pick up an abandoned machine. At the Muskellunge Motel," I added. "It's the division point between my turf and yours. Could you have a car drop by from time to time until it's gone?"

OPP told me they would. I thanked them and hung up. "Phone me if they show again," I told Jack. I didn't want to see them again any more than he did, but my oath of office tells me to protect the Queen's Peace. I thought she would approve of my coming back. Wales nodded and tried to say something but gave up and buried his nose in his rum. I left him and went out to the car. It was hot, early August. Sam wouldn't appreciate being kept in the car.

I got in and headed south on the highway to the turnoff that leads to Murphy's Harbour, my own personal bailiwick. This time of year it was packed with cottagers, soft pink people from Toronto or the States, anxiously turning red, then brown as they swam, fished for our big pike and pickerel, and tried to forget there were such things as offices to go back to in two weeks' time. I'd grown to like the place in the two years I'd been there.

Then the radio buzzed. It's the police-station telephone, coupled to the radio when I'm in the car. There was an anxious mother on the line. Her thirteen-year-old boy was missing. She gave me directions to the place she was staying, and I headed down there. I wasn't alarmed. Kids on vacation go missing a lot, usually playing somewhere that their parents haven't thought of looking. I get two or three a day at peak season. Only one of them had ever drowned. It didn't seem like anything to get excited about.

TWO

The missing kid's father was a belligerent semidrunk, a college professor, he told me unnecessarily, adding, "in film," at one of the middlebrow campuses in Toronto. I guessed he was insecure about something, because he gave me all this before he allowed his wife to go into detail about the missing boy. I decided I didn't like him. He was running to fat, although he would probably have considered himself sturdy or something equally flattering, and had rimless glasses and a mouth that turned down at the corners as if there were a bad smell around. Apart from stale gin on his breath I couldn't detect anything.

"When did you last seen Kennie, and what makes you think he's not just gone for a walk?" I asked. He just snorted. It's the obvious questions that infuriate people; they think policemen are psychic.

"Around ten. He said he'd be back by lunchtime. He doesn't usually say something to us and then not do it," the mother told me. She looked younger than her husband, fitter and more sensible. She was wearing a bikini under a Beethoven T-shirt.

"Where was he going?"

The father jumped on that one, both feet. "If we knew that, for Christ's sweet sake, we'd be looking there instead of asking you," he said. He took a big slug out of his glass. It was clear, with the faint bluish tint of gin and tonic.

"You're saying you don't know where he was headed?"

The wife said, "No, Officer. Usually if he's going anywhere, he tells me. That's why I called you. I mean, he's such a dependable boy." With Sam and me standing there, she was beginning to feel foolish, I guess, as if she'd gone to the dentist and then found that her tooth had stopped aching.

"Could he be visiting a friend? I'm not trying to downplay the concern you're feeling, but four hours isn't very long for a teenager to be away on his own."

"We're telling you it's not normal. All right?" The father barked. "If we thought it was normal, we wouldn't have called you." He set his drink down, making a slow, purposeful motion of it—some scene he must have remembered from his film course, proving how sensible he was, how sober.

"Tell me what he was wearing, what he looks like, and I'll start looking," I said.

It took them five minutes to remember that he had been wearing a white "Camp Sunrise" T-shirt, blue jeans, and running shoes, and to find a photograph. He was an ordinary sandy-haired kid, around five feet, ninety pounds, and he would be carrying his camera.

"A Nikon," his father said smugly.

"Is he a keen photographer?" I started, but he cut me off.

"What would you think? I told you, he's carrying a Nikon. You've heard of Nikon, have you?" The father sneered, and his wife made a shushing sound and frowned at him.

"Ken, really," she muttered.

I turned to her. "Does he go off on photography expeditions a lot, Mrs. Spenser? And if so, does he have a favorite subject, boats, flowers, what?"

"Anything at all," she said, rushing to head off her

husband before he could say something else snotty. "He's really quite talented."

That was my last chance of detective work shot to hell. I now had to search the whole photogenic world for him. "Okay, then. I suggest the pair of you split up and go opposite ways down the road behind the cottage, calling out for him. Meantime, I'll check places where kids gather around town. If you find him, don't forget to give me a call. If I find him or don't hear from you in a couple of hours, I'll come back and check with you."

The father finished his drink and stood up. "Great," he said. "We call for help, and he tells us to do it ourselves. Just great."

I didn't bother arguing with him. Drunks are part of the job. These days you can't get a conviction even if they're reeling around the center of town. You just send them home to sober up. But any policeman knows it's a waste of time arguing with them. I got back in the cruiser and drove down the narrow road behind all the cottages, keeping an eye out for his son. As I drove, I called the OPP and gave them the report. The kid was probably still in my bailiwick, but it's policy to alert them. If he'd gotten tired of his family, he could be out on the highway hitching a ride someplace. The guy at the dispatcher's desk took the call without comment. Missing boys generally come home when they're hungry.

He wasn't on the road or at the lock, where a crowd of youngsters usually hang around, golden little teenyboppers with cans of pop and squeals of laughter and gruff, shy boys trying out their newly breaking voices. They were doing all the standard thirteen-year-old things, shoving one another, giggling and joking. It restored your faith in kids. I lingered a minute or two, talking to the lockkeeper. He's an older man, a World War II veteran with one leg gone who used to be the mister at the police station until he stepped on the wrong side of the law. I couldn't talk him out of the mess he was in, so he was put on probation and lost his job. I managed to get the township to give him this one. It keeps him busy all summer and supplements his pension. I guess he's grateful for it, but he's always a bit shamefaced around me.

"Okay, I'll watch for him," he promised, then reached down to pat Sam, who still remembers him from the old days.

"Thanks, Murph. I'll take a run through town, check around. Call if you see him." I nodded and hissed at Sam, who sprang to my heel and followed me back to the car. I let him in, and he sat tall on the passenger side, looking out of the window as I drove off, over the narrow bridge and into the center of Murphy's Harbour. You have to brake fairly smartly or you could drive right through it. There's a marina and the Lakeside Tavern on one side, a small string of stores on the other.

There were more kids here, older this time, one of them even with a car. They were sipping Cokes that were probably laced, or at least flavored with rum from the mickey I'd seen the oldest one buy that morning when I checked the liquor store. They were listening to rock music and trying out the tentative mating patterns they'd progressed to after a few summers of squealing and shoving down by the locks. The town is small enough that I knew most of them by sight.

None of them had seen the missing boy. The boys were elaborately casual about telling me, showing how grown-up they were, but the girls, as usual, were more sensible. They studied the photograph and promised to watch for him. One of them was the daughter of Nick Vanderheyden, the man who runs the Lakeside Tavern. He'd been there since spring, after the previous owner had been murdered and the place was bought by another man with a string of hotels and taverns.

She was fifteen, and I figured she had a kind of crush on me. If she was waiting table in the Tavern when I dropped by, she always shuffled positions so that she

11

served me. And I got my meal faster than anybody else in the place, even the big spenders from the cruisers tied up outside. She's young enough that her comments usually choke themselves on giggles, but she's a nice kid, dark haired and pretty in an intense way. She'll be a looker when she grows up.

"That's the Spenser boy," she told me, and giggled. "He's always around here. He usually tries to take my picture." She blushed at the thought and amended it. "Our picture, any girl's picture."

That was interesting, and I followed it. "Is he a pint-sized ladies' man, Beckie, would you say?"

That convulsed her, and her friends. I waited until the laughter had petered out. "He thinks he is," she said. "He always acts, oh, you know, King Cool."

"Has he made friends with anybody, boys or girls, that you've noticed?"

She looked at me, shading her eyes with one hand. "Not really. Oh, he tries an' that, tags along, but generally one of the guys tells him to get lost and he goes away."

"Thanks. If he shows up, call me, please, would you, and tell him his folks are worried about him."

"Sure will." She beamed. I left, listening to the chorus of laughter behind me. Maybe her crush wasn't as secret as she thought. I checked the restaurant. He wasn't there, either, hadn't been in, Lee Chong said. That left the grocery and the bait store. I struck oil in the grocery.

"Yeah, he was in here around noon, bought some film," Dorothy told me. "I know for sure it was him. He's been in three times this week for film. Lord knows what he's takin' pictures of; he's only a kid." She threw her hands up. "Four fifty plus tax an' he doesn't turn a hair. His old man has to be loaded."

"He says the kid's a camera buff," I told her. "He's carrying about five hundred bucks' worth of camera round his neck. Did you talk with him?"

She frowned. Some vacationer was behind me, carrying a case of pop and a bag of ice cubes, as tense as a combat medic waiting to dress somebody's wound. I figured he had an emergency situation back in the cottage with his lady. I beamed and nodded at him to let him know this was official and waited while Dorothy scratched her rusty-looking head of gray hair.

"No, I didn't. But now you say it, Carl Simmonds was in—you know, the photographer." I nodded, and she went on, more thoughtfully. "Yeah, he made some comment about the camera the kid had on. Him and the kid went out together."

"Thanks." I smiled at her. "I'll talk to Carl."

She turned away to ring up the refreshments for the other guy. "Yeah, good idea," she said matter-of-factly. "Makes a lot of sense."

The tourist was anxious to show what a good citizen he was, how he didn't mind delaying his tryst while the law sought the truth. "Why's that, then?" he asked brightly.

Dorothy, who is a generously built farm-wife type, gestured casually with one hand. "Oh, you know," she said disarmingly. "What with Carl bein' queer an' all."

I didn't wait to see the guy do his double take. I've known Carl for a couple of years now. He's gay, but I've never heard of his doing anything about it in town. He's a nice guy, kind of lonely, like a spinster aunt. But if he was the last one to see the missing boy, it was worth a call. Maybe he and the kid were talking photography.

Carl's place is small, a winterized cottage, really. He keeps the front neat, a couple of flower beds and well-trimmed grass behind a picket fence. His Toyota was in the driveway, so I parked behind it and walked up to the front door with Sam at my heel. Carl must have seen us coming. He was at the door before me. "Hi, Reid," he said. "Got time for a cold one?"

"Yeah, please, Carl." He waved me in, and I sat down in one of the cane chairs he'd installed since a militant feminist group had smashed his place up one busy night last winter. Sam flopped down beside the chair, and we waited. Carl came back quickly with a couple of light beers and a glass for me, which I waved away. "By the throat's fine; save washing up."

He gave me the beer and sat down. He had an empty glass on the coffee table in front of him and a pile of wedding shots he'd taken. "I'm trying to find one where the best man's squint doesn't show," he said. "I hate to confront people with their faults."

I sipped my beer a moment, then told him, "The Spenser boy is missing. Have you seen him at all?"

He looked up, holding a photograph in each hand. Suddenly serious. "Missing?"

"Yes. His folks are worried. He's been away since ten or so. He's usually home for meals, like most kids."

He set his pictures on the table and looked at me anxiously. "And you think I had something to do with the fact that he's missing?"

"No." I shook my head. "Of course not. But you were the last person to see him that I've traced so far. I wondered if you got any idea where he was going."

"He didn't say. I assumed he was going home." Carl crossed his knees, then uncrossed them again and stood up. He was tense, but he didn't seem guilty of anything. There's a difference. "He said he was interested in shooting some boats. He'd seen some shots in a book. It's hard to say, but I feel he's got a good eye for composition. He mentioned trying to get the curve of the bow into it." Carl's voice ran away on him, going nervously higher until he stopped and cleared his throat. "He could be anywhere is what I'm saying."

I nodded and sipped again. "Was he here, in this house?"

He flushed and bit his lip, then spoke in a rush. "You don't think I'm interested in children, do you?"

14

I shook my head. "No, I'd be asking anyone the same question if they were the last person to see him. Was he here?"

"Yes." He nodded and blushed, then sat down angrily. "Dammit. Why would I feel embarrassed about that? Yes, he was here. I showed him my darkroom equipment. We chatted for half an hour. He had a Coke and left. That was all there was to it."

In the moment before I could answer him, he rushed on. "I would have done the same for any enthusiast regardless of how old they were or what sex."

"Look, I don't suspect you of anything, Carl. I'm just trying to track the kid's movements. I'd ask anybody the same questions."

He held up one hand apologetically. "I should know better. I'm sorry, Chief," he said formally. "But we have some very square people in town, and they get strange ideas about anybody who's gay."

"They're mostly kind," I said. "Murphy's Harbour isn't a really redneck town."

He picked up his glass, then set it down and looked at me levelly. "I've always kept my private life away from town," he said. "I have friends who wonder why I live here, away from the action. They wonder why I don't have them up here to visit. I just don't. This is my home. When I'm home, I'm just another guy, the one who isn't interested in peering down the waitress's front at the Tavern."

I put the beer bottle down. "I know. Don't get upset; I'm just following procedure. I'll finish my beer and go look around some more. I only have one more question for you. Did you see which way he went when he left here?"

"No. I started processing a roll of film, and in the middle of it he said he should be going and let himself out. I was in the darkroom a couple of minutes more, and when I came out, I looked up and down the street, but there was no sign of him."

15

"Them's the breaks," I said. I swallowed the last of my beer. "Thanks for the drink. I'll go earn my pittance."

He followed me to the door, looking anxious but not speaking. I waved to him and got into the car, with Sam beside me. He didn't wave back, just stood there, looking worried. It seemed like overreaction, and I put it into my memory and wondered what past experience this was bringing back to him.

The radio in the car called me, and I picked up the receiver. It was Wales at the motel. "Been trying to reach you, Chief," he said. "No need to come back up. Two o' the bikers came back with a spare wheel. They changed it and left, no problems; never even came in here."

"Fine, that's one worry over," I told him. "Don't lose any sleep about them. I think they were just moving through."

I hung up the receiver and drove to the marina. Walter Puckrin was working at the engine of a big inboard. He stopped when I got there and swore at Chrysler for a while, then offered me a beer, which I turned down, and told me he hadn't noticed the kid around.

"Maybe he went down the dock in front of the Tavern—there's boats there if he wanted pictures—maybe to the lock, maybe anywhere. Not here, though," he said.

"Fine, Walt, keep on cussing. I'll look around." I still wasn't worried too badly. The boy could be anywhere. It was coincidence that Carl had seen him last, nothing more. Right now he was out somewhere around boats, taking pictures.

I walked over to the Lakeside Tavern and strolled out onto the docks behind it. The usual crowd of pleasure boaters was standing around, comparing routes up and down the waterway and trying not to be too obvious about ogling one another's girl friends. None of them had seen the kid.

Nobody had at the north lock, either, so I crossed the bridge there and drove back down the other side of the

16

lake, the side his cottage lay on. I met his mother, about two miles up from their cottage, still calling. For the exercise more than anything, I walked back with her as far as the lock. It was only about a quarter of a mile. Sam needed the airing, and she was getting anxious, more because of what her husband would say, I thought, than for her son.

"He's Ken's stepson," she explained nervously. "It's just a coincidence that they're both named the same. My first husband's name is Harry."

"Does your son get on well with his stepfather?" I asked her, and she shot a glance at me.

"What makes you ask?" Her mouth was a straight line. I could read the tension in her face.

"A standard question. If they don't get on, Kennie might be tempted to stay away longer for fear of a licking when he goes home, that's all."

"That won't happen," she said firmly. She glared like a lioness protecting her cub. "I won't let him beat Kennie."

"Has he tried it before?"

"He did once, when we were just married. Kennie threw a tantrum at dinner, and the next thing, Ken pulled him away from the table and whacked him, hard, before I could stop him."

"Then you stepped in?"

"Yes," she said, and then suddenly closed her mouth on her next word and shook her head, angry at herself.

"And did your husband stop right away?" I let the question dangle a moment before adding the one I really wanted answered. "Or did he take a swing at you."

She gasped. "I've never told a soul," she said. "I told my friends I'd walked into a door."

We came around the last bend in the road that led to the lock, and I stopped. "It's a story I've heard a lot of times, Mrs. Spenser," I said. "It won't go any further. I just needed to know so I can be around when your son turns up. It won't happen again then."

She looked up at me and smiled, a nervous little twitch at the corners of her mouth. It lit up her whole appearance. "Thank you," she said. "But I'll be fine. Just find Kennie."

We walked down to the lock together. There were a couple of fishermen there with an illegal case of beer open beside them. They put a coat over it as we came up, and I ignored it. Beer and fishing go together, and these were steady-looking guys, not drunks. I asked them if they'd seen the boy, and they hadn't. Neither had the lockkeeper, so we walked back to the car, and I drove her to the house.

Her husband was already there, with a fresh drink. This time he made an effort to be pleasant. "I've walked all the way down to the lock," he told us. "Called and called, nothing."

I had Sam in the backseat of the car, and I let him out. "How about giving me something Kennie's worn—a dirty shirt would be fine—and I'll turn the dog loose to look for him."

The husband shook his head. He didn't look worried at all. "It won't help. He's been missing since I dropped him off in town, the other side of the lake. He could be anywhere." He didn't look at me, just lifted his gin and sipped, slowly, shutting me out.

"I understood he'd left from here," I said. He was beginning to be a pain.

"Yeah, well, I thought about it. Carol was off painting, and it got too quiet for me and Kennie, so we took a ride around to the town." To the liquor store, I thought, but didn't speak. He waved one hand casually. "The facts are still the same. He's always home by lunchtime, and today he isn't."

"Where did you see him last?" I cracked the question at him, trying to shatter the glassy haze he had set up between us. He looked up in surprise. I guess film students don't talk that way.

"Like I said, in town." He spread his hands apologetically. "I'm sorry if I've wasted any of your valuable time. I'm sure you've got better things to do."

I turned to his wife. "Do you have that shirt, Mrs. Spenser? I'll head over to the liquor store and turn my dog loose there."

Her husband sat up, sloshing some of his gin overboard. "Now just a goddamn minute," he started, but she cut him off.

"That's where you went, isn't it?" she said quietly.

"I don't like this cop's attitude," he said, and stood up to face me.

"And I don't like yours," I told him. "So sit and drink your gin and try to remember where you saw your stepson last."

He whirled at the woman. "So you've been whiling away the afternoon giving this guy your pedigree, have you?" He thumbed at me over his shoulder. "Your type, is he, tall, dark, rough trade. You'd like that, wouldn't you?"

She stepped past him, not looking at either of us, and went into the cottage. I stood there and he turned back, but not to face me. Instead, he finished his drink in three quick gulps and reached in his pocket for car keys. "Nothing to it but do the goddamn job myself," he said, and headed for the car.

"Forget it," I told him, and he paused for a moment, then turned back and stood with both hands on his hips like a little girl, facing me down.

"Are you telling me not to drive my car?" he bellowed.

"Yeah." I walked over to him and spoke softly so that he had to pay attention to hear me. "And I'm also telling you to keep your voice down and stop acting like a common drunk or I'll take action. Understand?"

He looked at me for a moment, debating whether to go the distance and take a swing. I guess he thought better of it. He dropped his eyes and threw his keys on the ground. "You go to hell," he said. "I'm damned if I'll

19

help you anymore." Then he turned and walked away into the cottage, letting the door bang.

He couldn't have helped me much less, but I was glad he'd quit. I picked up the keys and stood tossing them in my hand until his wife came back with a sweatshirt. "Kennie wore this last night when it got dark," she said. "Everything else is clean."

"That's fine. Thank you." I took the shirt and handed her the keys. "Your husband dropped these. Maybe you should keep them for a while."

She looked at me and gave her fleeting little smile again. "Thank you. I'm glad you were here." She stood for a moment, then said, "I think I should stay with him. He gets kind of jealous sometimes, for no reason."

"Good idea." I hissed at Sam, and he came to heel. "Now don't worry. I'm sure Kennie's gone for a walk with some other kids. This isn't any kind of big deal, tracking him. It just gives me a chance to give my dog some exercise."

She nodded without speaking and went back to the house. I could hear him shouting at her as soon as she went through the door. Who says it's only the working man who gives his wife a hard time?

I drove back to the town lock and dropped in on Murphy. He still hadn't seen the boy, but I could tell he had some news for me. It came out after he'd rolled one of his homemades and lit up. "We've got a pair of bikers in town," he said. "They went over the bridge and then north without stopping. Two of them."

He took his cigarette out of his mouth and examined the tip. "I hope they're not scouting the place for one o' their shivarees."

THREE

♦

Murphy gave me the description. He was with the police office long enough that he's a solid eyewitness. Both thirtyish, grubby, leather jackets, one with no sleeves over a bare chest, the other long sleeves over a T-shirt, the first with a black helmet, the second wearing a Wehrmacht steel pot. "I've put bullets through a couple of hats like that," Murphy said grimly. "I wouldn't mind with this bastard, either."

"Don't take it personally. This guy hates everybody, not just veterans," I said. "Thanks for the information. I'll check the Tavern and the beer parlor, see they're not up to any tricks."

There were no bikes outside either place, so I didn't bother going in. Instead, I went back to the liquor store and parked. The usual string of sunburned visitors were threading in and out, and they all nodded or acknowledged me as I called Sam out of the car and let him sniff Kennie Spenser's sweatshirt. Then I told him, "Seek." He ran in quick circles, then scratched at the door of the store. I let him in, nodding to the help and the customers, and watched as he followed the trail and went to the other door. Outside he circled some more, then ran a little way to a spot on the parking lot. There was no knowing whether the kid had started or ended his visit there, getting in and out of the family car, or maybe both, so I walked Sam around the whole area. No matter where he picked up the track, he went to the same place. Kennie had both started and finished his visit in the same car, which meant that his stepfather had taken him on somewhere else. I wondered if that other place was close enough that the guy hadn't remembered clearly or if I was going to have to talk to him again. The guy might have been boiled enough that he had trouble remembering all the details. So I walked Sam down to the store, and he picked up the track again just outside. I didn't go into the store with him but coaxed him on, from the doorway off to the side of the road. This time he followed for about a hundred yards, around the first corner to the street of inexpensive insul-brick-covered houses with their "Rooms for Rent" signs in the windows. But again Sam ran into a dead end, about six feet from the curb. And this time I was certain: the boy had gotten into a car. But there was no knowing whether it was the same one or somebody else's.

I heard the crackle of my car radio and went back to get the message. I connected, and a girl's voice said, "Are you in private, or am I coming over the airwaves?" The voice made me grin. It was Fred, an actress I got involved with after a hassle the previous winter. Fred, for Freda, thirty-two with Rita Hayworth hair, the color of a pint of English beer. I hadn't seen her for six months, but she phoned me often. I liked her a lot, but she had her life, and it didn't center on a place as small as this.

"You're on the air, kid. You want to try one of your radio parts for me."

She laughed, brightly enough that a visitor to the liquor store heard and whirled to see where the pretty girl must be. I turned the volume down on the radio, and she went on. "Then I'll keep it wholesome. Remember that key you gave me? I just used it. I'm here for the weekend, looking for some sun and games."

"There's some stuff in the fridge. Pretend you're doing

that Mexican-food commercial and put some tortillas together. I'll be there in five minutes."

"Chauvinist," she said, and hung up.

I put Sam in the car and got in, grinning. She was too good an actress to be happy for long playing house in Murphy's Harbour, but we had made a real twosome for the month she'd been with me. And now she was back. Good news.

I checked my watch. It was four-thirty, eight hours since I'd last eaten. I'd take a half-hour lunch break before getting back to work, although I didn't know what I was going to do about tracing the boy. Perhaps I should go back to the house and see if his stepfather had sobered up enough to remember anything else. Otherwise, there wasn't a lot more I could do besides walking around looking for him, like any other citizen.

The radio called again as I was putting the car in gear. I picked up the receiver. "Police chief."

"Chief, can you come up here right away?" There was panic in the voice, but I recognized it. Joe Davies, who ran the township's only campground and trailer park, up north of the far lock. I wondered what was making him tense.

"Can do, Joe. What's the problem?"

He spluttered a little, nervous and half embarrassed. "I've, er, got a couple of gennlemen here who wanna stay an' I've told 'em no but they won't leave."

My bikers had landed by the sound of it. "Be there in five," I said.

Davies was waiting for me at the gate, a big archway built of cedar logs that he'd cut when he cleared the site. Beyond him I could see the neat rows of trailers on their hard standings, plus some tents. A bunch of little kids were playing with a Frisbee, and there in the daisy chain were the two bikers, like a couple of ugly bears at a picnic. Except for the anxious faces on the parents in the background, nothing could have been cooler.

23

"It's them bikers," Davies told me. He was sunburned and lean from all the outdoor work but nervous as a bank teller during a holdup.

"What do they want? Just to stay?"

He nodded. "Yeah, they say there's fourteen o' them. But shit, they'll scare off all my regulars. This is a family place."

"They look harmless enough right now."

"Now's now," Davies said quickly. "But three o'clock in the morning, when they're all drunk an' tearin' the place up, they won't be harmless."

"Do you have any rules for this place, something we can hold them up by?" Civil liberties are a pain sometimes; laws are made for oddballs like these. Their freedoms are worth more to the lawmakers than the peace of mind of a hundred ordinary people.

"No booze," he said. "No booze at all."

"Then why's that citizen holding a beer?" I pointed to one of the dads in the background who was sucking on a Labatt Blue, getting his guts together for a fight if the bikers turned nasty.

"Oh, shit. I'll throw him out if I hafta. He shouldn't be drinkin'." Davies was trembling with anxiety.

"Won't stand up. But I'll have a word with them." Again I left Sam in the car, his head sticking out of the open window so he could be with me in a second if I whistled. I walked into the ring, caught the Frisbee, and tossed it to the nearest biker, the guy I'd flattened. "Hi. Got your tire fixed okay?" I asked.

"Yeah," he said, and whipped the Frisbee on, then stepped out of the circle to come over to me. On his feet he was less of a menace, about five six and dirty, but I could always get a tetanus shot if I had to bust my hand on him. "Yeah," he said again, growling at me in that same cultivated tone his boss had used. "We're lookin' to make a reservation, but the little guy says no." He paused and grinned, showing a complete set of brown

24

teeth. "I guess he ain't heard of our civil rights."

Out of the corner of my eye I saw Davies talking to the beer drinker, who immediately hid the bottle and turned away. "Yeah, well he's got this rule here, no drinking. And you guys aren't exactly charter members of the Temperance Union."

He accommodated me with a laugh, from the mouth only, his eyes drilling into me like the knife he would have preferred to use. "Seems like there's a lot of it goin' around," he said. He hooked his thumb back over his shoulder. "That fellah in the blue T-shirt is boozing right out here in front of these poor little suggestible kiddiewinkies."

I nodded. "Agreed, and the same camper is right now being kicked out. But that's not the problem. The thing is, where are you guys going to camp?"

The other one had joined him, not threatening me, standing alongside him, almost shoulder to shoulder, friends with a common problem. This one's eyes were calmer. It wasn't his tire I had shot away. "Yeah," he said easily. "Now you got it."

"Well, that's not hard to solve. There's a patch of township land, close to the water, flat, no trees, just what you want. Hell, we had a bunch of Boy Scouts there in June."

They looked at me in surprise. They hadn't expected civility. They were looking for a confrontation.

"Where?" the one in the German helmet wanted to know.

"Well, it's not a glamorous place, but it's quiet, and if you wanted to party, you wouldn't have the neighbors complaining."

The other one said, "Sounds good to me, Jas."

"Get on your bikes. I'll take you up there," I said. German helmet stood his ground. "Al said the campground," he growled. I could see he didn't want a campsite; he wanted my head on a charger.

25

"Naah, get a campsite was all he said." The other one wasn't as uptight as German helmet. He would have kicked me, happily, but it wasn't high on his agenda at that moment. "Let's go see," he said amiably. He tugged at Jas's arm, and after a second he broke off eye contact, and they walked away to their bikes, starting them up with a roar that sent the mothers scuttering like hens to round up their children.

I got back in the car and waited for them, then drove the half mile farther to the town dump site. It's not fancy—there are car bodies sticking out of the ground and piles of earth placed over each day's collection of garbage to discourage the bears that used to scavenge the place in the evenings—but next to it is a flat, gravelly meadow that runs down to the road that divides the place from the water's edge.

I saw the bikers exchange looks as I drove in through the gates and on to the meadow, where I cut the car motor and got out. They had stopped behind me, and Jas was looking at me through eyes as tight and angry as arrow slits in a castle wall.

"This is the goddamn dump."

"It's also the overflow campground. Like I said, we had three hundred Boy Scouts here last June. They didn't object."

"Yeah." The other one laughed. "Us an' Boy Scouts on the same field—ain' that a howl."

I waited, trying to look calm. I didn't want them near my turf at all, but this was a compromise that would offend the fewest people. It might even make them calm enough that they wouldn't bother hoorahing the town.

Jas cleared his throat and spat. Then he said, "Let's go see Al," and turned to rocket away, standing up on the back wheel with the torque of his acceleration. Impressive. The other one grinned at me and did the same, roaring down the road at speeds I should have summonsed them for if I hadn't been hoarding my tiny victory.

26

I didn't see them anymore on my ride back. My place is on the north end of town; they would have passed it before I got there. Freda's Honda was parked under the silver maple in the yard, so I honked and got out of the car. She came running out of the house, red hair flying. She was wearing a pale green shirt and stylish baggy white pants. Her smile was a yard wide.

"Hi, Reid." She threw her arms around me, and I swung her off her feet and kissed her. Then she wrestled free. "Come on in, let me feed you." She stooped and patted Sam and whisked ahead of me, up the steps to the front door.

I followed her in, liking the way she walked. She's on the tall side, around five eight, and she moves nicely. It was going to be good having her along, even just for the weekend.

I still hadn't spoken, but she didn't give me a chance. She took my cap off and sent it wheeling onto the couch. "Now, let's have the other half of that kiss," she said brightly, and that took us the rest of a minute.

"Welcome back," I said. "What's the occasion?"

"You can thank my rat-fink agent," she said. "I was accepted for *Prisoner of Second Avenue* in Calgary. I was going to be Edna. But he told me he'd got a TV part, bigger money, better exposure, so I let it go. Then I found he's screwing Aggie Cassidy. He sent her for the TV role, and I was out in the cold."

"Can you sue, change agents, what?"

"Monday," she said. "But in the meantime I wanted to get out of the city, out of context, and work out what comes next."

"This," I said, and kissed her again. Not everybody's kisses match, but ours do, and we lingered over it until I found myself needing her, immediately. She pulled away from me and laughed.

"You don't change," she said. "Before or after the tortillas?"

"I don't think it's romantic to make love on a full stomach," I told her, and she took my hand and led me upstairs.

We kissed again beside my sunken-centered double bed; then she stood back and shucked her shirt. She was wearing a creamy brassiere, almost transparent, and I could see her nipples engorged under the fabric. She unzipped the slacks and let them fall, then kicked them away like a lazy child. Her panties were the same fine fabric, and I stood looking at her like a farm boy at his first vaudeville show.

She flopped down on the bed, on one elbow. "You can look or you can play. It's up to you," she said, and I reached down to unbuckle my gun belt, holding my holster with one hand as I slipped the belt out through all the loops in my pants, then put belt and gun on the floor. She looked at me, her face tightening with need. "The rest has got to go," she said thickly. I unlaced my boots, then slipped quickly out of the shirt and pants. She lay back. "You big bastard," she said softly. "I've missed you in the damn city."

I finished undressing her, very slowly, and we made love, gently at first, building the anticipation almost to the point of pain. Then I rolled her flat and pulled her toward me. She groaned as we came together, and we were the happiest people in Murphy's Harbour.

Afterward we showered together, contented and slow, then I got dressed again and left her sketching in the little makeup she uses by day. Down in the kitchen Sam was lying on the cool old tile floor, and he looked up at me and wagged his tail. I patted him and turned the heat on under the mixture Fred had stuck in the frying pan.

Being a policeman is a condition, like having blue eyes or being afraid of heights. Where a civilian would have accepted Fred's return as plain good fortune, I couldn't help wondering what had happened to bring her back to me. The last time I had seen her, after she went back to Toronto in the late winter, she had been with a guy about my age, a creep, I thought, with a California tan that he wore like a suit of golden armor among all the pallid Toronto faces. She had called him "darling," but then, she was an actress. Everybody is darling to an actress. My guess was that he must have been her agent and wasn't darling anymore. Part of me wondered how much of a darling he had been.

She came downstairs a minute later, and I opened a bottle of Iniskillin rosé she had brought from Toronto and put in the freezer compartment of my rattly old refrigerator. I had just poured the wine when the phone rang. It was Murphy. "Bad news, Reid. They just found the kid."

Freda was holding up her glass in a toast, but she must have read my face, because she sat down, slowly lowering the glass as I looked at her, through her, and asked, "Where?"

"Just north of your place. Some pickerel fisherman snagged the poor little bastard in that weed bed south of Indian Island."

"Keep him there," I said. "I'll be right over."

FOUR

♦

By the time I got to the lock there were about a hundred people there. Everybody within running distance of the scene plus the occupants of all the cars that had crossed the bridge since the body was brought in. Most of them seemed to have cameras, and they were jostling one another for the chance to take long shots of the area above the lock. It's a one-lane bridge, and it was jammed with cars with their doors hanging open, but when I switched on the siren for a few seconds, the drivers ran back to move on and let me through.

I drove over and out onto the grass beside the lock-house. The siren hadn't affected the people here. They were clustering as close as they could to the edge, talking and pointing, one kid even laughing, proving to himself how cool he was.

I let Sam out of the car and told him, "Speak." He bounded forward on stiff legs, snarling and barking, and the crowd peeled open like an onion, layer on layer, until I could walk through and join Murphy and the two young men standing with him. I paused to tell the crowd, "You're not helping. Stand back, please." The people closest to me did back off a foot or two, but the pressure from the back of the crowd was building again, so I patted Sam and told him, "Keep." He paced around the area, snarling if anyone advanced, keeping the closest

30

people pushing back angrily against the pressure from behind.

Murphy pointed to one of the men, who was wearing a flowered shirt and pale blue slacks. "He found the boy."

I nodded and went out to the water's edge to look into the boat. The small body was laid out in the bottom of it, hands by its sides, as peaceful as if the boy were asleep. His hair was still damp, drying from dark brown back to gingerish in the sunlight, and his Camp Sunrise T-shirt and blue jeans were black with water. There was an injury on the left side of his head, about the height where he might have been hit by somebody taller than he was, somebody right-handed. There was no shoe or sock on the right foot. Possibly he had been trying to kick his shoes off so he could swim better, but then again, I doubted if he could have been conscious after a blow like the one he'd taken on the head. It looked far too severe to be an accidental bump.

I turned and asked the man, "Where did you find him?"

"South of that big bare rock, you know, up to the left of the channel, this side of the narrows." He had an intelligent face, pale under the ruddiness of his new tan.

"Was he floating?"

The other one answered, "No, Off'cer. He was down in the weeds. We were drifting for pickerel, and Fred's hook caught him."

He stopped, and the other one gulped and went on. "Yeah, in the pants, thank God. I don't know how I'd have felt if I'd snagged the poor little guy." He thought for a moment and went on. "I was hooked into the belt loop of his jeans. I thought it was a rock at first; then, when he came, it was kind of steady, almost easy, like when you've got a big pickerel on and he hasn't started fighting."

"What test line are you using?" I asked him. The strength of the line would give me an idea how great the strain had been.

31

"Thirty pounds," he said, then gave an apologetic half grin. "I know that's heavy, but I hooked a muskie last year and lost him. I didn't want that happening again."

"A good job you didn't lose this," I reassured him, "Now, how long ago did you find him?"

They looked at one another, and the first one said, "I didn't check the time, but it must have been about twenty minutes ago. We came right here. It was quicker. There were boats jammed up all around the marina or I'd have gone in there."

"You did right," I assured him. Then I took out my book. "Can I have your name and address and where you're staying up here?"

"Sure, Fred Dobos, one fifteen Davisville, Toronto." He gave me the apartment number, and I wrote it all down, then the lodge where he was staying in town. His friend's name was Jack Innes, also from Toronto, staying at the same place up here.

I shut the book and turned to Murphy. "Could you phone McKenney, please, Murph, and the doctor. Ask him to come to the funeral parlor as soon as he can."

"Sure thing." Murphy turned away, stumping through the crowd on his artificial leg, shoving angrily as people jostled him, scared of losing their places at the scene. Around me cameras were clicking, some of them even flashing, their lights pallid in the bright sun. I turned back to the two men.

"Which side of the island, do you remember?"

"Mid-channel side. Maybe thirty yards out."

I nodded. "And did you see any boats going up or down through the narrows before this happened?"

Dobos shook his head. "Sorry, Off'cer. We'd just got there. We went right up there from the marina."

"Well, did anything pass you, coming or going, as you went up the waterway?"

They looked at one another, trying to remember. Then Innes said, "Nothing much. There was a water-skier out, just this side of the island—three kids. The one who was skiing was good. He was going on one ski, you know, slalom. We were watching him. I didn't see anything else."

Murphy had returned, and before he could report, I asked him, "Any idea who three kids with water skis might be, Murph? Did they come through here?"

He shook his head. "Not today. Could be anybody."

"The one kid was a bit of a hotdog apparently, going slalom."

Now he nodded. "That could be young Cy Levine; he's pretty good." He turned to the two men. "What kind of boat was with him, a blue Fiberglas with a big Merc motor?"

"Yes." Innes was certain. "A blue boat, the same color as his swimsuit. Remember, Fred, I made some comment about him being color coordinated."

Dobos nodded. "I remember that, yeah."

"Good." I turned back to Murphy. "Can you get back on the phone to the Levine house, please, Murph. They've got a place on the east shore, up past the narrows. Ask them to get the boy to call me when he comes in."

"Okay," Murphy said. "And McKenney's on his way down; should be here in a few minutes."

"Thanks," I said, and turned to the two men again. "I've got some things to do right away. I'd be obliged if you could wait until I can take a proper statement."

They agreed, and I stepped into the boat and took a close look at the boy's face. There was the ugly break of the wound, and the rest of his face was dull reddish and puffy. The eyes were half open, and the jaw had dropped. He looked as if he might have drowned, but I would have to wait for Dr. McQuaig to tell me for sure. In the meantime, I was juggling the obvious first questions. Had these two men killed him? They seemed innocent, but it's an axiom of homicide investigations that the body is often "discovered" by the perpetrator. Many of

33

them can't stand the tension of waiting for somebody else to find it.

I was also thinking about the geography they'd given me. To land up south of Indian Island the boy must have gone in at the west side of the narrows or from a boat. I dismissed the idea of his falling in at the narrows. He must have gone off a boat to have drifted as far as he had in four hours. And that meant that somebody else knew something about him, either his killer or the person whose boat he had fallen out of. Of course, he might have been out alone and fallen, banging his head on the way, but the wound looked more serious than something he could have done casually like that. And besides, the men who found him would probably have seen an empty boat.

I stepped back out and spoke to them again. Tossing the question out as if it had nothing to do with the case.

"You gentlemen up here alone or with other people?"

"I'm with my wife and daughter. They're at the house," Dobos said immediately. "So's Jack's fiancée."

"Well, we won't keep you long," I promised, feeling relieved that my judgment had been right: they were both straight. It didn't mean they couldn't have killed the boy, but it cut the odds considerably. I ignored them and thought over the information Kennie's parents had given me. "Was he wearing a camera around his neck when you found him?"

They looked at one another blankly. Then Innes said, "No, he was just like this. I never saw anything else, even before we got him into the boat."

I stepped back into the boat to look at the body again. The crowd was still shoving toward Sam's magic circle, waiting for me to do something brilliant, I guess. Only there isn't room for brilliance at a time like this. You move slowly. The investigation has to start with facts, and finding them takes time and patience, not car chases. Life can be a lot more boring than television.

Without moving the body, I saw that there was a round cylinder in the right pants pocket. A film container, possibly, hopefully the one he had finished before he put in the new film he had bought at the store. Maybe there's be something useful on it. Aside from that there was nothing else remarkable about the body, but I kept looking until the hearse arrived from the funeral parlor.

McKenney got out. He's short and round, and he never wears anything other than a black suit with white shirt and black tie. He was in uniform now, incongruous among the T-shirts and casual wear of the onlookers. He stopped at the back of the crowd, and I got out of the boat and moved the people aside so he could back the hearse up, close to the water's edge.

He opened the back door and took out a little trolley, like a hospital gurney, only flat-bottomed and squared, big enough to accommodate a coffin. It's not fancy, but we don't have a local ambulance. McKenney is the only person for fifty miles with anything suitable for moving a body. He nodded to me and glanced at the boy, as if he were wondering if he had the right size of coffin in stock. "Just a child," he said with practiced sadness.

"Thirteen years old," I agreed. "Can you give me a hand, please?"

The body was still fresh enough to be limp, and it weighed almost nothing as we lifted it out of the boat and set it on the cart. I helped McKenney lift the cart back into his vehicle. Some overanxious youth in the crowd started forward to help us, rolling his cigarette dead center in his mouth for the effort, but Sam snarled and he retreated, muttering. I glanced at him, storing a note of his description. The murderer of a child often turns up at the murder scene or at the funeral.

I got back into the boat and checked it, from end to end, especially where the body had been lying. The boat was a cedar strip, hired from the lodge where the young men were staying. They keep their equipment tidy, and there was nothing in the bottom but two fishing rods and tackle boxes, a minnow bucket, and a cooler.

I flipped open the cooler. It was full of beer, on ice. Somebody in the crowd said, "I'll have one o' them," and people laughed. Now that the boy was out of sight, the festivities could continue. I shut it down and opened the tackle boxes, which were full of the kinds of lure we use up here, Mepps and Daredevls and Williams Wablers—nothing unusual. I glanced at the ends of the fishing rods. Both men were using minnows that had dried and withered out of the water. Their story was holding up. The bait pail was almost full. The men seemed to be legitimate, a couple of ordinary fishermen who had stumbled on the body.

I got out of the boat and nodded to Innes and Dobos. "Thanks for what you did. Can I see you at the station around seven this evening, just to finish the paperwork?"

They both agreed, and I spoke to McKenney, who was standing at the door of his hearse, ignoring the crowds, like a chauffeur waiting for a rock star. "Shall I go now, Chief?" He smiled at me, uncovering store-bought teeth as white as a fresh marble headstone.

"Sure, Les. Can you take him to your place? I'll be up there as soon as I've visited the parents."

"Sure, Chief," he said in the same hushed voice.

"One moment, first." I stopped him as he went to shut the door of the hearse and reached inside to dig into the boy's right-hand pants pocket. As I'd thought, the bulge was a roll of film, in the little black cylinder with the gray cover. I should have waited until I'd formally searched the body, but I wanted to get this to Carl for processing right away.

I spoke to the crowd. "Okay, everybody, that's it. Go on home now." They looked at me as if I were Moses pointing to the Promised Land, but nobody moved.

Murphy was still standing in the same place, ill at

ease. I turned to him. "Thanks, Murph. If anybody comes down the lock who might have been in the vicinity between noon and now, hold them and call me at the station, would you, please?"

"Sure will." You could tell he was wishing he was coming with me, still part of the police department, privy to all the answers I would try to find. He turned away, hiding his bitterness, and said, "I'll just open the lock now. Mustn't keep people waiting."

Sam came with me to the car, and the crowd started to disperse, the younger people laughing, kidding one another, brave again now that death had been put out of sight. One kid around seventeen puffed up beside me as I walked and asked, "What happens now?"

His face was a posy of acne blotches, and he was bursting to ingratiate himself, a lonely loser. Behind him I could see a couple of others his age, ordinary-looking boys who probably figured he was going to get his ears burned for talking to me, hiding their sniggers as they watched. I told him, "I have to do a few things. There's a procedure, you know."

"Is there?" He was screwing his courage up tight, and he blurted out, "Do you ever deputize guys, like when you need help?"

"Doesn't happen often," I told him, "but if it does, I'll keep you in mind. What's your name?"

"Ron Lacey," he said eagerly. "I'm at Bass Rocks Lodge—you know where it is?"

"Sure. Thanks." I nodded to him and went on. I'm not in business to play games with people, but lonely kids get to me. The car seats were scorching hot under the August sun, and I wound all the windows down before setting out on the errand I hated to make. It's the worst part of a policeman's job, breaking bad news. I went over a couple of approaches in my mind, searching for a way to soften the worst words a parent can ever hear.

Their car was still parked where it had been before,

and there was nobody in sight, but the moment I got out of my car the screen door burst open and Mrs. Spenser ran out, her face anxious. "Have you heard anything?"

I waited until I was close before I said, "Yes, Mrs. Spenser. I'm sorry to tell you I have, and it's bad news."

She buckled at the knees, and I grabbed her elbow to stop her from collapsing. She was sobbing helplessly. "He's hurt. That's it, isn't it?" God, I hate my job at times.

"Shall we go inside where you can sit down?" I suggested, but she toughened at once and jerked her elbow away from me. "What is it? Don't play games with me."

Behind her the screen door had opened, and her husband came out, his hair ruffled as if he had been sleeping. He shouted something, but I didn't listen. I told her, "I'm sorry, Mrs. Spenser, but a boy answering Kennie's description has been found drowned."

She turned away from me, blundering toward the cottage, both arms pumping as she wailed, "No, no," over and over. I stood for a moment, expecting her husband to try to hold her and console her, but he didn't. He stormed out at me, finger pointing like a gun.

"You useless, stupid bastard. Why didn't you find him before this could happen?"

I said nothing, and suddenly he collected himself and turned away, still not holding his wife but walking beside her as if she were a stranger in distress. "It's a mistake. I'm sure it's a mistake," he said, and turned to me and shouted, "It's a mistake, isn't it?"

I shook my head and said, "No, I'm sorry. A boy was found by two fishermen. I'll have to ask you to come and see if it is your son."

"You're not sure?" He roared it at me, posturing again.

"It's a sandy-haired boy wearing a Camp Sunrise T-shirt and blue jeans," I said, and he closed his mouth abruptly. After a moment's indecision he went to his wife, who was leaning against the wall of the cottage, her face buried in her hands. He stood for a few seconds, then reached out to touch her shoulder, moving cautiously, as if he were afraid she would brush his arm aside. He spoke softly. "It still might be a mistake, Carol. I'll go with the cop and see."

She whirled and held his sleeve. "I'll come, too." She had bitten back her tears now. Her face was desolate, but she brushed her hands across her eyes and repeated, "I'll come." He hesitated, and I could sympathize with him for the first time. He wasn't the boy's father; there was almost nothing he could do to soften her grief. I could see his mouth working, and I guessed he was craving the comfort of his gin.

She came toward me, with him a pace behind her. "Where is he?"

"In town," I said. She'd see the location soon enough. I didn't want to hurt her anymore.

"I'll drive behind you," she said, and turned to her husband, quiet and strong. "Get the keys, Ken. They're on the table."

We waited without speaking until he returned. She swiped at her eyes once more with the sleeve of her T-shirt and sniffed. When her husband came back, he was calmer. I wondered if he'd given himself a quick snort. He gave her the keys, and they got into the car.

We drove back, them twenty yards behind me. There were still a lot of people at the lock, but I could see in the rearview mirror that she didn't even glance their way. She followed me as if I were leading the funeral procession that would start in a few days' time.

I took them in, through the front of the funeral parlor. A small crowd had gathered outside, and they fell silent when we arrived. Mrs. Spenser didn't even look at them. She walked stiffly up the steps a pace in front of her husband.

Inside it was cool and smelled of flowers. Organ music was playing softly, and a couple of elderly women were standing in the doorway of one of the two rooms where McKenney laid out his clients. They looked at the Spensers and then at one another, and one of them nodded.

I sat the Spensers on chairs in the passageway and asked them to please wait. Then I went in through the double doors at the back, to McKenney's workroom. It's a sinister place with stainless-steel tables and a big sink and bottles of chemicals on shelves. McKenney was there with his assistant, a not-too-bright local kid who probably took the job because nobody else wanted it. His biggest assets are a permanently sad face and a total lack of imagination. They were standing over the boy's body, staring at it with professional interest.

McKenney said, "You know, Chief, he didn't drown."

"Are you sure?" I looked at the body again, comparing it with the very few drowning victims I've seen. The only thing I could see, beside the injury, was the absence of one shoe and sock.

McKenney put his pudgy white forefinger down close to the boy's mouth. "Most times, if the body's fresh, like this one, there's froth around the mouth. The doctor says it's something to do with the lungs being full of water."

"The guys who found him said he was deep. He'd have been closer to the surface if his lungs were empty," I said, not arguing, just looking for facts.

McKenney nodded. "Yes, I agree. I'm just saying, it's unusual."

I thought about what he was saying and then reached out and pushed the cuff of the boy's jeans up on the bared foot. The ankle was scraped raw.

McKenney pointed to the scrape before I could speak. "Look at that. His foot must have been snarled in something—rocks, maybe."

"Maybe," I said thoughtfully. It all jibed with what the fisherman had said. The body had been slow to move. Dobos thought he had struck a rock; then it came easily. He must have pulled it free of the encumbrance, pulling the shoe and sock off at the same time. "Look, I want Dr. McQuaig to see him as soon as possible, but first we have to get the identification done. I've got the parents out front. Can you bring him out? Put a sheet over him first and give me a half minute to settle them down."

They both nodded, and the kid reached for a sheet. I went out again into the hall where the parents were standing, apart, like strangers on a subway platform. I spoke to the mother. "I'm going to ask you to tell me if the boy is Kennie," I said gently. "I'm afraid it most likely is, but I have to ask you to look at him."

She nodded without speaking, and her husband came over to her, timidly, and took her elbow. Behind me the doors swung open, and McKenney came out with the trolley. He brought it up beside her and gently moved the sheet away from the dead face.

The mother fainted, her weight slipping away from her husband's hand on her elbow as she collapsed. I caught her and laid her flat on the floor. The husband crouched down beside her, trying to lift her head and cradle it in his arms. It was the first real tenderness he'd shown, but I had to stop him. "Leave her flat, please, Mr. Spenser. The blood's gone from her head. We have to let it circulate back again."

He let go, and I lowered her flat again. She lay still for about thirty seconds; then her eyes opened, and she tried to sit up. I restrained her, gently, pressing on one shoulder. "Lie still a moment, please. You've had a shock."

She lay still, and then, as consciousness brought memory back, she began to weep silently. After a moment or two I helped her to sit up, and McKenney brought a chair. Her husband lifted her to her feet and sat her down. McKenney's assistant appeared with a glass of water. "Sip this," I told her, and she did while the tears ran down her face.

I turned to her husband. "I think you should take her back to the cottage, Mr. Spenser. I'll be over to see you both later, in about an hour."

He nodded, and then he spoke quickly, so softly that I had to lean close to hear him. "Listen, Chief, I'm sorry I was difficult earlier on when you came around. I'd been drinking."

I was surprised but gave him a formal little smile and said, "Don't worry about it; you're on vacation."

He nodded, grateful for the out. "I know. But I drink too goddamn much."

He stooped and put his arm around his wife's shoulders and eased her to her feet. I watched them leave and wondered why he was apologizing, and to whom.

FIVE

♦

Dr. McQuaig must have passed them as they left. He
came in thirty seconds later, carrying his scuffed leather
bag, head down and hurrying as he always is. He's a lean
old Scot who settled in the Harbour because he likes to
fish and can be on the water in two minutes from his
big old house on the shore.

He smiled when he saw me, a businesslike flicker of
the mouth. "Hi, Reid. Is that the kiddie under there?"

"I'm afraid so, Doctor. Shall we take him out back
again?"

"That would be best," he said, slipping out of his
jacket as he walked. McKenney's assistant pushed the
gurney back into the preparation room, and we all followed. The doctor flung his coat carelessly over an empty
coffin and flicked the sheet back from the dead face.

He grunted. "How long since he was in the water?"

"About forty minutes."

McKenney's soft voice said, "There was no frothing at
the mouth or the nostrils that I could see."

The doctor glanced at him, then back at the boy.
"That bump could have killed the wee lad." He opened
his bag and took out his stethoscope. He put it into his
ears, rolled back the Camp Sunrise T-shirt on the dead
boy, and put the little cup on the chest, low down. I
wondered if he was checking for signs of life, but he

tapped the chest with his free hand, keeping the cup pressed down while he did it.

We watched him as he rolled the body over and did the same thing low on the back, at the bottom of the ribs. Then he took the stethoscope out of his ears and stood looking at the body for a few seconds. Nobody spoke. He rolled the body right side up, moving as gently as if the boy were asleep, and stooped to check the face, tilting his bifocals up with his left hand so he could come in close. Then he picked up the boy's limp hand and studied the fingernails.

At last he lay the hand down and straightened up. McKenney and his assistant were watching him, poised like birds of prey, waiting for him to speak, but McQuaig's lived in Murphy's Harbour long enough to know that McKenney's one vice is gossip. McQuaig smiled the same tight smile and said, "I'd like a word with the chief in confidence, if you'll excuse us, Les."

McKenney cleared his throat and paused for a moment longer while the doctor kept on smiling. Then he gave in and turned to his assistant. "You may as well go for supper, Irwin. I'll see you back at seven."

The assistant straightened himself up, just as reluctant to move, but said, "Yeah, okay, Mr. McKenney," and ambled out, with his boss a slow pace behind him.

When the big metal-covered door had swung shut, the doctor said, "I don't want this getting around town, you understand."

"Of course," I said. "What do you see?"

He turned back and picked up the dead hand. "There's marked lividity in his face—you can see that—but it's also in his fingernails." I waited, still not certain what he meant. He rolled the boy's shirt back and tapped the abdomen with his fingertips as if it were a bongo. "See that?" He glanced up at me. "There's a lot of spring in the abdomen, as though his lungs were still filled with air."

"He didn't drown, then?"

44

"No. If you want my first opinion, I'd say he was smothered. That would be after he was struck in the head." He pulled down the boy's right eyelid, pointing at the white of the eye. "See those rusty-looking marks there? They're petechial hemorrhages."

"And that wouldn't have happened in a drowning?"

Like all medical men, McQuaig was cagey. "It could have, but it's not likely. If you ask me, and you did, I'd say somebody put a cloth or something over his face and held it there."

"Wouldn't his bowels have emptied?" I'd investigated the usual number of homicides while I was in the Toronto police. In most of the cases you had to hold your breath when you found the body.

McQuaig nodded. "Normally, yes, the sphincter relaxes. I imagine that he was too far gone after the blow to the head."

He was looking at me without focusing, his mind working on the evidence he had found. Then, still moving gently, he unzipped the blue jeans and slipped them half down. I watched as he rolled the body over and checked the buttocks. "He's clean," he said. He bent over and examined more closely. "And it wasn't a sexual killing."

"No marks on him?"

He looked up at me sharply. "Here, look for yourself."

"I'll take your word for it."

We stood and looked at one another for a long moment. I was going over all the things I had to do, trying to set some priorities. He spoke first. "You ought to have a proper autopsy done. The best place is Toronto, the attorney general's department. I could do it but—" He waved one hand awkwardly. "It's a special skill, forensics. They'll find things I could miss."

I came out of my trance. "Right. I'll have McKenney ship the body down there right away. But before it goes, could you take a look at the foot, the bare one?"

45

He turned back to the body and pulled the cuff of the blue jeans up on the bare leg. The graze I had seen earlier made him stoop again and stare long and hard.

"It looks like a rope burn," he said softly. "If you look closely, there's a loop effect, as if whatever was holding him down was right around the leg. No rock would have done that."

"That's what I thought. Can you see any fibers?"

He dropped the foot and went to his bag, rummaging in it for a magnifying glass. I held the dead foot for him while he looked it all over. Then he said, "Ah."

"Find something?" I couldn't see anything myself, but he was pointing to the deepest part of the scrape.

"There. Almost buried. I can't see a lot, but it looks to me like a piece of yellow fiber. You know the kind. Half the boats in town use that kind of rope for tying up."

He lent me the glass, and I stooped and stared until I could make out what he was pointing to. It was tiny, barely a sixteenth of an inch long.

"Leave it where it is," he instructed me. "The boys at the lab will know what to do with it better than we do. All you have to go on for now is the fact that he was tied down with a yellow rope."

"Then it's up there still, in the water below Indian Island." I straightened up. "Thank you, Doctor. Now I'd like to search the body. Then, if you could take care of the transportation arrangements with McKenney, I have to make some phone calls in a big hurry."

"Of course." He nodded and quietly pulled the boy's jeans straight again and zipped the fly. "Would you like me to stay while you go through his pockets?"

"Yeah, I'd like you here as a witness. Would you pull everything out, please?"

He nodded again and dug deep into the pockets. "Pocket knife, Swiss army pattern. Three dollars and fourteen cents. Kleenex," he said as I wrote the items in my book. "That's all in the left. In the right, one small pebble, pink color. One red-and-white Daredevl spoon."

I looked up sharply. "Is the hook still on?"

"No. No hook, just a ring on the broad end to attach a hook. There seems to be a portion of a broken hook shaft attached. Maybe he found it somewhere." He dug deeper. "There's a foreign coin of some kind." He looked at it and handed it over. "A ten-peso piece, Mexican. Could have been his lucky coin. Although it didna do him any good."

He dug on silently. "Short piece of casting line, black. Looks like heavy test. That's it. Now the back."

He rolled the body and went into the hip pocket. "Ah," he said, and pulled out a soggy bundle of paper. "Maybe this is something."

There may be nothing sadder than the things a dead child leaves behind. I didn't like going through his papers, but I had to. It helped to have the doctor there so I could stay objective and call out what I'd found. "A sales slip for almost five dollars from the grocery. That's probably for the film he bought. Two photographs. One of some boy about seventeen. The other—yes, it's his stepfather getting out of his car outside their apartment."

I stopped and looked at the photographs more closely. First the boy, blond and handsome in an English public-school kind of way. He looked as proud as a young soldier, standing in tennis clothes, holding a cup. There was an inscription on the front. "To the brat from David." The photo was well composed, a close-up, just wide enough to include the boy's face and body and the cup. Most amateurs stand off to make sure they get your feet in. If young Spenser had taken this, Carl was right. He'd had an eye for composition.

The second photograph was less impressive. It looked as if it had been taken from across a city street. A car was just driving by on the far side, but beyond it was the Spensers' car, with the stepfather rising from the seat. There was another person in the lobby of the apartment, partly obscured by the brightness on the lobby glass. I checked it through the doctor's magnifying glass. As far as I could tell, the person was a woman, blond, with short hair.

I put the glass and the photographs aside and looked at the last item. It was a letter, with the address of the Spensers' summer cottage at the top and yesterday's date. There was no name at the top; it burst out at once into angry words. I read them aloud, ignoring the childish misspellings. " 'You said we were friends and I thought we were but we're not. Don't say I'm making this up like you always do. I was there and I saw and you promised you weren't going to see him anymore and you did. I saw you. That's not what being friends means, I don't think so anyways and when I get back from this rotten place I'm never going to speak to you again. Kennie.' "

Dr. McQuaig gave a little humph of embarrassment more than amusement. "Passionate little beggar, wasn't he."

I looked at him, then at the body on the table. The Vanderheyden girl had said he was always hanging around her and her friends, shy and awkward, trying to break in but not sure how to do it. And yet this letter wasn't shy. It was the kind of letter a man might send to an unfaithful lover. It was angry, filled with hurt of the kind that a timid boy would never put into words, not even in the privacy of a letter he hadn't addressed or mailed.

"It's a precocious letter," I said. "It doesn't fit with the kind of picture I had of him."

"Aye, it's precocious," McQuaig said. "When you say it. Not many boys his age would be that vehement. It was as if he was writing to some girl he was intimate with. Somebody older, maybe, who was amusing herself with him but still had other guys she was serious about."

"But that seems a bit unlikely. I mean, a girl even of his own age, would likely be taller than him. Somebody who'd matured enough to fool around, even without going the distance. She'd be too big to want a little freckle-faced kid tagging after her."

We stood staring at one another, frowning, until the same thought came to both of us at once. McQuaig put it into words.

"There's always the possibility that the letter isna addressed to a girl at all. Maybe it's to a boy."

"Like a schoolboy crush kind of thing?" I wondered.

McQuaig nodded and rubbed his chin, making a brisk little sound. "Call it a crush, but it's love."

"Do you think it was physical?" The answer was important; it would change the way I investigated the case. I might start by finding out more about the David who inscribed the photograph to him.

"It could be." McQuaig was being clinical again. "It could be, maybe, just the kind of clumsy fumbling you see in puppy dogs, or maybe, if the other boy is older, it was the real full-dress thing."

I straightened up. "Okay, thank you, Doctor. That's all I need to know for now. Could you ask the forensics people to give you an opinion about it. I'm not sure if they can, but knowing it might help."

He nodded. "Aye, I will. I'll do them a wee letter explaining what we think. And ask them to check for hairs and fibers and all the other things they can do. I'll get on with it now."

"Good. In the meantime, I've got some calls to make, and I think I should do it from the station."

He raised one hand mutely, and I went out the back door and around to my car. The crowd outside was starting to thin. It was hot, a perfect blue August day, and the dust on the unmade roadway scuffed under my feet, dry as flour.

In three minutes I was at my office, with Sam flopped on the floor beside me as I took out the office phone directory. The first person I rang was a former partner of

49

mine in Metro Toronto, a detective by the name of Irv Goldman. I was lucky. He was just in, and he hadn't picked up the evening's headaches yet.

"Hi, Reid. How's everything going in God's country?"

"Busy for once, Irv. I've got a homicide on my hands, a boy hit on the head and smothered."

He made sympathetic noises and asked, "So what can we do in Hogtown?"

"I'd like to see if a few guys have got sheets. It'll be faster if you do it for me. D'you mind?"

"Shoot," he said, and I stared at the top of my list.

"First off, a Fred Dobos, one fifteen Davisville. Next is Jack Innes." I gave him the address and waited while he wrote everything down. "Also, the dead boy's stepfather. He's an odd fish, name of Ken Spenser."

Irv grunted. "Odd, what way?"

"Well, nothing certifiable, but he's a two-fisted drinker, miserable with it."

"Hmm. Worth a check," Irv said. "What's the address?"

I gave it to him and then added the last name, the one that had me feeling a little guilty for encroaching on the man's privacy. "And the fourth name is Carl Simmonds, around thirty-eight, address West Shore Road, Murphy's Harbour."

"Be back with you in an hour," Irv said.

I thanked him and hung up, then called the local office of the OPP. The guy on phone duty was Jack Reinhardt, a friend of mine. I told him to take the boy off the missing list and then explained about the bikers and asked if he could contact the OPP special unit that'd been set up to deal with them. They might be able to give me a lead on where this gang came from. It was more direct than working from their descriptions, finding their names from mug shots, and then going through the criminal-records process I'd set in motion with Irv Goldman.

Jack said he'd do it for me, taking the notes himself and calling me back. He knows I'm alone here and need all the help I can get. Then I rang the third number, the insurance office in town. The secretary answered and put me through right away to her boss, Wolfgang Schneider.

He was with a client but took the call, anyway. "Yes, Chief, what can we do for you? Maybe increase the contents coverage on your house?"

"Next time, thanks, Wolf. No, it's not insurance this time. I've got a drowned kid, and the guy who pulled him in thinks he may have been tied to something up south of Indian Island, maybe thirty yards towards mid-channel, just off the southern tip. I was wondering if you could call out your scuba club for me and go looking for whatever it was." I added the same statement I always made when I used his services. "We can't pay for your time, I'm afraid, but we'll cover any out-of-pocket expenses. Could you do it for me?"

"Sure, I was just closing up. Do you know what we're looking for?"

"Whatever it is, there's likely a loop of yellow boat cord attached to it. I'd like your guys to bring it in if they can without touching it. I want to try for fingerprints."

"I'll get them some gloves," he said, his German accent hissing gently on the "s." "That's deep there, over thirty feet, I think."

"Yeah, and the bottom's weedy, so it may be hard pinpointing the place. I've got a few things to do now; then I'll come up to the point in the police boat, bringing the guys who found the kid. They'll know where you should look first."

"That would be good. When will you be there?" He hesitated and added a respectful "Chief." All the Germans I've ever met love rank.

"Two hours," I told him. I checked my watch. "Let's say seven-thirty."

His voice became dubious. "We would have light only for an hour. I'll get Roger to bring his underwater light."

51

"Thanks, Wolf. At least we know we're looking for a fixed object. It won't be drifting away from us."

"That's one good thing," he said. "See you there at seven-thirty."

The phone rang at once, and I answered, "Police chief."

A teenaged boy spoke at once. "Yes, Chief. I'm Cy Levine. My mother said you wanted to speak to me."

"Thanks for being so prompt, Cy. I hear you were going slalom up near Indian Island this afternoon."

The voice was cautious. I remembered that Levine senior was a lawyer. "I was skiing safely, Chief," he said. "We stayed away from other boats, had an observer and a driver."

"I know, Cy, and I hear you're pretty good. The reason I'm calling is to ask if you saw any boats up near the narrows while you were out."

"Oh." He was relieved and eager to please. "Lemme see. There were a couple of guys fishing. They caught something, then left."

"I know about them. Anybody else?"

Another pause and he said, "There were boats, you know, but if they're not in your way, you don't notice. Like I was working pretty hard at the time." I could feel his ego swelling up, blocking out his memory of anything other then himself flashing over the waves. I burst his bubble to get at the truth. "The reason I'm asking is that those fishermen found a boy drowned and I believe he came from a boat. What you remember may be important to me."

He gasped, and his voice went up a fifth. He was a kid again, not a star. "Wow. Drowned. Yeah, well, that's different. Let me see." He thought about it and said, "There was a sailboat up above the narrows. It had a red sail. Not a big boat—holds two, you know."

I scribbled this down and waited. He went on. "Oh, and there was a green aluminum johnboat, the kind they use at the lodge near us to take the garbage over to the dump."

52

I wrote that down as well and asked, "Where was it?"

"Coming north through the narrows. As if it was coming from the lodge. Heading over towards the dump."

I probed to see if he remembered any garbage bags in it or who was driving, but he didn't. He had seen a biggish inboard/outboard with a canvas cover. He didn't recognize it but remembered it was green. And a canoe. The canoe had only one man in it. It was gray aluminum, and he didn't remember what the man looked like.

"Okay. Now I've got some other things to do. Could you please round up your friends and see what else they can remember? I'll drop by your cottage at dusk, in the boat, to check. If you could have them both there, I'd appreciate it. It's important."

"Yeah. Sure will." His voice sank again to its teenage masculinity. "Is this, like a homicide, Chief?"

"We treat them all that way, Cy," I said ambiguously. "So it's important. Thanks for calling. See you at dusk."

The next call I made was to Freda. It rang five times before she picked it up and answered, "Hello there."

"Hi, it's your landlord," I said, and she laughed.

"I've been meaning to talk to you about the deer-fly situation. Here I am, a defenseless woman in a bikini, trying to get some sun, and they're gnawing on me."

"Understandable. You looked very bitable the last time I saw you," I kidded, then came to the point. "Listen, can you throw some clothes on and come down to the station? You know where it is."

"I ought to. You locked me up in it once." She laughed. "You want me to pay for my keep now?"

"Yes, this drowning is getting complicated. I need somebody to answer the phone while I play cops and bad guys. Can you help me?"

"Sure will. Be there in ten," she said, and added the typical actor's afterthought. "It'll give me a chance to practice my accents."

I hung up, grinning. What Murphy's Harbour would think when the phone was answered by an East Indian, a Mexican, an Irishwoman, or a Cockney, I didn't know. But Fred has a good mind, and she wouldn't play games with the facts.

It took only a few minutes for her to arrive, and I used the time well. I rang the lodge and asked who had been using their johnboat around four o'clock. They told me it was the owner, a guy in his fifties, straight as an arrow, to my knowledge. He had gone to the dump on his own. Right now he was in town at the hardware store, but he would call when he came back.

The other two boats were harder to trace. I called both locks and gave a description of the pair of them to the keepers, asking them to detain any boat of that description and call me, then rang Walter Puckrin at the marina and picked his brains. He knew the sailboat. It belonged to a Toronto schoolteacher and his wife. They stayed at the cottage up above the narrows. They had no phone, and I decided to call on them later. The cruiser might be any of a dozen he could think of or a stranger passing through our stretch of the waterway. He would make a list of the locals and leave it for me.

Then Fred arrived, wearing a peasant blouse and a light skirt that swirled when she walked. She came over and kissed me. I wasn't in a mood for kissing, but she compensated for that and told me gravely I was going to have to work on my pucker. Then she got down to business, and I explained what messages I was expecting and how to reach me on the radio. She did a nice Katharine Hepburn good-bye, and I took Sam out to the car. First I would drop the boy's film in at Carl's and wait while he developed it. Then I would visit the Spensers and try to find out more about the mysterious David whose picture had been in their son's pocket.

As I reached the car, I heard the whooping and revving of the gang of bikers speeding up past the station, filling the whole road as they roared by me. At the back of the procession there was a General Motors van with two people in it, a man and a woman. I thought they were visitors or thrill seekers following the bikers for the excitement. Then the driver turned his head my way, and I recognized him as the head of the gang.

I may have been overly cautious, but I've always found it pays to be prepared for trouble, so I went back into the station and told Fred to call the OPP and let them know the bikers were in town. And while I was there I unlocked the station shotgun and propped it under the counter beside her. She laughed, but I told her, "Just don't use it on any little old ladies. In the meantime, it gives you firepower if they decide to hoorah the place."

She slipped into a southern-belle accent. "Whah, Mistah Bennett, Ah'll take good care. Y'hear?"

I rolled my eyes up, and she laughed and punched me in the arm, but not hard. Then I kissed her on the nose and left.

SIX

♦

The bikers had stopped at the government beer and liquor store in town. Murphy's Harbour is small enough that we don't rate separate outlets for each, like you find in the cities, so the gang didn't have to stop twice to fill their van with wine and beer.

They put in three dozen bottles of white wine and a dozen two-fours of Molson Export. It was a heroic amount of booze for fifteen people, but at least they hadn't included any hard liquor. That probably meant they intended to party, maybe doing a little grass along with their wine, but not to get ugly drunk. I hoped so, anyway.

They worked quietly, ignoring me and not disturbing the other shoppers, most of whom waited outside until the bikers were through. Then they saddled up and rode off up the side road, going two by two like animals into the ark, moving at the limit.

I wondered if they were on their best behavior because I was there to see. Probably not. From time to time bikers play this kind of game, behaving like choirboys instead of the hoodlums they really are. People fear them, anyway. They can afford to walk softly occasionally. It makes the public more likely to come down on their side if some poor bloody policeman has to wade into them. If I was real lucky, they would be on good behavior all weekend, but I wasn't holding my breath. I was glad I'd informed the OPP.

I sat for a minute or two longer while the last-minute shoppers went into the liquor store, which closes at six. That would be the classic time for a holdup, before the day's take was stashed in the safe. But, as usual, nobody tried anything, and when the manager closed the door, I started up again and drove to Carl's house.

There was a polite sign over the doorbell—typical Carl. "May keep you waiting a couple of minutes. I'm in the darkroom. Please ring and wait."

I rang and waited, settling Sam down on the step. Carl's voice came from inside, singing up in the campy way he uses with customers. It's his way of letting them know he's more creative than the other people who live in the Harbour. "Thank you for waiting," he yodeled. "I'm coming."

Behind me a car went slowly up the road. I turned and saw the shopper who had been in the grocery store with me earlier on. He had a girl with him, heading back to town. He half waved at me, and his girl turned a plain face my way. I waved back and turned to greet Carl, who had opened the door.

"I'm sorry to tell you, Carl. The boy's been found dead."

He gasped. "Oh, no. That's terrible. How did it happen?"

"Can I come in, please?"

He stood aside. "Yes, of course."

I went in, leaving Sam out on the step. "Look, Carl. I don't think you're involved in this. But I've got two things to ask you, one off the record, one on."

"Glad to help," he said, and reached for the film. I kept hold of it, and he checked himself and met my eyes.

"First favor. Can you tell me, off the record, if the boy seemed like he was gay?"

"No." He said it quickly, and I cocked my head without speaking as he hurried on. "Not the least. No. He was anxious to talk, but just about cameras. He was a perfectly ordinary little boy." He hesitated and went on in a voice that had a hint of a tremor to it. "You're not saying this was a sex case, are you, Reid?"

"The doctor says no. But tell me, what did you talk about?"

Carl shrugged. "We just discussed photography. He was keen to ask me questions because he thought I was an expert. He wanted to know things about depth of field, and I gave him some advice."

I pushed the film toward him. "The second thing I needed—I was wondering if you could develop this film for me. It was in his possession."

"Of course." He took the film and turned toward the back of the house. "I'll do it right away. It's warm in the darkroom, but if you want to come along, please do."

We went into the little room with its trays and machinery. He turned on a work light, then closed the door. "Kodacolor. I've just been working with it. That's good; everything's set up."

He had a commercial tank that ate the film out of his hand so he could keep the light on while he worked. I suppose I could have asked him about the process, but I didn't have time to waste. I was working out what to do next. Spenser was the key. He may not be the prime suspect yet, but there was something about the picture of him outside the apartment building that intrigued me. Perhaps he had some guilty secret that the boy had discovered. He wasn't the boy's father. If the secret was big enough, maybe he had taken the boy out in a boat and killed him to ensure his silence.

Carl had taken out the roll of negatives and was holding them up to the light. I looked over his shoulder, unable to make out much in the reversed colors. He held them against a light and skimmed them. "Nothing very exciting so far," he said as he reached the halfway point. "Six—no, seven—shots of the gigglers who hang around downtown. A couple of boats."

"Is one of them a cruiser with a canvas cover?" I was looking at them with him but could see only red. The angle was wrong for me.

"One is," he said. "It would be green in the positive." I said nothing, and he turned to me. "Does that mean anything?"

"It could," I said. "What else is there?"

"Let me see . . . more boats, a chipmunk eating peanuts. He must have used a long lens for this one; the little rascal is full frame. Then there's that miserable dog of Walter Puckrin's. See, a good composition, head hanging out of his doghouse. He looks like an old French trollop in her bedroom window."

"Could you pull me a quick print of these, please? I can't read negatives the way you can."

"Right away." He fiddled with his other machine. "I'll do straight contacts. They're small, but it's faster."

"Good." I nodded. "I appreciate it."

He went to work with his other machine and was absorbed for a moment or two, then asked over his shoulder, "What happened? Was he drowned?"

"No," I said, and he looked up in genuine surprise.

"I assumed . . ." he said, and trailed off.

"So will most people. His body was recovered off Indian Island, but the doctor thinks he was smothered, and he'd been hit in the head first."

"Good God," he said angrily. "That's sick."

"It's murder. And whoever did it wanted the evidence hidden. The body was dropped into the deep hole off Indian Island."

He straightened up from his machine and looked at me. "Doesn't that tell you that whoever did it knows the lake very well?" he asked.

"Yes. That's what I think. That's why I want this film. I think he may have known the man who killed him. Maybe there's a photo on the film."

"I hope so," Carl said savagely. "I hope to God there is."

He worked silently for another five minutes before

pulling out the contact sheets from the drier and handing them to me. I looked at each in turn. Nothing jumped out and spoke to me. The girls at the tavern were laughing and pointing at the camera as if it were a joke. Beckie Vanderheyden was one of them, and her pretty young face was no kinder than any of the others. Then there were animal pictures, a couple of the chipmunk, one of Walter's old shepherd dog, another of a tortoiseshell cat. And then there were boats.

I studied these more slowly. Carl had a magnifying glass on a little stand, and he handed it to me, pulling down a high-intensity lamp for me to use. The pictures were arty, made up of the curves and shapes of boats, several boats in each picture. Some were from low level, taken as he lay full-length on a dock somewhere, I guessed, looking for the effect he wanted. Others were high shots, from where? Up a tree possibly. Or! The thought came to me like a bolt of lightning. From the second-story balcony of some cottage set above the water. Which meant they had been taken from one of only about a dozen places around the lake.

I pointed out one of the pictures for Carl. "When would you say this was taken, morning or evening?"

He moved the glass away from me and examined the shot carefully. "The light is yellowish. The shadows are getting long. I'd say this was taken around seven in the evening."

I took the glass and contact sheets back from him and studied the shadows. "In that case, looking at the run of that dock against the sun, it was taken on this side of the waterway, from a balcony. And that means it could be the Corbetts' place."

He looked at me and nodded. "Right. I covered a party there once, a twenty-fifth anniversary. The balcony is about, oh, say, fifteen feet above the dock. The angle's right."

I straightened up, tapping the contact sheets together

so they were square. Carl found an envelope for me. I shoved them into it, and he opened the door.

He switched off the light as we left, and I walked through his living room to the front door.

"Thanks, Carl. Keep the negatives, please. If something comes up later, I might need an enlargement or two."

"Will do," he said, and then added impulsively, "Catch the bastard, Reid. It's a terrible thing, and it means more to me than anybody else in town. The tongues will be wagging, and the trouble will pile up against my door."

"I know. If anything should start, call the station. I've got someone at the telephone, and I'll get back to you."

"Thank you," he said firmly. "I will. You're a good policeman, Reid."

There was nothing to say but Aw shucks, so I just nodded and went out onto the step. Sam was lying there, and I let him sniff the boy's sweatshirt again and set him seeking. He ran to the door, then out to the road, directly opposite the door, then trotted off northward. Carl was watching from the step, and he said, "Does that mean he went that way?"

"It could. I'm going to follow Sam's nose. Stay in touch if there's any trouble."

He nodded grimly and shut the door.

I let Sam lead me up the roadway, keeping behind him in the scout car. He jogged on, nose to the ground, once taking a side trip toward a tree. I waited while he sniffed around the base, noticing that it had a grotesque bump on one side. Maybe the boy had stopped to photograph it. But Sam soon resumed his trot up the road, staying on the left-hand side. The kid had walked safely, facing the oncoming traffic. I was assuming that this trail had been laid after the boy left Carl's house. He might have gone back, but his time had been running out. He must have been killed soon after leaving Carl's house. And he must have left there alive. This trail was proof.

61

The road to the Corbett's cottage took me past the dump. I slowed as I passed and looked out at the bikers who were setting up on the flat field. They had their bikes in a line and were drinking beer and setting up a couple of big tents, laughing and swearing together. One of them stopped and pointed at me, and the others laughed. Then another one held up a bottle of beer invitingly. I waved and drove on, their laughter drifting after me.

Sam led me another quarter mile, straight to the Corbett place. It's right on the water, down a slight slope from the roadway, almost hidden in a stand of poplars planted years ago when the cottage was built. I got out of the car and followed him down to the back door, where he stopped and sniffed. I watched him and waited, glancing up at the cottage. It's more than a cottage, a grand summer residence, really. Mrs. Corbett's parents owned it. Now they're dead, and she comes up here alone through the week in the summer months. Her husband commutes from his business in Toronto and its surroundings. He runs a number of hotels, and I had heard the local gossip that he was trying to open a big marina hotel near here, out on the shore of Georgian Bay, where he can cater to the summer boat traffic.

After a minute or so Sam moved away from the door, out to the side of the cottage and down to the dock. There was a cruiser tied to the dock. It was green, with a canvas hood, the same kind the Levine boy had seen. Sam followed the boy's trail right into it, but tentatively at first, nosing the air more than the ground. But when he reached the side of the cruiser, he didn't hesitate. He dived right into it and snuffled around the center, not on the seats but on the bottom of the boat, what I'd have called the deck if I'd still been in the marines.

I followed him down and checked the boat myself. It was empty, and there were no obvious new scratches or bloodstains to guide or to confuse me. The first fact I picked up was that the rope at bow and stern was the same common yellow plastic that the boy had been tied with. I checked both lines closely. The one at the bow had been sealed with heat, the way most nylon lines are sealed after being cut, either with an electric heater at the store or with a match if the owner cuts and reseals it. The stern line was cut, unsealed, and was beginning to unravel slightly. There was about a yard of slack, and I cut the end of the line off, making a knot in the original cut end. If we did find the object the boy had been tied to, the crime laboratory in Toronto would compare the ends of it with this cut. Often plastic material shows the marks of the machine that formed it. Perhaps we would have further evidence to tie this boat to the dead boy.

My next observation was that the boat had been hot-wired. A bird's nest of wiring was hanging down under the dash, and when I checked further, I found that the wires to the ignition lock had been torn away.

I stood up again and thought through it all. My next move was fingerprinting. The best way was to impound the boat and take it down to the police station, where I kept my kit. But that meant getting a trailer, and if I did, I might smudge the prints, if any. I decided to spare the ten minutes necessary to fetch my gear. This place was private enough to do my printing, and if I found anything, I could cover it with clear tape before moving the boat. I brought Sam to heel and fussed him, thanking him for his work. He wagged his tail and lolled his tongue out happily. Then I went back up the dock, taking out my notebook, where I keep a couple of found property tags. I wrote on one, "Do not touch the cruiser at the dock. Will be back in a few minutes, Chief Bennett," and went to the door, where I tied it on the handle.

The knob was loose in my hand, so I took out my handkerchief and turned the handle gently. The door swung open, and I walked in.

I called, "Police here. Anybody home?" but nobody

answered. It was dark behind the closed drapes over the window, but after a moment I got enough night vision to look around. And what I saw stopped me from moving further. The place had been vandalized. Flour was dusted everywhere. Plates and cups were broken underfoot, and ketchup and mustard and jam had been hurled against the walls. Instinctively I glanced down at the flour all over the floor. I was right. There was a footprint in the flour, and I stooped to look at it more closely. It was the mark of a boot, with a horseshoe-shaped steel cleat around the heel. A biker's boot.

SEVEN

♦

I felt like a cat in a basement full of mice. No murder I'd ever investigated had thrown so many clues at me so fast. I didn't know what to do first. Obviously, I had to print the cruiser. The boy had been in it at some time over the last couple of days, and he hadn't sat down on the seat. He had been on the deck, which probably meant he had been in it today, already dead. That meant his killer's fingerprints might be on it, too, along with those of the Corbetts and whoever else had used it.

But the debris in the cottage was another lead. Somebody had vandalized the place. It looked like bikers, judging from that heel print. And if it had been, the chances were excellent that the kid had been here with them and that one of them had killed him. I had no proof, but when facts pile up this high around you, any policeman has to believe they're connected.

I stood for a moment, thinking hard. There was nothing else for it. I had to call in the OPP Criminal Investigation branch. They come to the aid of places like Murphy's Harbour when the load of investigation gets too heavy for the staff of the local department to handle. A couple of years ago I would have resisted calling them. But the people in town knew I was doing a good job. I had nothing to fear anymore from some councilor arguing that the OPP should take over the town's police coverage completely.

I went outside, backing up carefully so that I stepped in my own boot prints going out, not disturbing anything more. Sam was waiting for me, wagging his tail, anticipating more work. I patted him and sat in the front of the cruiser, calling in on the radio.

Fred answered at once, in a thick German accent. I told her, "Hi, it's Reid. Will you patch me through to the OPP, quickly, please."

"Vait, I vill," she said, staying in character.

I heard the phone ring, and then the OPP corporal answered.

"Hello, Corporal, this is Chief Bennett of Murphy's Harbour. I have a homicide investigation going on, and I need some help from the C.I.B. people. Can you scare them up for me, please?"

"Hold on, Chief, I'll connect you."

There was a pause, and I got the C.I.B. office, Sergeant Landy. I knew him, and that helped get through the formalities, but then he gave me the bad news. There had been a blazing crash on the highway outside Gravenhurst, and the boys were down there with the coroner. They wouldn't be free until ten o'clock at the earliest, and they'd been on duty since morning.

I asked him to give them the message and have them call me first chance they got. Then I hung up and thought some more. I was going to have to proceed alone.

The first thing I did was take the flashlight from the glove compartment and go back into the cottage. I crouched a pace inside the door and memorized the outlines of the boot print. To guide me further, I sketched it in my notebook, taking rough measurements overall and marking in the prominent features I could make out. It was rough, but it would have to do for now. If I came up lucky with my next move, I wouldn't need anything any more fancy.

I closed the door and hung a tag on it. "Investigation in progress. Do not enter. Call the police station," and signed it. Then I put Sam in the car and called the station on the radio.

This time a Cockney answered. I told her, "Hi, Fred, it's your nemesis. I'm at the site of a break-in that may be important. I'm expecting a call from a family, name of Corbett. If they ring, have them come to the station and wait for me. Tell them not to touch their house, or the boat out back."

She switched to a normal voice to answer. "Sounds heavy, Reid. You sure that's all I can do for you?"

"Over the radio it is," I said, and she laughed and I hung up.

I thought about my next move for a couple of minutes, trying to find something smarter to do than stick my head in the lion's mouth. But finally I faced the fact. I had to do this and I had to do it now, before anybody got time to leave. So I went ahead, psyching myself up for the confrontation.

I drove down to the dump site and very slowly pulled the car in onto the field. The bikers had lit a fire and were standing around it with beers in their hands. The leader was in the center, holding court. Most of the others were listening, paying attention. It reminded me again of the marines.

I parked about thirty yards short of them, respecting their space, and got out. The talk stopped, and they turned to look at me, stone faced. It was going to be as hard as I'd expected. I waved and came forward. Nobody spoke. I said, "Hi, how's the accommodation?"

"It ain't the Royal York," the leader said, and the others howled and slapped their legs like movie stars when a friend is breaking in a new act.

"It's the best we've got in town," I said. "And you've got it looking real homey."

"Not bad," he admitted, showing me his broken smile. "Wanna beer?"

"Yeah, thanks, it would go good." Manners cost nowt, my father always said.

One of them threw me a beer, putting a spin on the bottle so I had to snap it out of the air. Fortunately I've done that before; nobody passes anything in boot camp. I nodded, unscrewed the cap, and let the foam fizz away from me. They watched as I raised it. "Good health."

I pulled down a good mouthful and then lowered the bottle. The formalities were over. "I have a favor to ask," I said amiably.

"Don't press your luck," the leader said, and the others nodded. That was the way to talk to pigs.

"No big deal. I wondered if I could take a look at your boots." I stood and waited while they looked at one another. Then one of them laughed. "You're lookin' at 'em a'ready."

I smiled politely. "Yeah, but I meant the soles."

That stopped the laugh. One of them said, "What for?"

"Curiosity." I grinned, nice and boyish, and waited. And then German Helmet tossed away his beer bottle, sending it spinning underhanded into the fire. "You piss me off," he said.

I shrugged, letting my own beer bottle fall between my fingertips so I could upend it and use it as a club if I had to.

"Yeah," he said. He turned to the leader. "Me an' him got something to settle. That okay?"

I waited for the leader to interfere. But he just grinned. "Guess you do, Jas," he said. "Go ahead."

I held up one hand, mild mannered. Looking calm up to the last second. It's always the best tactic. "Look, I didn't come for trouble. I came to ask if I could look at the boots on you guys, that's all. Simple enough."

"I'll show you mine. Give you a real close look," Jas promised. He was reaching for his waist, and I saw his fingers unfastening the length of chain he had around him.

I kept my voice cool. "Yeah. So, okay. Me and you

sort this out. If I'm still on my feet, you let me look at everybody's boots."

They all roared with laughter, but the leader spoke first. And as he did, I realized I was in the middle of a power struggle. He and Jas were tussling for command of the gang. If I beat Jas, I would have their leader for an ally. It might stop the others from kicking my head in. "Yeah," he said in his gravelly voice. "Sounds fair to me. Only you ain' gonna be on your feet." He paused and then grinned again. He looked like a big, happy, ugly baby. "You're carryin'. Like, that'd spoil the fight. So you pull that thing and I blow you away. Okay?"

"No." I grinned. "But if that's the rules, I'll have to play by them." I could see the sawed-off shotgun one of them had produced from a saddlebag. Concealed weapon! I could arrest him. Hah!

They all laughed, and Jas grinned at me like a hungry bear. He had his chain unwound now, and he was swinging it in a figure eight, slack at first, then tightening it so it stuck out in front of him, a defense I couldn't get through. I spun the beer bottle at him, but he ducked, quicker than he had looked, and grinned again, still advancing. I knew he would flick the chain when he got closer, snapping the end in my face where one rap would rattle me hard enough to let him win.

I reached my right hand back and drew my stick from the right hip pocket. It's lignum vitae, heavy as metal. I held it in front of me as if it were a saber, turning my body. The stick would give me a chance, a slim chance.

He picked up the speed of his whirling, moving the chain with an almost invisible hiss in a line two feet out from his fist. And then I moved, slamming down on the chain with my stick, hitting as it came up on its curve so it wrapped itself around the stick. It was my instant, and I used it, tugging hard, trying to pull him off balance so I could block him across the face with the stick. But he was ahead of me. He let go of the chain and hit me a

69

solid left hand that connected on my right cheekbone, making the stars come out and play. I backed off and shook my head as he came for me, swinging another haymaker at my head.

I dropped stick and chain and ducked under his arm, hitting him a straight left, on the point of his nose. It splattered, gushing blood down his face, but he didn't hesitate. He came at me again, lashing out with his left foot. I hopped back, slamming my boot down on his rising instep. It would have stopped anybody in light shoes, but his boots saved his shin, and he grinned again, through his mask of blood.

Slowly we circled, and his right hand went down to the pocket of his sleeveless leather vest. I wasn't placed right to hit him, so I watched as he brought out the flick knife. And I knew I could win.

I learned knife fighting from Leroy Winston, a kid from Harlem. He was small and fast, and he showed me how he'd survived the gang fights that made up his block's social life. His biggest lesson had been switchblades. "When some dude touch that button, he God, man. He touch somethin' an' like he got a hard-on, jus' like that. Man, when he touch that click, you gotta second while he still groovin'."

Jas moved to the same choreography. He drew the knife and pressed the button, and for perhaps a half second he was motionless, feeling all that steel power pouring through the handle into his wrist and up into his whole body.

And that's when I hit him, smashing him right-handed in the face while I batted the knife away with my left. He staggered back, and I kneed him, three times, faster than Nureyev could have moved his feet, hammering his padded crotch so hard he didn't even have strength enough to moan. He fell facedown, clutching both hands to his testicles.

I glanced around quickly. His brothers were motionless, faces hanging open, beer bottles dangling slackly from extended arms. I took charge, moving like a copper, rebuilding the authority I had given away by brawling. I pulled the handcuffs from the pouch on my belt and tugged his arms behind him, cuffing him quickly while he lay convex on the grass, knees and head on the turf, moaning.

I straightened up and spoke to the leader. "Fair, right?"

He nodded, trying to conceal his grin. "Fair," he growled, and the others began to nod. They weren't afraid of me, man for man, but they liked to see efficient fighting. I turned and picked up my stick, the chain still coiled around it. I put the stick in my pocket and held the chain coiled in my own left hand. If they decided to renege on our bargain, I wanted my right hand clear to get at my gun.

"We had a deal," I said. "I'm gonna look at Jas's boots first, then the rest of you guys. Fair?"

"Fair," the leader said again, and I realized that if any one of these ugly men had killed the boy, he wasn't aware of it.

I checked Jas's right boot as he gave up trying to bury his face in the grass and rolled onto one side, showing tears mixed with the blood on his face. For a moment I almost felt sorry for him, but I was still in danger, so I kept it out of my face.

His boot was studded on the heel, a row of iron studs that would have killed me but that didn't match my drawing. I let the foot fall and turned to the others. "Just the right boot, please. Can you hold it up behind you?"

A couple of them swore, but the leader looked at them, and one by one they lifted their right feet and let me examine the underside of their boots. I came to a boot with the characteristic all-around bar on the heel, but it was too big to have made the print I had found at the Corbett place. Then I found three more, one after the other, but each one had breaks or nicks that would have shown in the footprint I'd seen. I made mental notes of them in case I turned up a print like any of them later. But for now I said nothing until I'd finished.

I stood up after I'd looked at the last of them. "Thanks, guys. 'Preciate your help."

The leader pointed to Jas, who was trying to sit up while one of the others wiped his face with the kind of tenderness a normal man might have shown to a child. I noticed it was the one who had ridden into the campsite with him earlier, a special buddy, I guessed, the one I would have to watch for from here on.

"Wha' happens to Jas?" he asked me, and again I could read the self-interest. Any normal biker would make a stand here, demanding his release. The leader apparently didn't want him around any more than I did.

"He needs to see the doctor," I said. "After which he's gonna need some rest. I figure he can stay at the station overnight unless you want to take him down to Sundridge to the hospital."

"We look after our own," the leader said. "Take them cuffs offa him."

"And you're taking him to the hospital." I was on a tightrope, the diplomat expecting the barbarians to respect the rules of cricket.

The leader looked at me. His eyes were cold, but I could see through that gaze as if it were glass. He was going to talk tough but not cause any more trouble than would seem necessary to his crew. I wasn't safe, but at least the fuse on the dynamite wasn't smoldering right this minute.

"I'll ask him when he can talk," he said.

I shrugged. "Might be smart, but he's a tough son-ofabitch."

I turned and half crouched to unsnap the handcuffs and put them back in my pouch. Then I waved to them all without speaking and went back to the car, hoping that my trembling knees didn't show.

The mirror told me that I was going to be wearing a mouse for the next little while. I didn't like it, but I've been hurt a lot worse, so I turned and backed out of the parkground and drove down toward the town. If the C.I.B. people couldn't help me, I had plenty to do over the next few hours, starting with a trip over to the Spenser place to have a calm talk with the boy's stepfather. But first I stopped in at the station.

Freda was on the telephone, sounding like Lady Di. She looked up and winked, then saw my face and gasped. I waved her concern aside, and she returned to the phone call, still in character. What a pro.

She hung up and came out from behind the desk on the run. "Reid, what happened?"

"I walked into some knuckles."

She came over all maternal. "That needs a cold compress, something to get the swelling down. Otherwise it could leave a permanent lump."

"I'm lumpy enough nobody is going to notice," I told her. She stood in front of me, her hands on my shoulders in a businesslike stance, looking into my face as if it were a TV screen showing hot news.

"How on earth did that happen?" she asked again. "What I've seen of you, I figured you were unhittable."

"Unstoppable," I corrected. "This is no big deal. I won the showdown. And I'm up to here with work. Has anybody phoned?"

On cue the telephone rang again, and she darted back and picked it up, answering in a bright, normal voice. She looked up over the receiver and waved to me, an urgent hand flap. I came forward, and she covered the phone. "It's for you. Somebody called Irv Goldman. Says it's important."

"Thanks." I took the phone from her. "Hi, Irv. What'd you find out?"

His voice was slow and cheerful, the voice he always used unless things were desperate. "Drew a lot of blanks, buddy. Those two guys, Dobos and Innes, nothing. Spenser, he's had three arrests for drunk driving. Two squeaky

73

dismissals, one of them under our goddamn crazy Charter of Rights, no justifiable cause for stopping him. He's out on remand on the third one. I spoke to the traffic cop, and this one looks solid. He's going to lose his license."

"Interesting, but it doesn't tie in with the case too tight."

"Hold your horses. I haven't finished yet. That other guy you asked about, Carl Simmonds—now that was where it paid off."

"Yeah? I didn't know Carl had a sheet." Fred was looking at me fascinated, as if I had started speaking Greek in front of her. I saw her eyes widen.

Irv's voice rolled on, soft and calm. "A sheet. You bet your—well, I know there's a lady present; she answered the phone. You bet what you want, buddy. Your boy's done time, heavy time. In Kingston."

Kingston Penitentiary is a maximum-security joint. Nobody goes there unless he's a guaranteed menace, to society or to himself. I phrased my question carefully. "What did he do?"

Irv laughed. "Ten years, less good behavior. He got out in six."

"Come on, now." My face ached, and I was in no mood for kidding. I wanted facts. Carl, in Kingston? I couldn't believe it.

"Okay. He was involved in a gay murder. He and his roommate were burglarized by some kid. The roommate came home early and surprised him. The kid knifed the roommate, and he died. Carl saw the kid, reported the crime—that was all kosher enough. Then three weeks later he was out on St. Catherine Street."

"This happened in Montreal?"

"Of course, M'real, where the elite meet to eat." Irv was enjoying himself. "Yeah, so he sees the kid, or someone he thinks is the kid, so he pulls out a blade of his own, and he stabs him in the kidney. Only this isn't the right kid. This is some choirboy from Trois-Rivières. He may or may not have been cruising for the same kind of action Carl likes, but he ended up dead, and Carl ended up inside and very sorry."

I blew out a long gusty sigh. "Poor bastards, all three of them," I said.

Irv dropped his bantering voice. "Why in hell they call them 'gay' is beyond me," he said. "They sure lead lousy lives. Anyway, I figured you needed to know."

I was silent for a moment, and he went on. "Listen, I'm off the weekend, and it's summer and all like that. I wondered if I could bring Di and the boys up there for a couple of days."

"I'd like that a lot, Irv. There's a couple of spare rooms at my place where you can stay. I'm gonna be too busy to take you fishing, though."

He laughed outright. "Fishing? I'm Jewish, you schmuck. The last Jew went fishing was Jonah, and you know what happened to him."

I laughed with him, and he said, "Nah, Di and the boys can catch some rays. Maybe if you need a hand I could pitch in—kind of a busman's holiday."

I looked down the telephone as if I could somehow lock eyes with him over the wire. "If you were single, I'd propose to you. That's the kindest thing anybody's said to me for years."

"See you around noon," he said, and hung up.

EIGHT

◆

I left Fred still fussing about my bruise and drove to the Spenser place. Already time was tightening up on me. I had to visit the divers in an hour, then go on and talk to the Levine boat party. By that time the two men who had found the body would be waiting for me at the office. I needed to take an hour to get a formal statement from them. It would complete the book work, but it wouldn't solve the case. I'd already picked their brains. Their best leads had been the location and the presence of the Levine boat. Perhaps either one of these second rungs on the ladder of investigation would be helpful. I checked my watch. Time was running out. Dobos and his friend would be back at the station long before me. Talking to them was fairly routine. On impulse I lifted the microphone and called Fred. I guess the punch I'd taken had made her serious. She answered crisply in her own voice, and I told her I wanted her to get a statement from each of the men.

"I remember that," she said cheerfully. "You took one from me last time I was a guest in this hotel. And besides, I've played a policewoman on 'Night Heat' since. Where do you keep the statement forms?"

I told her, gave her the rundown on the rest of the formalities she needed to know, and then hung up, grateful that she was there to help me carry the extra load.

Not the holiday weekend she'd planned for, but she was a lively woman, always looking for new experiences. Taking the statement would delight her. She wouldn't let it get her flustered like some people might.

In the meantime, I would talk to the Levine party. I had high hopes for them. What I needed was a good description of the man in the boat. I was sure the body had been dumped from it and not from the other boats young Cy had seen around the narrows. Sam's nose had given me a lead that would otherwise have taken days to track down. If the kids could describe the man who'd been running the green cruiser they'd seen, I'd be half-way home.

I put that thought aside. There were other things to do first. I wanted to talk to Spenser, preferably apart from his wife, to try and find if there was any reason why the boy would have taken photographs of the Corbett place. And whether there was any special meaning to the photographs and letter he'd been carrying.

I drove over there and found the Spensers inside the cottage. The stepfather came to the door when I knocked, but his wife followed him when he said, "Hello, Officer."

She stood without speaking. Her eyes were red with weeping and held the thousand-yard stare I've seen in combat-fatigued buddies in 'Nam.

I took my hat off and said, "I'm sorry to have to intrude on you, but there are a few things I have to ask." Neither of them spoke, and I put the question as carefully as I could. "Perhaps if I could have a few words with each of you in private—would that be possible?"

She said nothing, but her husband licked his lips quickly and said, "I suppose so. If it will help."

I nodded at her and backed out. He followed me, and I walked slowly away from the cottage, down the slope over the thin grass and out on the rock that dropped off sheer into the black water.

He walked beside me, half turning his head my way,

not sure whether to speak. I stopped, out of earshot of the house, and turned to face him. He met my eyes for a moment, then looked away, out over the lake, shading his face with his hand.

"I'm afraid that your stepson didn't drown," I said quietly.

He dropped his hand, gaping at me, horrified. "Didn't drown? But we saw him. Are you saying there's been a mistake?"

"Not a mistake in identity, but the doctor doesn't think he drowned. There are some marks on his face that indicate he was smothered."

"God." He gasped it. "Are you saying he was murdered?"

"It's starting to look that way, Mr. Spenser."

He turned away from me, balling up his fists, curling his arms, the helpless contractions of a man at the end of his ability to cope. I waited without speaking, and when he turned back to me, I could see tears in his eyes. "That's unspeakable," he said, spending the word like it was a silver dollar. It rang phony, but the guy was a professor, I reminded myself, and people always sound rehearsed when they talk about crime. It's as if they're preparing to be quoted in the newspaper.

I made a sympathetic gesture. "Yes, but I'm afraid it's true. And the doctor has asked that your son's body be sent to Toronto for an autopsy by the forensic specialists at the attorney general's department."

He worked his mouth as if he wanted to find enough saliva to spit. At last he said, "I can't tell her all this. Can you do it?" I stood, wondering at the state of his marriage that he would think a stranger better able to break the news. Then I nodded.

"I'll do it in a moment, but first I have a couple of questions to ask you, if you don't mind." He looked at me quickly, then away, the kind of look petty crooks give when you've locked them up for the umpteenth time. He was wary, and I wondered why. Had it been him in that boat at the narrows?

"They're pretty much routine, nothing you have to worry about. The thing is, I found a couple of photographs in his pocket and wondered if you had any comments on them."

He tried a hollow little laugh. "Photographs! He lived for his camera, that boy." Or perhaps died for it, I thought. We might know better if we found his camera with the new film in it. Maybe. Spenser held up his hands, palms toward me. "Anything I can do, I'll be glad to."

"Good." I took out the pictures of himself and David and gave him the one of the boy first. "Would you happen to know who this is?"

I was watching what I could see of his face, but he had pulled all his feelings inside and slammed the door. He looked at the picture without a flicker of feeling. "That's a boy called Reg something, a friend of Kennie's."

"But the picture's signed 'David,' " I pointed out.

He shrugged. "I know, but the boy's name is Reg. Kennie met him last year at camp. He was a counselor, I guess. He was also into photography, and the two of them struck up a friendship. They go—went, that is—on photo expeditions together."

"A counselor? That would make him older than Kennie, wouldn't it?"

"He's around sixteen, seventeen." Spenser shrugged. "Like I said, they were both into cameras. It was innocent enough."

I frowned. "Of course I'd thought it was innocent. Why would you have thought anything else?"

He almost roared the answer. "I didn't think anything else. It was two kids with cameras, plugging along together, taking pictures and developing them. Innocent. Of course it was." He shook his head as if the anger he was feeling could be spun loose, like water in your ear. "Christ, I only said that because you insinuated something about the age difference."

"I didn't mean anything sinister," I said. I took the

photo back and handed him the one of himself getting out of the car. "Is this your apartment?"

He answered without looking at the shot. "We don't live in an apartment. We have a house, in North York." I didn't answer, and he glanced down at the photograph, and I saw the flicker in his eyes.

I asked him, "Where was this taken? Do you remember?"

He thrust it back at me angrily. "No, I don't remember anything about this shot. It's me, somewhere, in my car. Why Kennie would have taken a picture of me I don't know. Maybe he was doing some kind of kiddie investigative journalism, prying around getting candid shots. He picked me because I was a handy subject to follow."

"But you were driving, and he's too young to drive, so he couldn't have followed you and then taken your shot from across the street. He had to be waiting. That's why I asked if it was your apartment." I kept my voice almost apologetic, wondering why he was reacting this way.

"Look, he's—he was a teenager. You should know you can't keep tabs on teenagers. They're all over the place."

"He was only just a teenager. Just thirteen. Tell me, what was he like? Was he difficult? Was he into drugs or trouble of some kind?"

"Drugs." He looked me straight in the eye and spat the word out. "You're sick. That's the trouble with you cops. You live with garbage, and you expect nothing else anywhere."

He was closer to the truth than I like, but I persisted, anyway. "Mr. Spenser, I don't know anything about your stepson except what I've learned today. If he had some secret or other, some friends or habits that were out of the ordinary, I need to know. If he didn't, then I hope you'll excuse my asking. It has to be done."

He jammed his hands in his pockets angrily and pivoted away from me to look back at the cottage. It was

80

the move of an angry, impotent man, pinned by something he couldn't handle. Finally he said, "You're right. I'm sorry. This is all very unsettling."

"I know. I only have two more questions for you."

He turned again, trying to calm himself. "Go ahead."

"I found a letter he'd been writing. It was kind of a love letter, not addressed to anyone but obviously very sincere. Did he have a special girlfriend?"

"Girlfriend." He snorted. "No, he didn't have a girlfriend." He dragged the word out, making it a slur. "Except for this buddy of his, he was a loner, never asked anyone home, never went anywhere without a camera in his hand." He sniffed and softened his tone. "It's not easy being a stepfather, you know. I did my best with him. When I saw what kind of kid he was turning into, a little hermit, I bought him a camera, something he could maybe make some contact with, something to get him out of his room and away from the science fiction he was forever reading."

"Okay. Thank you for your help. Now, my last question. Did Kennie have anything to do with the Corbetts, across the lake, just north of the narrows?"

His head shake was genuine. "I don't think he knew anybody up here."

"Well, thanks again. Now I'd like to talk to your wife and ask if I can look through Kennie's things. That okay?"

He didn't answer. He looked down at the ground and scuffed one foot in the sand that showed through the grass like an old man's scalp through his hair. I paused and then moved away to the cottage. He followed me, walking slowly, like a truant being brought back to face the schoolteacher.

Kennie's mother was standing just inside the door. I knocked, then took off my cap and went in to speak to her. I saw her looking at the bruise on my face, but she said nothing, and as gently as I knew how, I broke the news about Kennie's death.

She gave a little shriek of horror, then gathered her strength and said, "Catch the man. Tell me you'll catch him and punish him."

"I'll do my best, Mrs. Spenser, and a lot of people will be helping." Spenser had come in behind me, and he moved past me to stand next to his wife and put his hand on her arm. It looked like a gesture that would drain her strength rather than help, but it was well meant, and she reached out and clenched her other hand over his fingers.

I took out the photograph signed "David" and showed it to her. "Do you recognize this boy? Kennie had this picture with him."

She looked at it, then at me. "You don't think he did it, do you?"

"I don't think anything. I'm just trying to tie up all the loose ends, that's all. If you know this boy, it will be something."

She handed the picture back. "That's Reg Waters. He has a camera, and he and Kennie were friends."

"But it's signed 'From David,' " I prodded.

"That was a joke. Kennie took the picture last month, after Reggie won the tennis championship at his club. He was up against a much bigger and tougher boy, so they were calling the match the battle between David and Goliath. I remember Kennie telling me about it."

"Thank you." I debated with myself whether to bring out the other photo, but I could see the tension in Spenser's face, and I didn't do it. She had enough on her plate already without my asking if she knew her husband was two-timing her, which was the most obvious reason for the way he was acting. Instead, I asked if I could look through her son's belongings. She led me to his bedroom. It was a typical rented bedroom, furnished with the least possible number of items.

She watched without speaking, clutching her husband's hand as I went through the boy's few belongings. There was nothing to help me. A drugstore envelope from Parry Sound with another set of photographs in it, the same variety as he'd had on the reel that Carl had developed for me. There were no more letters or anything else that might be useful. I finished inside ten minutes and thanked her. There was no need to remove anything.

"If you want to go home, it will be all right," I told them. "There's nothing more for you to do here. I'll contact you with any news as I get it."

She nodded, and Spenser growled that they would leave in the morning, and I nodded and put my cap back on and left.

I called the station and told Fred where I was going. She answered crisply in her normal voice. I wasn't sure if she was getting bored or just running out of accents. "Hi, Reid. Nothing new for you. A lot of people have called, but they were mostly just nosy, asking for particulars. I told them there was an investigation going on, like you suggested."

"Thanks, Fred. I'm afraid this isn't the weekend you'd planned. We don't get busy often up here, and they had to pick today. I'm sorry."

"Nothing's wasted," she promised. "After today I can audition for the Judy Holliday part in *Bells Are Ringing*."

"Stay away from casting couches," I told her, and she laughed and signed off.

I parked the cruiser by the marina and unlocked the little boathouse where we keep our beat-up old cedar-strip. The township had sprung for a new motor a couple of months earlier, a Mercury 25-horse that skipped the boat along at a good clip. It wouldn't take me too long to get up to Indian Island. Sam settled into the bow, and I backed out, past the cruisers where long, cool women were sipping long, cool drinks while their red-faced men talked routes and weather like hardened sailors. One or two of the women had that restless, bored look you see in singles bars. They looked me over with more interest than they were giving the conversations around them. I guess isolation will do that.

The breeze was cool out on the water, and the few mosquitoes that had started to gather at dockside dropped away. It was the time of day I usually head out to fish for pike, and a couple of regular fishermen waved to me in a puzzled way when they saw I was still in uniform.

The divers were working off Wolfgang's big inboard/outboard. It was flying the red/white "Diver below" flag, and in case anybody around hadn't learned what it meant, he had a big double-sided sign on the deck. "Keep Away. Diving."

I slowed and waited about forty yards off his stern until he saw me and called me alongside, indicating the path he wanted me to take. I came up slowly, and he reached over and took the bow line and secured it. I tied my stern line to his rear mooring cleat and got into his boat.

"Nothing yet," he said. "But they've only been in the water fifteen minutes. They're over there." He indicated a spot about halfway to the rock. A stream of bubbles was crinkling the surface of the water. They moved slowly ahead, toward the rock.

"It's deep here, right?" I asked.

"One of the deepest spots in the whole lake." He nodded. "If somebody put the boy here, they didn't expect him to be found for a while."

"Fisherman's luck," I said.

A powerboat came south through the narrows, pushing a three-foot bow wave as it raced toward us. The driver saw us and veered off, not slackening his speed, and we bounced on the wake.

"Dumb bastard," Wolfgang said automatically. "Kids. They don't consider anybody."

We stood looking at the stream of bubbles for a couple more minutes; then the stream split, one side turning toward the west. After a moment the second half of the stream turned after it.

"They've seen something," Wolfgang said. "Look, they've stopped." We waited another thirty seconds, and then a small orange float popped up to the surface and bounced there.

"That's it." He started the motor and pulled in the anchor rope; then we inched toward the buoy. As we approached, a head bobbed up next to it, black and slick, with the diving mask pushed up on top like the mouth of some strange aquatic mammal. He waved to us and pointed down. Wolfgang motored up close enough to talk, then put the engine in neutral and called down, "What've you got down there?"

The man pointed down again. "I think this is what you're looking for. It's got yellow rope on it with a loop, about yea big." He made a circle of his middle finger and thumb, opened slightly. It looked as if the loop were about four inches in diameter.

Wolfgang looked at me, and I nodded. "Could be it. What's it fastened to?"

The man shook his head and pointed to the hood over his ears, then swam closer and clung to the side of the boat. I leaned down to him and asked him again. "What's the rope tied to?"

"The guts of an old engine block. No pistons or sump or crankshaft, just the block."

Wolfgang reached down and shook his hand. "Well done," he said heartily. I nodded, and Wolfgang glanced at me and grinned. "How about that, Chief. Good work, huh?"

"Fantastic. Thanks," I said. "Can you bring it up for me?"

Wolfgang turned to the diver again. "How heavy is the engine, roughly? Fifty kilos?"

The diver nodded. "Yeah, a hundred pounds, I'd say." He waited while Wolfgang looked at me for guidance.

"Great work," I told the diver. "Can you get a rope through it and we'll hoist it in."

"Gimme the rope," he said. Wolfgang stooped and unshackled the anchor rope, handing the end to him. "Tug when you're ready," he said.

The diver held the rope in his left hand, adjusted the mask with his right, and then sank out of sight, trailing bubbles.

Wolfgang looked at me. "I have a little brandy in the medicine chest for when the divers come up. Would you like some?"

I grinned. "That's my kind of first aid, Wolfie. But no thanks. I have to go and talk to some kids who were here at around the time it all happened. It wouldn't do to breathe firewater on anybody."

"You decide." He turned back to the rope, feeling it carefully through finger and thumb, like a fisherman waiting for a rainbow trout to start mouthing the bait. Then it jumped in his hand, and he said, "So, let's pull."

We worked together, feeling the strain even under the buoyancy of the water. "This thing weighs a ton," he said. Sweat was forming on his forehead in beads, and he dashed it away with his forearm.

"Yeah, let's not scratch up your boat. I'll get in the police boat and take it. Okay?"

"Yeah. I'll come with you." He supported the dead weight on the line while I climbed down into the cedar-strip. Then I took it and he joined me. Together we horsed the engine the rest of the way in, scraping it lightly against the side of the boat until I could lean down and hold it away from the hull while we struggled it in.

"There," Wolfgang said. We sat each side of it, me in the stern, him in the middle seat, looking at it. "Looks like a Ford V8," he said. "Out of a truck, something."

"Yeah," I said. "And it's in good shape. This is out of somebody's workshop. There's not a speck of rust in it."

86

"See." Wolfgang waved his arms expansively. "Now you have a nice shiny new clue, maybe with fingerprints."

"Good. I need one."

He was triumphant, savoring the pleasure of finding the block so quickly. "Maybe this one will solve your homicide," he said, and grinned. I grinned back. I hadn't told him it was a homicide, but you didn't need to be Sherlock Holmes to work out that much for yourself.

I asked him if his guys could spend a few more minutes checking around down there for the kid's camera. It was a long shot, I told him, and he agreed, getting technical on me. The weeds were bad, but they would do what they could.

I thanked him, and he got back into his own boat. I changed my plan and headed back to the marina. The Levines would have to wait. I wanted to get this block under cover until it could be fingerprinted. It was the first real key to the case. Anyone could have used the Corbett boat to dump the body, but this block had to have come from somewhere. If I could identify its source, I would be a whole giant step ahead. It had come from a shop; otherwise, it would have been rusty. How many people would have had a V8 engine block handy? Not as many as know how to hot-wire a cruiser. I ran through a mental list of possibilities as I drove. It was a car or truck motor, not a marine engine. That narrowed my scan considerably.

By the time I got to the marina, the big light was already burning, turning the purple shadows of dying daylight into bright blue-tinged visibility. In it I saw the OPP cruiser parked to one side of the marina, and next to it the two-year-old Cadillac that belonged to the town reeve. I wondered if there had been some scare about the bikers while I was gone, and I didn't slow as much as I usually do when entering the dock, but the motor reversed neatly for me and brought me in to the mooring without a bump. I ordered Sam out at dockside, then pulled forward into the boathouse. I would have the OPP crew check for prints in the morning. For now I would drive up to the Levine place and take statements.

As I came out of the boathouse, locking the door carefully, the reeve came up with another man. I recognized him at once. He's the OPP inspector in the district that embraces ours. We've crossed swords once or twice, and I could see by the smug look on his face that his visit wasn't meant to make me feel comfortable.

I nodded to the pair of them. "George, Inspector."

The reeve cleared his throat nervously. "Hi, Chief. Inspector Anderson has had a complaint about you."

Now it was Anderson's moment, and he milked it. "A very serious complaint," he said slowly, pitching his voice low.

I straightened up to my full height, any man's reaction under threat. Anderson was shorter than me, and he bristled a little harder. "What kind of complaint?"

"Brutality." He dragged the word out to its full length, loving it. "You knocked down a man with your stick and kicked him in the testicles."

I couldn't believe him. "You could be talking about a fight I had with one of those bikers, but you've got your facts wrong. I didn't hit him with the stick or kick him. But I put him down. I had to."

"Oh, I'm sure you have a story," he said primly, "but there's no justification for violence. I'm here to tell you that you're suspended, pending a hearing."

NINE

♦

Anderson was smiling like a bad poker player with four aces. I spoke slowly. "Who laid this complaint?"

He composed his face. "A citizen, on behalf of James Murdoch, who is in the hospital in Sundridge."

I remembered the other biker, crouching by Jas as he lay and groaned. I'd expected violence, but he'd been smarter than that. He'd attacked my livelihood instead.

The reeve spoke. He sounded apologetic, for however much good that was going to do me. "I'm sure there's an explanation, Chief."

"There is, but Inspector Anderson doesn't want to hear it," I said carefully.

Anderson leaped on that one. "Oh, yes I do. You're a regular police officer, a little unconventional, I'm told, but you'll get the same hearing as any other policeman." He waited, and when I didn't answer, he prodded, politely. "What happened?"

"I had occasion to visit the camp where the bikers are staying overnight in connection with the homicide investigation I'm conducting. This Murdoch character insisted on fighting. I had no choice. I didn't hit him with my stick. I defended myself against a chain and a switchblade. I put him down and never touched him from the moment he hit the deck."

Anderson glowed. I could almost see him swelling.

"And, of course, you arrested him for assault with a deadly weapon."

"Oh, sure. Just the same as you would have done, single-handed against a whole gang of bikers." I turned away in disgust. There it was. I had failed to work by the book. It made no difference that the other bikers would have jumped me, maybe even blown me away with their sawed-off shotgun if I'd tried to take Jas in. I hadn't followed the procedures, and it would cost me my job. It was that simple.

Anderson thundered out the question. "Where do you think you're going, Bennett?"

"I know where I'm going, Inspector. Back to the station to turn in my badge. You can notify me who's taking over the investigation and I'll brief him. Then you can tell me when the case against me will be brought before the police commission and I'll attend."

He was still talking, and the crowd of vacationers that had formed quietly around us, at the edges of the pool of light from the marina, were soaking it all up. "You'll do as you're ordered," he said.

"Why? I'm not working here anymore, am I?" Sweet reason itself. So why did I slam the door of the car after I'd placed Sam inside and got into the driver's seat? I had the same sense of disgust, at authority and at myself, that had driven me out of the Toronto Police Department two years before.

I drove out, past the people who were crouching to peer in at me, anxious for a glimpse of news in the making. Behind me in the mirror I saw the reeve get into his car, and then Anderson got into the OPP cruiser on the passenger side. That much was good news. He had someone else with him, somebody to take over the search for whoever had killed young Spenser.

Fred's car was at the station, with another OPP car parked alongside it. I got out of my cruiser and locked it, then went inside. A young OPP constable was operating the radio. Fred was sitting on a bench in front of the counter. She jumped to her feet when I came in. "Reid, what's going on? Some man came in and told me you weren't in charge anymore. He put this officer on the phone."

"I've been suspended," I said. She gasped, and the young constable got to his feet and came to the counter.

"I'm sorry about this, Chief. The way I hear it, some hairy goddamn biker laid the charge. I dunno why anybody would believe one of them over a copper."

"Thanks for your concern." I smiled formally and started emptying my pockets of police material. First thing to go was the plastic ID from my wallet. Then I took out my notebook and stood at the counter, entering the details of the engine block found by the divers. Fred was a good enough actress to know when the best line is silence. She stood and waited for me to finish.

When I'd brought my book up-to-date, I told the constable, "There's the investigation details so far. I also want to talk to the detective who takes over from me."

The door opened behind me, and Anderson came in, along with a sergeant I recognized. I ignored Anderson and said, "Hi, Sergeant Kowalchuk, isn't it?"

He stuck out his hand. "Yeah, Wally. Sorry to be here under these circumstances, Chief."

"You taking over the investigation into the Spenser boy's death?" I asked as we shook hands, and Anderson pursed his lips.

"That's none of your concern," Anderson said before Kowalchuk could answer. "You're off the case. Go home."

"What a professional," I said, smiling at him. "Throw away all the work that's been done just to treat me like a naughty boy."

He began to speak, but I cut him off. "A real copper works from facts. Your man hasn't got any. I have. Now why don't you drive back to your nice, comfortable office and start preparing the book you're going to throw at me while Sergeant Kowalchuk gets on with some police work."

Anderson knew he was out of line. He drew himself up to his full five foot ten, his cheap summer suit darkening and lightening as his movement changed the creases around the chest. "Sergeant Kowalchuk, you're in charge. If you want to talk to this man, that's up to you. I'll send the detectives out as soon as I can. In the meantime, take his ID and his gun."

"No dice," I told him, and he stopped in mid-turn, a double take from a silent movie.

"What did you say?" he spluttered.

"The gun is personal property. I had to buy it when I took this job, and I'm licensed to carry it within this jurisdiction. The ID you can have."

"Check for sure that he has a license for it," Anderson told Kowalchuk. "If he hasn't, take the gun."

He left, and Fred broke her long silence. "Who the hell is that guy?"

Kowalchuk made an apologetic little shrug. "He's the duty inspector. He lives and dies by the damn book."

"Well, I hope he drops it on his foot," she said.

We all grinned, and then I sat down with Kowalchuk and brought him up-to-date. He was over his head, as he soon admitted. He didn't normally do detective work, but at least he could keep tabs on things until the detectives showed.

"When will that be?" I wondered.

"Not until tomorrow now. There's nobody closer than Gravenhurst, and they're working on a stabbing at the Magnetawan Indian Reserve. But forget about Anderson. If anything breaks while I'm here, I'll call on you." He paused and cleared his throat. "Like, it'll have to be off the record. That guy would have my job quick as winking if I didn't play along with him."

I stuck out my hand. "Well, it's an ill wind. We'll go home and make like this is a normal weekend."

"Good enough. Enjoy it. This nonsense isn't going to come to anything," he said.

I hissed at Sam, and he came out after Fred and me to her car. "I hope you don't mind a few dog hairs on the seat," I said, but she didn't play along.

"Why aren't you mad?" She was blazing now, her hands up in a half-fighting stance. "Why didn't you tell Anderson what a nerd he is and ignore him?"

I puffed out a slow breath. "That's not the way it works, except in the movies," I said. "The guy has right on his side. I should have arrested that biker after the hey-rube. I didn't, so his story is the authorized version."

"Well, why didn't you arrest him?" We were standing now on opposite sides of her car as she shook out her keys from the little leather holder.

"It wasn't going to help," I said, and left it at that.

She opened her door and sank out of sight into the driver's seat. Then my door clicked, and I let myself in, putting Sam into the rear seat first.

Freda was facing forward, wriggling the key into the ignition. I reached over and put my hand on her wrist. She stopped fiddling and looked at me. In the gloom of the car interior her face was nothing but a pattern of angles and shadows, but her perfume was light as summer. "I'm sorry, kid. I'm mad as hell about all this, but it doesn't help. So let's just go home and kick back. Okay?"

"Sorry, Reid," she said, and bent toward me. We kissed, and when we stopped, she said, "Let's go right home and have a drink. Maybe you've got a steak in your fridge for a hungry woman."

"You've been peeking," I said. "Did you find the bottle of wine under the sink?"

"Pouilly-Fuissé," she said approvingly. "Was that intended to loosen some other lady's elastic?"

"You mean that stuff works?" I asked, and she laughed, and the knot in my gut slackened a little. So I was suspended? I'd been through this before. So what? I wouldn't quit this time, the way I had in Toronto after I'd killed those other bikers. This time I'd sit in my little house and live on my savings until the hearing, and then I'd decide, in cold blood. And then I'd quit. My gut tightened up again, and I reached out and patted Fred's arm as she drove out onto the roadway.

"Well, at least we can try out the wine without my having to rush off and play cops and robbers."

"Good," she said. "If you're not doing that, I was going to suggest we play nice. How does that sound?"

When we got to the house, I put Sam in his pen on the front lawn, making sure his water dish was full; then we went inside. Acting the clown, I carried Fred over the threshold, and she didn't laugh or protest. She put her arms around my neck, and we kissed so hard I almost stumbled on the top step. "No wine for you," she whispered. "Forget it, anyway. Let's go upstairs."

I tightened my grip on her, but she laughed and swung her legs down. "I don't want you with sacroiliac problems. I'll walk up. You can carry me down later if either of us has got any strength left."

"Brave talk," I said. And then the phone rang.

It was Carl Simmonds, his light voice squeaky with alarm. "Reid, what's happening? I phoned the station, and somebody told me you were off duty."

"It's a long story." My mind was still on Fred, who was standing three steps up the creaky old stairs, slowly pulling off her blouse as if a saxophone were playing "Night Train" somewhere.

"But can you come? There's people all over the place, and they're calling out all kinds of things." He sounded almost in tears. Fred was reaching around to unsnap her brassiere, but I held up one hand and shook my head. She gave a stagy pout and stopped.

"Where are you? At home?"

"Yes, and nobody will come from the police station. They said they'd call a patrol car in off the highway, it

94

would be here in half an hour. I don't want to worry you, Reid, but half an hour could be too late."

"Are they threatening you?" Fred had dropped her acting and was slipping back into her blouse as efficiently as if she were trying it on in a store.

"Yes." His voice was almost a squeal. "They've already ripped up half my picket fence, and they're all over the lawn. I need protection." For the first time since I'd known the guy, he sounded petulant.

"I've been relieved of duty, but if you've got a problem, I'll come and help." And then, through the metallic filter of the telephone, I heard the unmistakable music of splintering glass.

I put the phone down and said to Fred, "Be back in a minute; there's a riot going on." I tossed my hat on the table and pulled my light windbreaker off the back of the door and slipped it on over my uniform shirt and Sam Browne belt and the gun. Then I ran out. Fred pattered down the steps behind me and out onto the lawn.

"Where are you going?"

I let Sam out of the cage and tapped my back pocket to make sure my stick was in place as I ran toward my own car. "North of here; there's a guy being assaulted. Stay here."

But she was at the car beside me. "You bloody chauvinist. I'm not staying home knitting if you're in a mess. I'm coming."

I opened my mouth to argue, but she waved one finger at me. "Forget it. I'm coming with you."

"Okay. Just stay in the car until I tell you to get out," I said. I whistled to Sam, and he jumped in behind the wheel, then over the seat into the back.

There must have been forty cars around Carl's place, and I could hear the noise even before I switched the motor off. They were a little drunk, standard for Saturday night, but angrier than I've seen a crowd since I came here. Carl's fence was flattened, and they were gathering around his front door, hammering on it, shouting. He had his yellow porch light on, and they all looked jaundiced. I stopped the car in the middle of the road and jumped out. "Stay here. If there's trouble I can't handle, drive down to the station and get the OPP man," I said, and Fred squirmed behind the wheel as I got out and let Sam out of the back.

I didn't waste time. I told him, "Speak," and the crowd split apart, letting me through, to the front step. I stood there, the light behind me playing on all their angry faces. "Go home," I said. "Go home before you all end up in jail."

Someone at the back shouted, "What about this queer? He killed the little boy?"

"If he had, he'd be in jail," I said. "You're all breaking the law. Take off now before you end up in big trouble."

A young guy in a T-shirt pushed through to the front. He was bigger than the others, macho as hell, with his cigarette pack stuffed up his left sleeve. "You can't give orders. You've been fired," he said, and the crowd roared. I was watching them; there must have been close to a hundred, all men, all fired up. The crowd from the beverage room, I guessed, plus whoever else they'd been able to rope in for the razzing. I wasn't afraid of them. Canadians are peaceful mostly. These would be when the beer staled in their bellies.

"I'm telling you to go home," I said to him, but he laughed.

"I was down at the marina when they fired you, copper. You're just the same as the rest of us now. You go fuck yourself."

The roar built, and they started pressing forward again, the men at the back more eager about it than the ones closest to me and Sam but still menacing.

I stepped down and moved in on the big guy. He was a touch taller than me and proud of his strength—gymnasium muscles by the look of him, useless in a fight. I pressed in on him, invading his space, so he drew back a fraction of an inch.

"You can go peacefully, or you can go in an ambulance," I told him in a whisper, smiling as I said it. "Yes, I'm suspended, and so it won't make any difference if I take your head off."

"Just try," he said, and I saw the punch coming, in his eyes. I swayed away from it and sank a solid right into his gut. The wind went out of him in a rush. I said, "Speak," and Sam did, rushing at the closest man, excited now that he'd seen the beginnings of a fight. They broke and scrambled away, yelping with alarm. I stilled Sam with a whistle and waited until the bravest one of them had stopped running and turned to face me again.

"Take this man with you," I told him, and turned away, walking up the steps and ringing the bell.

Carl opened the door immediately. He was almost babbling, but I put a finger to my lips and pushed the door shut behind me. "Cool it. They're all going home now. You'll be okay."

He drew in a breath that was almost a sob. "Whatever you say, Reid."

"Good, I'll step outside until they've gone. You stay out of sight for a few moments."

I opened the door again and found two clones of the guy on the floor picking him up. One of them looked up at me and then spat, but I ignored it. He was backing down. He didn't have to like it.

I folded my arms and waited, and they supported their buddy over to a big green Mercury with splashes of brown primer paint on it. It started with a roar, then turned, running insolently over the grass of Carl's front lawn before spinning its rear wheels and heading back down into town. Then the other cars followed them, noisily at first, but with more and more decorum as the number dwindled and the drivers knew I would be able to identify them.

I walked out to my car and spoke to Fred. "Park this thing on the side, please. We'll go in the house for a few minutes, make sure nobody comes back."

"You've got it, Chief," she said. "I wouldn't want to get hit as hard as you hit that big guy."

"He's fine," I said. I was coming down off my combat high, angry with myself for not having been able to silver tongue my way around the problem. Sometimes you can't. But dammit, a policeman is supposed to try, even a suspended policeman.

Fred parked the car neatly against the grass verge and got out to join me. I took her by the arm and led her up the steps past Sam, who was lying there quietly, his tongue lolling in the heat. We both stopped to pat him and tell him he was a good boy. Then Carl opened the door again.

"Do come in," he said, smiling as wide as he could manage.

Fred gave him a smile back, and we went in. I introduced them, and they shook hands and said they were charmed. Then Carl asked if we'd like a drink.

"Why not, I'm not on duty," I said, and Fred said she'd like a glass of wine if he had one.

"In the fridge," Carl said, and went out to the kitchen. He came back with wine for the pair of them and a rye straight up for me.

I thanked him and asked about the broken window. "It's in the kitchen," he said. "Fortunately nothing's damaged, but the mosquitoes are simply pouring in."

Fred sipped her wine. "What a bunch of losers," she said. "Imagine doing that to somebody."

Carl tried a laugh. It was shaky. "That's what you get for being gay."

I raised my glass to him and sipped. It was Crown Royal by the taste of it, far more expensive than the Black Velvet I usually buy. "Tell me, what did they say at the station? There's two guys down there. I'm surprised one of them didn't come."

He shrugged, pulling his head right down into his shoulders. "The man said there was nobody to spare. The other officer was out at a car accident, and he had to stay by the radio."

"Busy night," Fred said. "Riots, accidents. Where will it end?" She said it lightly, not wanting to spook Carl anymore, but he was serious.

"The whole town's gone mad. First that boy is killed. Then this foofaraw here." He looked at me. "We need you on duty, Reid."

"Don't worry. The OPP are good guys; they'll take care of business." I didn't want to give him any details of my suspension. It would be all over town by morning. Churchgoers would exchange the gossip on the chapel steps. Fishermen would pick it up along with their minnows from the bait store. He'd get it somewhere.

A car pulled up outside. We heard the door slam, and Carl looked up nervously. Then Sam barked his "Keeping" bark. I put my drink down. "I'll see who it is. Sit tight."

Sam was on the porch, barking at two men in uniform, OPP constables. One of them was the kid from the station. The other was a stranger. I hushed Sam and called out, "Come on in."

They walked up, stepping around Sam very warily and into the house. Carl was on his feet, and he stopped and waited for me to speak. "Here's your policemen, Carl. You want to lay a complaint?"

He shook his head. "I don't know who threw the stone."

"What stone?" the new constable asked.

"Somebody broke my window. There must have been a hundred people out there, at least. Then Mr. Bennett came, and they went away."

The officer from the station spoke first. "Thanks, Chief. I couldn't get away. The sarge was called away to that Mrs. Spenser's house."

"What happened?"

He cleared his throat nervously. "I'm not exactly clear, but it seems that the dead boy's father committed suicide."

TEN

◆

I looked at Fred. "Do you mind if I follow this up?"

She gave me a wry smile. "I'd be disappointed in you if you didn't."

I winked at her and asked the OPP man, "What happened—pills, he hang himself, what?"

He looked at Fred first, making sure she looked robust enough not to shriek at the news. "No, simpler than that. He just drove his car off the rock in front of their cottage."

Guilty! my brain shouted. He'd chosen the same grave he'd put his stepson into. It was classic. I asked the next obvious question. "Did he leave a note?"

"I don't know. I got a call from his wife; she was hysterical. Seems she'd been resting. He'd given her a pill of some kind, and she was lying down. Next thing she heard this great roar outside, and she went out the door just as the car went in."

"That doesn't add up," I said automatically. "A great roar means he must have been racing the engine. Then she has time to go outside and see him go over the rock. He'd have been in the lake before she could reach the door if he was gunning it."

The OPP man shrugged. "That's what she said. The sergeant's gone over there. He told me to call you and

101

let you know. Then this gentleman calle 1 for help, so I had to call in a mobile patrol."

"Sergeant Kowalchuk asked for me to see him there?" I wanted reassurance. There would be enough of a crowd at the Spenser place without my cluttering up the scene. If he hadn't asked, I wouldn't go.

"For sure. He said to get you down there as fast as possible."

I turned to Freda. "Would you come with me, please? That woman must be going out of her mind. She needs somebody to take care of her."

"Surely." She set her wineglass down and turned to Carl. "Thank you for the drink. It was lovely to meet you."

He took her hand in both of his, impulsively. "Likewise. I hope Reid will bring you again, very soon. And Reid, thanks again."

I nodded and led Fred out to the car, bringing Sam with us from the stoop. "This won't be easy," I told her, "but I appreciate your coming along. This woman's taken the worst two pieces of news a person can get, in the space of eight hours. She needs somebody to hang on to, and a big hairy policeman isn't it."

"I know," she said in a tone that showed she really did. "She must be shattered. I'll do what I can."

"I knew you would," I said, and patted her hand.

One of the reasons I've always been fond of Freda, from the night I found her running naked over the ice, out of her mind with cold and fear, is her cheerfulness. That night she had started making jokes the moment she thawed out. Tonight she broke the mood immediately by changing the subject. "You're doing me a favor. If I'd stayed in town, I'd have been watching television by now, waiting for the phone to ring."

"A knockout like you? It should be ringing off the wall," I told her.

"Typical man," she said. "You think women have it all, that horny guys like you are pouring out of the woodwork to take us to dinner and work their wicked way with us."

"Well, it has to be easier for a good-looking woman than it is for a man." Only half my mind was on the conversation. I was wondering what the roar had been that Mrs. Spenser had heard. Had her husband wanted her to rush out and plead with him? A lot of suicides are tentative. This one sounded real enough, but that roar bothered me. I'd heard her car start up earlier in the day. It didn't roar unless you tramped on the gas, and if he'd done that, he would have been off the rock before she reached the door.

Fred was oblivious to my thoughts, carrying on with the conversation as if we were any two people on a date, friends who knew how to make one another laugh. "I get my quota of calls. A lot of them are from smoothies, guys who think they're cool as hell and don't know the world can see the word c-r-e-e-p tattooed across their foreheads. Then there's the sweethearts who want to tell their friends they laid the girl in the Caliente Tortillas commercial. And then there's the gays, who see a woman as a passport to the straight world where they can cruise for what they're really after in new company."

"It's a cruel world," I said, and took my hand off the wheel to pat her arm. "Here we divorced men are washing our own socks and warming up our own TV dinners, never knowing we're in short supply." The small part of my mind that isn't police equipment wondered how much of the truth she was telling me. Freda was beautiful. She was as close to a celebrity as a Canadian actress gets to be without a couple of Hollywood credits to her name. She must have had romances. But I didn't follow up with questions. Getting together with a woman in her thirties is like opening a book in the middle. You don't know what went before, and it's easier on your mind if you never find out.

103

She ignored my silence, laughing and squeezing my hand. "I can still remember how we met. I figure you rescue enough damsels in distress to manage just fine."

We'd reached town, and I glanced around as I drove slowly through it. There were fewer cars than usual for a Saturday night. Both the hotel and the beer-parlor parking lots were half empty. I guessed the crowd from Carl's house had gone home after the showdown. They couldn't sit and look at one another over glasses of draft, knowing they'd made themselves look foolish.

We drove over the bridge and up the road on the other side of the water to the Spenser place. Kowalchuk's cruiser was parked on the grass in front of it. He'd been smart enough to turn his flasher off, but already the neighbors were starting to cluster on the edge of the property, chattering and plucking up their courage to go and knock on the cottage door. They made way without a word for Fred or me—and Sam, who was shadowing us. If any of them knew I'd been suspended, they didn't say so.

I could see Kowalchuk in the kitchen, so I tapped on the door and entered. Mrs. Spenser was sitting at the table with a half glass of water in front of her. Her mouth was tight. She looked more angry than sad. "This place is evil," she whispered.

I said, "This is Freda Hollis, Mrs. Spenser."

Fred was perfect. She was transformed from the pretty kibitzer who had ridden with me. She was motherhood. She didn't say a word. She just went up to the woman and crouched and hugged her.

Mrs. Spenser sat motionless for a second or two, thawing out of her anger; then she softened and clung to Freda, dry-eyed and angry but holding very tight. I hooked my head at Kowalchuk, and he followed me outside.

"Thanks for coming over and bringing your girlfriend," he said. "This woman's had about all she can take."

"Fred's solid. She'll take care of her," I minimized. "What did you find out?"

He shook his head. "Not a hell of a lot. She was almost out of her mind. The neighbors tried to help, but she just broke away from them and ran back to her place. All I've got is she heard an engine roar, then she went out, just in time to see the car going over the rock into the water."

"Did she see for sure if he was in it? I've met the guy; he's a lush. Maybe he's pulled this stunt so he can take off and hide somewhere, play some kind of game on her."

"She says there were no lights on the car—she remembers that. For all she knew, the whole of the goddamn Rolling Stones were in the thing."

"I guess we'll know if he was in there as soon as the divers go down."

"I'll never get the divers until morning," Kowalchuk said. "The last I heard of them, they were diving for a tourist, some American who fell overboard at Tobermory. His widow's making a hell of a fuss, and they've been tied up all week looking for him."

"There's a scuba club in town," I said, "I've already had them out, but they'll turn out again if they have to. They're good people."

"Can you dig 'em up for me while I talk to the neighbors?" He was a good policeman, I decided, doing what I would have done in his place, fitting the pieces together and looking for those that were missing.

"Sure. The cottage next door has a phone. I saw the wires when I was out here earlier. I'll use it. Are your detectives on the way? We could use some more troops."

"They are, thank God," he said. "They've locked up the victim's wife in that Indian stabbing. They're on their way now. Should be here in another hour."

"Okay, let's see what we can put together for them." I left him and walked out to the cluster of people standing at the edge of the circle of light from the porch at the Spensers', like aboriginals respecting another man's camp fire.

105

Sam was with me, and when I approached, someone said, "What's happening, Chief?" I guess they'd have recognized Sam even if I'd been in disguise instead of plain clothes.

"There's been an accident, and I need to use a phone. Who lives in that cottage there?" I pointed to the one next door.

A man and woman stepped forward. They were fiftyish and dressed better than most of our weekenders. The man had white pants instead of blue jeans.

He spoke first. "We do. We're the Wilsons."

"How do you do, Mr. Wilson. Can I use your phone, please?"

"Of course." They fell in on each side of me and bustled me over to their door, talking in a torrent. "What's going on? We were sitting at dinner, and then we heard Mrs. Spenser scream, then a splash. Then we ran out, and she was standing on the rock, saying her husband had driven over," the husband told me.

The wife took over like a tag-team wrestler. "So we called the police station, and then this OPP man came down. I mean, we expected you. Are you off duty?"

"Kind of," I said. They wanted the whole story, but it wouldn't speed things up, so I just added, "Thank you for your cooperation. I need to call the diving club now."

They led me inside. I could tell by the way they eyed Sam that their home was not the kind of place to welcome dog hairs. I told him, "Sit," and he stayed on the porch. Their place was a transplanted city apartment except that the lights were propane instead of electric. It was filled with teak furniture and chairs upholstered in plastic that looked as if it would stick to the backs of your knees on a hot day. The phone was on the coffee table, next to a stack of *Financial Post*s and *Wall Street Journal*s. I picked it up and called Wolfgang at home. His wife answered, excited to hear from me. Yes, he was there. He'd just got in from Indian Island. Wasn't it wonderful that they had found the engine for me?

She put him on, and he boomed at me. "Hello, Reid. No luck with the camera, I'm afraid. We dived for another fifteen minutes; then the light went. We could try again tomorrow if you like."

"Thanks for the offer, Wolf. I hate to ask you, but I've got another emergency on my hands, and you're the only guy who can help. Do you have a couple of fresh divers?"

The steam went out of him. Like most people, he thought police work was finished once they'd done their little dash. "Well, I guess I could dive, and Dave Henderson, he was out earlier. If I can get ahold of him. What's happening?"

I told him and waited while he spoke to his wife in rapid German. Then he told me his wife would get the lamps out and he would be over as soon as he could, on his own if he couldn't get Henderson.

I thanked him and hung up. The Wilsons were hovering, waiting to be paid for their assistance with more information. I fed them a few crumbs. "It looks as if Mr. Spenser went off the rock. We have to check the car to see if he was in fact in it."

"I wouldn't be surprised," Wilson said sourly. "The way that man drinks. He was at the gin from breakfast time on, it seemed to me."

His wife had the important question. "Do you think he murdered that little boy? It wasn't his real son, you know. It's a second marriage." Her face was frank and honest, but I wondered how she had managed to round up that much information in the few days the Spensers had been renting next door. A dyed-in-the-wool busybody, I guessed.

"Yes, I know that. It's all very confusing, especially now," I said. There, a lot implied and nothing said. Well done, Bennett.

Mrs. Wilson looked anxious to go on talking, so I asked her the other question, the one that had been bothering me. "Mrs. Spenser said she was wakened up by the sound of an engine roaring. Did you hear that?"

I saw the look that flashed between them before he spoke, clearing his throat first, a dead giveaway. "I told you what we heard, Chief. We heard Mrs. Spenser scream, then a splash."

"Look." I stared down his eyes, through the one-way glass that stockbrokers wear over their souls. "This isn't a game, Mr. Wilson. The little boy was murdered. I don't want this getting around, but he didn't drown accidentally. Now his father is dead, and it's up to everybody who can help to come forward with everything they've got. What did you hear?"

His wife muttered the word "murdered" to herself, but he shook his head grimly. "I told you what we heard. That was all of it."

"I'll be back," I said. "Thanks for the use of your phone."

I kept my tone cold. The hell with him. I needed information, and the fact that he might lose some money by coming back to an inquest when he could be selling mining stock was his own problem. Being part of society means earning your keep every now and then. This was his chance. I figured his wife would work on him better while I was away. But I was coming back here for sure before the night was out.

I called Sam off the porch with a hiss, and he followed me out to where Kowalchuk was talking to the neighbors, unproductively, I judged from his tone. He thanked the woman he was talking to and came to join me. "What's happening?"

"The divers are on their way, should be here soon. And the folks next door heard something they're not talking about. I've thrown a little frightening powder around and left the wife to talk to the husband for a while, but they know something."

"Should I go over there?" He was eager. Detective work appealed to him, as it appeals to most policemen. He spent his days untangling torn bodies from car wrecks and straightforward stories from the lies told by the lawyers retained by the other drivers. He could taste the excitement in this case, and he wanted it wrapped up before the car from Parry Sound pulled in with the detectives on board.

"It won't help just yet, but when we've seen to the divers, then they'll talk. I can feel it."

"This Spenser interests me," he said. "From what the neighbors say, he was a heavy drinker. He was down the liquor store every day, just bought one bottle at a time but put most of it away before opening time next day. I've spoken to three people, and they all said the same thing."

"I met him. He was a loudmouth drunk, no doubt about it, but that doesn't give us much to go on. We have to see what the divers find out."

"Okay," he said. "I'll wait, but I want to talk to those people myself. It'll be faster than telling the detectives. He was high on the glamour of the investigation. You could sense it in the air around him, like after-shave.

"You keep talking to the neighbors for a moment. I want to see if I can follow Spenser's tracks."

"How the hell you gonna do that, you part Indian?" he asked.

I pointed at Sam. "He's got a better nose than Baker, the dog the OPP use for bomb sniffing," I said. "Trust me."

"See you here when the divers arrive," he said, and turned back to the thickening crowd at the edge of the property. A few cars had stopped there now, and people were beginning to act excited.

I went into the cottage. Fred was at the stove, making tea. She looked over at me and put her finger to her lips. "I've got her resting," she whispered.

"Good work." I nodded at her and looked around. A windbreaker that could only have fit Spenser was hanging over the back of a chair. I took it and went back out to Sam. I shoved it under his nose and patted his big head. "Remember this one," I told him. It's not a command, but sometimes I find myself talking to him as if he were a person. He's trained to sniff anything I put in front of him like this, and he did. Now I told him, "Seek," and he put his head down and ran at once to a point about forty feet from the cabin. As I watched, trying to place the Spenser car there from my last visit to this place, he stopped and whined for a moment, puzzled, then ran back to me and out again, toward the rock, the path Spenser and I had taken when I talked to him earlier.

"Good boy," I told him. "Come." He came to me, and I patted him again and told him, "Easy," then took the windbreaker back inside and dropped it over the chair back. No doubt about it, Spenser had walked out to the car. And the car had been pointing toward the rock, not ominously, just sitting at the angle they had left it when they drove back from the funeral parlor. That meant that the last walk he had taken had been out to the car, one way. Maybe he had jumped at the last minute, but if he had, his wife would have seen him, and Sam would have picked up his trail. No, he hadn't done that. But maybe he had been sober enough and cool enough to let the car flood, then push the door open under twenty feet of water, and swim ashore. Maybe. But Sam's nose had told me he had been in that car when it pulled away from its parking spot.

I saw headlights approaching and then heard the polite beep of a big car horn. The crowd at the roadway parted, and Wolf's big station wagon drove down in front of the cabin. Wolfgang got out with two other men. I went over, and Wolf said hello brusquely and set to work getting the equipment out of the back. In the gloom I recognized one of the other men, the face I'd seen in the water up at Indian Island. The other guy was a stranger, young and lean. Wolfgang introduced him as he pulled tanks out of the back of the wagon. "Dave Henderson, Chief Bennett. And you've already met Tim."

"Hi, guys. Thanks for turning out. We've got a car gone over the rock. I need to know if there's anyone in it, and if there is, exactly how he's positioned. Like, does he look as if he was driving, and are his injuries compatible with an accident. Know what I mean?"

"I drive ambulance up in Parry Sound," Henderson said. "I've seen plenny accidents."

"Great. You know what people look like after a smash."

"Do I?" he snorted. "Don't worry, I'll report."

I wasn't sure what I was looking for. I wanted to know if Spenser had been hurt, but if he hadn't, it wouldn't make any difference to the facts. If he'd decided to kill himself, he might just have braced for the impact, perhaps even fastened his seat belt, determined to take the water like a permanent anesthetic.

Henderson already had a wet suit on. Wolfgang slipped casually out of his blue jeans and pulled his own on over patterned bikini shorts. "What's the drop-off here?"

"Looks like it goes right down deep, but I've never been in, just glanced down off the top of the rock once in daylight," I told him.

"Fine. We go in carefully," he said. He switched on one of the two big lamps he'd brought and shone it down into the black water. A school of minnows stopped, paralyzed by the light, but below them the water was a cold black cave. "Take the rope, Tim. I'll go in easy," he said. He turned, big and awkward with his tanks on his back, flippers grotesque on his feet. He wrapped the rope around his hands, not wanting to snag his air lines, I guessed, and as Tim and I braced, he rappeled down the rock face and slid into the water with hardly a splash. He let go of the rope and trod water, calling up. "Now you, Dave."

111

Henderson did the same, keeping hold of the rope in the water.

"When we find the car, I'll give three tugs," he said. "Then, if the guy's there, two more, got that?"

"Three for the car, two for the guy. Gotcha," Tim said.

The two divers adjusted their masks, gave one another a thumbs up, and sank into the water, the big submersible lamps growing dimmer as the water closed over them. I stood on the top of the rock, watching, seeing the pair of bodies lying horizontal in the water, stark against the lights they were holding in front of them. Then the darkness won, and all I could see was two diminishing glows.

I turned to look at Tim, who was holding the line very carefully in both hands, paying it out a foot at a time. Then the line went slack. "They're on the bottom," he said, talking out of the side of his mouth as if he were afraid any noise would disturb the divers. The line went tight again, and he paid out another six feet, then stopped. I saw his hands move three times. "They've found it," he said.

ELEVEN

♦

We waited without speaking. The rope in his hand moved, then stopped. They had come to the side of the car, I guessed. I wondered how much damage had been done. Would the door be impacted by the shock of the six-foot fall? Would the pressure make it stick? Probably not. If Mrs. Spenser had seen it going off the rock, it must have been crawling. It probably hadn't suffered damage as bad as it would have taken in a ten-mile-an-hour collision. Spenser hadn't been racing to his doom. He had just driven over, as quietly as a man gliding into a parking space outside a church.

I ran through the physics I could remember from school. Gravity works at thirty-two feet per second per second. He'd fallen six feet, so it would have taken him less than a third of a second. That kind of impact wouldn't have smashed the car up. But why were they taking so long?

I took a long breath to calm myself. Tim was checking his watch, a big depth-proof diver's model. "How long have they been down?" I asked him.

"About a minute," he said. I straightened up and went closer to the edge of the rock. The bubbles were almost invisible, but I could make them out, a single cluster of silvered globes, lit from the dim light below, breaking at irregular intervals, showing that the two men were working side by side, probably opening the door. The two streams diverged for a moment, and then Tim shouted, "Two tugs—they've found him."

"Great." I ran back over the rock to where Kowalchuk was doggedly doing his job, talking to another person in the crowd.

"Can you come down the rock, please?"

He nodded and spoke to the woman. "Thank you, Mrs. Serrel. Now if you'll excuse me . . ."

He turned away, ignoring the calls from the people far enough back in the crowd to be faceless, the usual curious questions: "What gives?" "Don't you want to talk to me?" "What's going on?"

"They've found the body," I told him.

"Good. Are they going to bring it out?"

"They will if they can. The one guy is an ambulance driver. He said he'd look for any injuries and compare them with the inside of the car."

"What other kind of injuries would you expect?" he asked carefully.

"I'm not sure. But I would like to know that he did this himself before we cross it off as a suicide," I said.

"You're still thinking about the Wilsons and what they heard. Hearing doesn't amount to a hill of beans," he told me. I already knew that, but there was more to the Wilsons' exchange of glances than had been expressed so far. I was wondering whether they'd heard a fight between Spenser and his wife, whether she had hit him in the head with a skillet and stuffed him into the car and driven it off. She had no cause to like the guy. I'd seen that much in the time I'd known the pair of them.

We reached Tim, and he turned to give us the news. "The line just went slack. That likely means they're on the way back up."

"Good," Kowalchuk said. He crouched with me on the edge of the rock, and as we watched, the dim glow of the underwater lights grew brighter. Then the bodies of

114

the two divers became visible, arms and legs moving gently, and then at last, the loglike object they were carrying.

Kowalchuk turned to me, his voice hoarse with excitement. "They've got the sonofabitch, first dive."

"They're good; they found that engine block within minutes," I told him. Part of me was relieved at their find, but another part was angry that I was sharing it with another policeman, my replacement. I was a disowned, discredited copper, nothing more than a glorified spectator.

One of the lights broke the surface first, momentarily blinding the pair of us. Then Henderson's head appeared. He flashed the light around until he was sure he had found us. Shielding my eyes, I stared down the beam and saw that he had shoved his mask back. "Found him, got him out easy," he shouted.

"Good work," I called. "Is he cut up at all?"

Now the second light broke the surface, and it was Wolfgang's voice that came up to us. "Come to your right, about thirty feet. There's a ledge. We can give him up to you."

Kowalchuk and I scrambled over the rock and down to the ledge, about eighteen inches above the water. Neither of the divers spoke. They swam to us, the lights attached to their wrists waving in the darkness.

Wolfgang reached the rock and held it with one hand as Kowalchuk and I scrambled down to it. "Be careful," Wolfgang said, and handed me Spenser's limp arm. It was still warm through the water that it wore like a sleeve. I tugged gently until I had him with his back to the rock. Then Kowalchuk got under one arm and I got under the other, and we pulled him up on the rock, his heels dragging over the surface.

Kowalchuk had his flashlight stuck in the strap of his Sam Browne belt. He took it out and shone it down onto Spenser's face.

"No marks on him," he said.

"No, but there's no froth at the mouth, either," I said. "According to our local doctor, that makes it doubtful that he drowned."

"What do we do with him next? Is there an ambulance in town?"

"No, I'll have to call the funeral parlor, see if they've got any empty boxes." I was growing angrier by the minute as I realized fully what my suspension had done to me. I was not in charge of the investigation. Instead, I was the local volunteer, like Wolfgang and Henderson. When the real detectives turned up, they would pat me on the head and send me home.

Tim had come up behind us. "Wolfgang's got a phone in his car," he said. "You wanna use that to call McKenney?"

"Sure, great." I stood up, leaving Kowalchuk kneeling beside the body. Tim handed me the phone, and I called McKenney, giving him the details he needed and holding back those he didn't. Then I went back to Kowalchuk.

"I took a look at the back of his head. There's no marks there, either." He was excited, the way I should have been.

"I wonder what happened to him. He couldn't have just gone in there and held his breath until he died. He wasn't breathing; at least that's what no frothing at the mouth's supposed to mean."

I looked at Kowalchuk over the cone of his flashlight, aimed down, whitening Spenser's pale face to the color of paper.

"Don't ask me," he said. "I'm not the doctor."

"There is one other possibility." The thought came to me, "Maybe he was just plain drunk." I knew Spenser was a drinker. Maybe he had been drunk enough to go out and step into his car, and then he had started up and died, choked on his own vomit, maybe, before it rolled him down the slope and into the lake. It was thin, but I didn't have anything better to go on. Or maybe he was a drug user, as well. It was possible; anything was possible right now. I lifted his arm and glanced at the crook of the elbow. He didn't have needle tracks there, but maybe he was injecting between his toes, or even into his neck. Drug addicts are sneaky, especially if they've got a good job to maintain. It's only skid-row addicts who don't care who sees their needle scars.

There was nothing obvious, not in the light from Kowalchuk's flashlight, so I stood up and wiped my damp hands on my pants legs. Maybe the case was closed now. It had gone full circle. Murder, remorse, suicide. The hell with it. Let the OPP worry. I'd arrange for Mrs. Spenser to be attended by their people, and Fred and I would go home and play house, if I could get myself interested in it while the red-and-white flashers on the OPP cruisers were lighting up my territory.

The radio on Kowalchuk's car crackled again. He'd left it on, and there had been a number of calls that he had ignored. This time he responded, trotting over to the car door.

I heard the message clearly. It was a dispatcher from the OPP detachment down the highway from Murphy's Harbour. "Yeah, Sarge, got a message for you from Murphy's Harbour. A family called Corbett has just arrived at the police station. They wanted to talk to Chief Bennett. Is he there with you?"

Kowalchuk told him I was, and the dispatcher said, "Can you ask him to drop by the station right away. They want to go home, and he's closed their place up apparently."

"Will do. Out."

Kowalchuk turned to me as I approached him. "Did you get that?"

"Yeah, I'll take my car. Would you tell Freda I'll be away a while and then try to get a matron up here to take care of Mrs. Spenser?"

"Fine" was all he said. I knew what was happening to him. Kowalchuk was high on the investigation, full of the hunting lust that takes over once you start working on a good case. He'd started out apologetic for taking my job. Now he would have fought me to keep it. It was natural as breathing, but it made me sour inside.

I called Sam and went back to my car. People had started to drive up now. There is a real jungle telegraph in places as small as the Harbour. Within an hour you wouldn't be able to get up the road for the parked cars.

The crowd parted, letting me back out through the pack and down the road a piece, where I turned and drove back to the bridge and over to the side where the beverage room is located. And I noticed that there were half a dozen motorcycles outside. From the look of them they belonged to my bikers. I imagined the bar owner had already called the station, asking for some policeman to come and protect him, and I wondered if any had. I should have been there, with Sam by my side. It was what this town expected of me and I felt guilty as I drove by. I'd been suspended from my job, but not from my conscience.

There was a Mercedes coupe outside the station, I recognized it as the Corbetts' car. Stan Corbett, anyway. His wife has a beat-up old station wagon.

Corbett was sitting on the pew out in front of the counter. He was wearing a neat gray pin-striped suit. I guessed he had come right from one of the hotels or bars he owns. He was smoking a cigar that smelled expensive and he looked angry.

"What's happening, Chief? What's this OPP officer doing here?" he asked me. He's tall and tough-looking, as if he had personally built all those hotels himself.

"They've taken over, Mr. Corbett. I'm under suspension."

"What the hell for?" He glared at the OPP man. "Whose idea was this?"

"It's not important, just a formality. But before I was taken off the case, I was investigating the death of a boy and I had occasion to visit your cottage."

Corbett frowned. "My cottage? A dead boy? Just a minute, Chief, can you take this a little slower. What's happening here?"

"The victim, a boy, had a picture of your dock. He was a camera buff and he had a lot of pictures of boats, but I recognized your dock and from the angle of the shot it looked as if it had been taken from your balcony. So I went there."

Now Corbett interrupted me. His eyes had narrowed and he asked his question carefully as if he figured the answer might get him into trouble.

"You say it was a boy, a photographer?"

"Yes, Kennie Spenser. Do you know him?"

He nodded. "Twelve, something like that, sandy-haired?"

"That's him. Have you met him?"

"Yes, lots of times, he's a friend of my grandson."

My mind took a leap forward. "Is your grandson Reggie Waters?"

He looked at me, the same kind of look he might have given some extra-sharp salesman who knew too much about his business. "How did you know that?" he asked.

"Kennie had a photograph of a young fellow and his mother told me the name."

Corbett put his cigar back in his mouth. It had gone out and he relit it carefully. "This is terrible news. What happened to him?"

"He was found in the water, out by Indian Island. A fisherman snagged him."

He shook his head sadly. "Poor little guy. A nice boy, quiet, well behaved. This is terrible. Angela will be heartbroken."

Angela was his wife, she was softer than him, always ready to volunteer for fund-raising for the community or to pitch in with work on projects over at the Indian reserve. She would probably cry, then set to and find some way of helping Mrs. Spenser.

In the meantime, I had to add to their problems. "I'm sorry to tell you that's just part of the bad news."

119

"Oh?" he growled, frowning and puffing out cigar smoke.

"Yes, I have reason to believe that it was your cruiser that was used to dump the boy's body. The wires have been torn out of it and my dog tracked the boy to the deck."

"Goddamn." He took his cigar out of his mouth and looked around for an ashtray, then let it fall to the old linoleum. "I should have immobilized that boat, taken the rotor arm out of the ignition."

"I wish you had." I waited while he ground the cigar out under his foot. "And one last thing, Major, I'm afraid. Your house has been vandalized."

"Vandalized?" He pivoted on the foot he was using to crush his cigar butt, turning away from me angrily, then back. "Vandalized? What the Sam Hill is going on?"

"Vandalized!" He said it again, disbelievingly, rigid with rage, ducking from the waist and jerking his arms in tight little convulsions, a disgusted, helpless man. "That makes me vomit." He turned away from me, raising his voice as if he were addressing a meeting. "Do you know what I'm going through, right now, for the people of this town?"

The OPP man stood listening, trying to look respectful, although I could see he was amused at the show. He hadn't seen Corbett's house.

"I've sunk a million dollars of my money into the Bay Marina project." Corbett said. "Mortgaged every goddamn thing I own." His eyes focused on the OPP man and he jabbed at him with his finger. "A million dollars. To create jobs and prosperity for my fucking neighbors in Murphy's Harbour."

Now he turned to me, still furious, white foam forming in the corners of his mouth. "My own money. The Arabs and the bloody Hong Kong Chinese won't touch anything outside of Toronto. The banks won't. I've been on my knees, almost, to a bunch of church credit unions down in Quebec." He laughed out loud. "Yeah, promis-

120

ing the bunch of pious bastards I won't use the money to promote anything sinful." He laughed again. "Yeah. Kissing their black-suited asses for money for this town. And now this."

He stopped and I let him collect himself for a moment. When he stayed silent, I gave him the rest of the news.

"I don't think it was anybody from this town. I think it was a bunch of bikers. There's the prints of a biker's boot in the mess on the floor, and there's a gang of them in town."

He pinched his lips tightly together, bottling up his anger while he breathed in and out a couple of times, flaring his nostrils. At last he said, "Were these OPP clowns in charge when all this happened?"

"I found the damage today, around six p.m. It looked recent. But a couple of things. The door hadn't been forced. It was open and unlocked. Did you leave the key somewhere around?"

"Angie left a key somewhere, for the neighbor. He would come in and switch the heat on if we were coming up in fall. For some reason he didn't keep it, it was left hidden up at the house."

"And when were you there last?"

"Last Sunday night," he said immediately. "Angie was there until Tuesday, then she went to the airport in Toronto and flew out to Vancouver to see her sister, but I left Sunday night to be back in my office on Monday."

"So the damage was done between Tuesday last and now. Do you have any idea who might have wrecked your place, Mr. Corbett, is anybody mad at you?"

"No." He shook his head, then stopped and thought, then shook his head again. "No. Oh, I won't say I don't have people in business who don't wish me well, but nothing like this. This must be kids. Have you checked the local kids?"

"I'm going to," I promised. "In the meantime, I'm afraid I'll have to ask you to stay away from the house until I can get through and fingerprint it, and your boat. I'm wondering if the people who wrecked your house might not have been involved with the boy's killing as well."

He shrank, his shoulders slumping. "I can stay with friends, I guess. I'll call you in the morning."

"Okay. If I'm not here, one of the OPP constables will take the message and get back to you when you can go home."

"Then I'll say good night," he said and turned away.

"Oh, before you do that, could I show you a couple of photos, please, see if you recognize them?"

He straightened his back, like a man who has done a hard day's work. "Sure, why not."

The file folder containing the evidence I had assembled on the case was lying on the countertop. I opened it and took out the pictures, giving him the photograph of Reg Waters. Corbett looked at it and nodded. "I don't know why he's signed it 'David,' that's Reg Waters, my grandson."

Behind him the OPP constable was shifting from foot to foot, wishing he had the nerve to tell me I'd been relieved and let him take over the investigation. If he could have helped I would have let him, but it wouldn't, he didn't have the background I had and he didn't know Corbett.

I took the picture back and got out the other one, making conversation as I did so. "How old is your grandson?"

"Late teens," he said. "Lemme see. His birthday's May Day so that makes him a year older, right, he's just eighteen."

Old, to have a thirteen-year-old friend who idolized him. I got out the other photograph and passed it to Corbett. He studied it and nodded. "Yes, that's our apartment building, in Toronto."

"And do you happen to know who that man is, getting out of the car?"

He bent his head to look at the photograph closely, then shook his head. "No, doesn't look like anybody I know."

"Thank you then, that's all I need for now. I'm sorry about your house."

He stamped over to the door and paused with his hand on the doorknob. "Just be sure and lock up the sonsabitches who did it." Then he left as I was answering.

"I'll try my damndest." I put the pictures back in the folder and closed it. "Tell the detectives what's happened when they get here," I told the constable.

"Sure will." I noticed he'd dropped the "Chief." Rank has to be real before policemen take any notice of it. As far as he was concerned I was just another ex-copper.

The door opened again and a young woman came in. She was small and dark, wearing horn-rimmed glasses and an earnest expression that looked as if she put it on with her clothes in the mornings. I recognized her and groaned inside. She was the reporter from the Parry Sound paper.

She saw me and brightened. "Chief Bennett, isn't it?"

"Uhhuh" I said, not wanting to either lie or explain.

"Good. Just the man I was looking for. I understand you're suspended. Is it something to do with this drowning that occurred today?" She had her notebook out and poised the way they must have taught her in her journalism class. One of the skills that earned her two hundred bucks a week and all the aggravation she could stir up.

"My suspension has nothing to do with the drowning. Aside from that I have nothing to say, Miss Lafleche." There, me and Jackie Onassis in the same league.

"But what's it all about?" She was flicking her pencil over her book. Lord, she was keen. She was using shorthand for crying out loud.

"Nothing to say," I repeated. "Now excuse me, please." I hissed to Sam and he followed me, almost tripping her up as she scrambled out after me, following me right to the car, still throwing questions at me like balls at a coconut. I smiled at her, very politely, put Sam in the car and drove off, almost running over her feet as she leaned over the car, book in hand.

I kept my speed down by a conscious effort as I headed back, past the beverage room, noting that there were more motorcycles there now. The hell with it. Let the

123

OPP guys take their turn in the hot seat. I was going home.

The crowd at the Spenser place had grown some more. I parked at the end of the line of cars and left Sam inside while I went around them all and down to the front of the cottage. McKenney was there again, with his helper. Kowalchuk was over with him, and so were a couple of new men, tall and lean, the standard issue Hollywood gumshoes, OPP style.

I tapped on the Spensers' door and went in. Fred was sitting there with the Wilson woman from next door.

Mrs. Wilson started when I came in, fluttering her hand to her chest. "Oh, Chief, you startled me." She said in a faint voice.

I smiled at her, a tight-faced formality. "I'm sorry, ma'am, it wasn't intended."

Fred stood up and came over to me, reaching for my hand. "I think you should listen to what Mrs. Wilson has been telling me."

"With pleasure." I squeezed her hand and looked at Mrs. Wilson. "What was that, please?"

"My husband is quite angry with me," she said, "but I think we should tell you."

"Appreciate it," I told her, wondering what she had heard that was so significant.

"Well, when we said we heard Mrs. Spenser scream, that wasn't the first sound that disturbed us."

I sat down on the other side of the kitchen table, it's standard procedure, a standing man is menacing, my sitting made it easier for her to overcome her anxiety.

"No," she said. "No, the sound that we heard first was the noise of an engine racing away."

"You mean a car passing?"

She shook her head. "No, it wasn't passing. It started up, from outside their house. And it wasn't a car. It was a motorcycle."

TWELVE

♦

I took her over it again, three or four times, but she didn't have anything more for me. She hadn't seen anything, just heard a bike roar away. She was positive about that. It hadn't just driven by, it had roared away. I thanked her and left her with Fred while I went back outside to where the OPP detectives were watching the body being loaded into McKenney's hearse.

I waited until the doors were closed; then Kowalchuk noticed me and introduced me to the detectives. I didn't know either of them. One was called Kennedy, the other Werner. They shook hands, the way men shake hands with distant relatives at a funeral.

Kennedy said, "You sure left us with a mess," and Werner chuckled.

"Not my choice," I told him. "If you want me to fill you in, I'm here, but in the meantime, there's something I just heard that may be important."

"Yeah, what's 'at?" Werner was the prankster of the pair, I guessed; one partner usually is. He's the one who gives the long hours their light relief, making most of the wisecracks, setting up the occasional heavy-handed practical jokes cops play on one another.

"The neighbors heard a motorcycle roar away from here just before the car went over the edge."

"That's it?" Werner mocked.

"There's a gang of bikers in town. It could have been one of them who set Spenser up and rolled him off the edge of that rock."

"Maybe," Kennedy said. "But hell, that's nothing to go on."

"It's all you've got so far," I said. My suspension was hanging around me like a sour smell, embarrassing all of us. They wanted me gone almost as much as I wanted to be away from there.

"Yeah, well, we'll talk to her, I guess," Kennedy said. He turned away, concentrating on Kowalchuk. "See if you can break up the happy band of sightseers. Jack'll talk to this neighbor. I'll go down the funeral parlor and check on the stiff."

They all moved away, and I stood there angrily. "What about the bikers?" I asked.

Werner turned back. "We got enough on our plates without getting mixed up with a hairy bunch of trouble-makers. Why'nt you go on home? We'll drop by later when we're done at the funeral parlor."

"Okay, if that's what you want. But can you round up somebody to take care of the widow? A friend of mine is with her right now."

"We'll try," Kennedy said. And that was that.

I stood watching them, knowing how they felt. To them this wasn't the murder of a little boy. This was another chunk of duty added to a day that had gone on too long already. They were taking it the way I would have done, I reasoned with myself. What was past was past. They would enter the investigation at their point of contact, at the death of Spenser senior. If it led them back to the boy's death, they would pick up the threads of the investigation there; otherwise, they were as objective about this case as they would have been about any other. They would do the job their way. Examine the dead, question the living. That was the pattern.

126

After a moment I walked over to the cottage, Sam at my heels like a patient shadow. We went in. Werner was in the kitchen talking to Mrs. Wilson. I could see the weariness in his stoop-shouldered stance, but his tone was as bright as ever. I motioned to Fred with my head, and she came over.

"Has anybody lined up a replacement for you here?"

"Nobody's said a word so far, but somebody's got to stay here, and the neighbor doesn't want to," she whispered.

"Talk to Werner when he's through with Mrs. Wilson. I have a call to make, and then I'll be back, maybe half an hour. That okay with you?"

"Sure," she said, with no trace of annoyance. Maybe actors are more patient than the rest of us. They can wait two hours to deliver their line, then melt back behind the scenery so the show can go on. Maybe. I knew Fred pretty well from the months we'd spent together. We had become close then, had been close since, and now this spontaneous arrival of hers made me hope she wanted it to happen again.

I winked at her, and she winked back and turned her face up to me. I kissed her and left, Sam half a step behind me.

Kowalchuk was doing good work at the roadside. Most of the crowd had dispersed, heading up or down the road in knots, gossiping. The cars were filling up as well, and I had to wait for a chance to back up into a driveway and turn around before heading back to town.

I stopped outside the beer parlor. It's the Murphy's Arms Hotel, different from the real hotel, the Lakeside Tavern. It's the local watering hole, with a cocktail bar, frequented by the wealthier locals, and a beverage room, a beer hall, where most of the people in town do any serious drinking they have in mind.

The bikes were still parked outside. I left my car behind them and went in through the delivery door. It's big, covered with sheet iron to discourage shopbreaking. There hasn't been much crime since I took over here, but nobody was going to change a door for that reason.

I came in past the store area, with its mesh fence surrounding dozens of cases of beer, waiting to be whisked into the big cooler behind the bar, and walked down the short corridor.

Nick, the barkeep, was filling glasses, fitting them under the never-ending beer tap without pausing to turn it off. He looked at me and grinned and made to offer me a glass, but I shook my head, and he went on loading the aluminum tray in front of him.

I looked over his shoulder. The bar was a lot emptier than it is most summer Saturday nights. The music was as loud as ever, mindless rock from the local station interspersed with commercials for used cars and swell dinners at some hotel in Parry Sound. In one corner of the room the bikers were sitting at three tables they had pulled together and filled with glasses. I counted the men quickly. There were eleven, and no empty seats.

"Any problem with the bikers?" I asked Nick.

"Nah." He shook his head and went on filling glasses. "They're sure putting the beer away, but they ain't said a word outa line."

"Have they been here long?"

The waiter answered for me as he scooped up his tray and turned to leave. "About eight beers each, Chief. You figurin' to bust 'em for impaired driving?"

"Me and whose army?" I asked, and we all three smiled. If either one of them had heard I was suspended, they didn't comment. I'd cleaned up a few fights here that could have cost them money, or teeth. They liked me.

"Did they all come at the same time?" I asked Nick as he paused for a drag on the cigarette he had resting on the edge of the counter.

"That four at this end came in last," he said, nodding at the nearest table. "Oh, yeah, an' that guy with the red hair, he came in last of all, maybe half an hour ago."

I waited a minute longer, making sure I would be able to recognize the redheaded man later, wondering if it had been his motorcycle that had left the Spenser place earlier. When I'd made a mental picture of his appearance, including his bone structure in case he decided to shave off his beard, I nodded to Nick and left.

I stood outside for a few seconds, listening to the night sounds. Noisy music drifted out of the screened window of the bar, but under it I could hear the crickets and the repetitions of a whippoorwill and under that again the growly croaking of the bullfrogs in the reeds along the water's edge. A typical peaceful night except for the two unexplained deaths I had to solve. I corrected that one—the two deaths that had happened. Courtesy of that friend of Jas, I was off the job. Nothing to solve except a way of getting Freda back to my place. Only I couldn't content myself with doing nothing.

I got into the car and drove north, toward my house, then past it, up the side of the water to a spot about two hundred yards below the town dump. I parked on the side of the road and took out my flashlight from the glove compartment, then called Sam out with a hiss. After that I shut the door quietly and walked on up toward the dump.

Sam shadowed me, and I kept to the road for most of the way, then moved off into the sparse bush that crowds the roadside. I had a plan, and I wanted to put it into action, silently if possible.

It took me five careful minutes to make the last hundred yards to the back of the dump; then I worked around it to the back of the field where the bikers were camping. I pointed my finger at Sam, and he sank into a sit, still as a statue in the faint moonlight.

I crouched and looked at the tents in the field. There were three of them, two big ones, the kind Boy Scouts set up as mess tents, and one small one. I guessed they had established a dormitory in one of the big ones, perhaps their mess arrangements in the second. The third was a private tent for the leader of the pack. I thought back over the faces I had seen in the beverage room. No, he hadn't been there. He was probably back here with the woman from the van he had been driving when he came into town. I thought about it for a moment, then sank to my belly and began the crawl to the tents, about forty yards away.

It took me a couple of minutes, moving more and more carefully as I got closer to the tents and to the fire that still glowed, burned down now from its earlier blaze. Mosquitoes swarmed on my face and bare hands, and I let them bite, not wanting to risk the noise that moving them would make. Blinking kept them out of my eyes, and I moved my face muscles constantly, trying to shed them, the way a horse might flick its skin.

I was five yards from the nearest tent when I heard the voice and froze. The words didn't register as quickly as the tone. It was playful. "Hey, c'm'ere." The kind of voice a relaxed man might use to his girlfriend on an intimate evening.

There was an answer, high and light, pitched too soft for me to understand. Then the original voice growled again, gurgling over its playful laughter. "Aw, c'mon."

I inched closer, against the side of one of the big tents. And this time I heard the second voice clearly. It was coming from in front of the same tent, close to the fire. "You're terrible, you know that?" it said brightly, and my hair prickled on my neck. It wasn't the voice of a woman. It was a young man's voice.

The other man was still amused, but the words were sterner. "Now don' go playin' hard'a'get or I'm gonna have to wail the tar outa ya."

"Not again," the boy's voice said mockingly, and then the man laughed, and I saw a shadow grow on the tent wall in front of me as the boy by the fire stood up and moved away to my right, toward the small tent. I could make out his blond hair.

I waited until I heard the sound of canvas brushing over his back. He had gone into the small tent. Good. He would be there for a few minutes, most likely. I had a chance to look around.

I crawled around to the front of the tent I had reached and swore silently. It was the mess tent. The other lay to my left, away from the gang leader, who was laughing playfully now. I rose into a crouch and darted over to the other tent. It was sealed in front to keep the mosquitoes out, and I worked quickly to unfasten the net and slip inside.

Here it was almost totally black. The dim moon didn't penetrate the canvas, and except for some flickerings at the open front, the firelight didn't reach, either. I took my flashlight from the pocket of my windbreaker and covered the glass with my left hand, letting only a splinter of light come out between my slightly parted fingers.

In its glow I could see that groundsheets had been laid out all around the tent. There was no bedding, but that didn't surprise me. Bikers, along with Shriners and every other male group at a convention, pride themselves on staying awake for the whole session. They would drink until they dropped. But I wondered about the groundsheets. If they weren't going to sleep, why would they need groundsheets? There were no women here, no apparent reason for comfort.

There were saddlebags, however, and I went to each one in turn, checking the contents, looking for a boot with a heel that matched the mark I had seen in the Corbetts' cottage. My heart was racing as I worked. The gang could swing into the field at any moment. If they did, I was in trouble.

I didn't find any boots, just clothes and oddments, until I came to the last bag. This one didn't have boots, either, but it had a TV camera, a Panasonic with another machine with switches and dials. It held the tape, I guessed. I squatted, frowning. Why would they have it with them? To take pictures of their weekend to screen at the clubhouse on the long winter evenings? That was doubtful. Puzzled, I dug deeper and came up with a videotape cassette, VCR format.

Not quite sure why, I slipped the tape into the pocket of my windbreaker and repacked the bag.

I switched off the light and went to the mouth of the tent. It was still quiet outside, but I wasn't sure the man and boy in the other tent hadn't come back outside. I slithered out, keeping low to the deck. Nobody shouted. Nothing moved that I could hear. I was still safe. I began fastening the flap of the tent just as the sound of motorcycles hit me. The gang was coming back.

I fastened the last of the ties and ducked around the back of the tent, not bothering to check around me. It was too late for much stealth. Keeping on tiptoe, I ran for the cover of the bush as the headlights of the approaching bikes pulled around the last corner south of the camp. I rolled the last three yards into the undergrowth and lay for a moment, heart pounding, watching the play of the lights over the tents behind me. Then, one by one, the motors died, and voices took over, noisy half-drunk voices. And then I heard the other voices mixed in, quieter but shrill. Women. They had women with them. Maybe that was what they had been waiting for at the beer parlor. Their van had gone somewhere to pick up their womenfolk. Now they were ready to party. It was time to get away.

I sat up and hissed to Sam. He came to me, staying perfectly silent, looking at me, then back to the tents, wondering what work I had for him next. I rubbed his neck softly, then stood up and made my way back around the dump and down to the road.

My car was still in place, with all four tires inflated. The gang hadn't been feeling playful. They hadn't slashed or scratched it. I got back into it with Sam beside me and started up as quietly as I could, then turned and headed back toward my own place. But as I drove I realized I would have to take one more step in my illegal procedure. To complete the circle of investigation I had to look at the cassette I'd captured. It might bring me a step closer to the solution to the boy's murder.

By now it was after ten o'clock, early by city standards but past the bedtime of most cottagers and even of most of our locals in the Harbour. That left me wondering who might still be up and would also have a video player to lend me.

The answer was Jack Wales. Ever since his wife ran off with some salesman, Jack has lived for his TV. He was the first person around to get a dish aerial installed, and I guessed he also had VCR of some kind.

I drove down the side road, through town, and out to the highway. The motel had its "Vacancy" light still shining in the front office, although most of the units already had their lights out.

I rang the bell and waited, and after a minute Jack appeared, surprised to see me. "Hi, Chief. What brings you up here so late?"

"I've got a favor to ask, Jack. I've got a videotape to view. It's evidence."

"Oh, sure, come on in." He ushered me through the office to his living quarters behind. They were like the rooms of a million other single men, including me. Tidy, because tidy is easier than dirty in the long run, and sparely furnished. His TV was playing some rock video. He apologized for it. "I was just watching a movie on the machine. Here, I'll take the tape out for you."

I watched him as he fiddled with his machine, happy as only the real gadget lover ever gets. He laid his tape on top of the TV set and held out his hand. I gave him the biker's tape, and he put it in. Then I told him, "This may be rough, Jack. Maybe you shouldn't see it."

"Rough?" He laughed shortly. "You should see some of the films these days."

"Yeah, but this is evidence. Maybe for your own sake you should step outside for a moment while I take a quick look."

He sniffed. "Well, you're the copper an' all that. If you think it'd be smart, I'll go make some coffee." He turned, then paused. "Got time for a cup?"

"Please," I told him, and he left. I pressed the start button, and the rock video mercifully died. There was a black-and-white flutter, and then the tape began, no titles, no credits, just action.

It was the kind of action I'd seen before as a young marine on liberty in San Diego. A pretty, hard-faced girl was undressing. She turned to the doorway and put her hand over her mouth. A man came in and began to undress, and she started to get excited, and away went the familiar pornographic story. At nineteen I had found them exciting. Now it just looked ugly. I flicked to fast forward and endured the howling of the rock video for thirty seconds before trying again.

They were still together, and I was about to fast forward again when suddenly the camera moved, revealing the open door. A young man came through it. The man on the bed stood up, and then the scenario changed its sexual orientation.

I was looking at it, horrified, not at the action, it was as false in its own way as the girl's seduction earlier. Then I heard Jack Wales's chirpy English voice behind me. "Stone the crows, Chief. You said it was gonna be rough, but this is really rough."

I stood up and pressed the stop button, then the rewind. "It could get a lot rougher, Jack," I told him quietly.

The rock video thrashed around us like a storm, and I flicked the volume down. There was no doubt about it. The boy in the second sequence was the same one who had autographed the picture for Kennie Spenser. Reg Waters.

THIRTEEN

♦

Jack was holding two cups of coffee, and he collected himself and handed one to me. I thanked him and sat down on the couch.

Jack cleared his throat harshly. "Where'd you get that tape? I mean, they got some pornie stuff in Parry Sound; nothing serious, you know, but hot. But, I mean ..." His voice died away, and he took a slurp of his coffee.

"Like I said, it's evidence. If you can forget you saw it, you'll be doing us both a favor."

I sipped my coffee, and my stomach growled, reminding me how long it was since the Mexican food with Freda. I glanced at my watch. Quarter to eleven. Ideal timing if we wanted to raid those bikers and search their camp. They would be awake but off balance from the beer plus the uppers they would be taking to stay awake. It would take a couple hours before I could get a search warrant. I corrected myself—before the OPP could get a warrant. The bikers would be woozy by then, vulnerable.

Jack pumped me, glad I was there. I was more exciting than *The Cotton Club*. "Sure, I won't say anything, Chief, you know that. But what's it evidence of? Is somebody in town selling this stuff?"

"Yes." It was simpler than the whole answer. "You don't know their name, but it's all got to be kept quiet." Especially the fact that I had appeared on his doorstep

135

with the tape two hours before the police could officially raid the biker's camp, but he didn't have to know that, either.

He gave up on playing detective. Instead, he started telling me about pornie shows he had seen, in the British army, in Hamburg after the war. He described them lovingly while I sipped coffee and nodded and thought about what had to be done.

I set down my cup, and stood up, and retrieved the videotape. "Well, I have to report this. Thanks for the coffee and the use of the machine, Jack."

He stood up with me, smirking. "If you wanna go through the whole thing or if you've got any others, feel free. I mean, anytime, eh."

"I doubt it, but I'll keep it in mind. Meantime, thanks again." I went ahead of him, out to the front door. A station wagon with a canoe on the top was pulling in. "Your lucky night," I told him. "Here's another customer."

"Good. Then I can put the sign off and watch the rest of the movie in peace." He slipped behind the counter of the office as I went out, passing a tired-looking young man in the doorway.

There were two OPP cars outside my police station. I parked beside them, leaving Sam in the car, and went into the office. The two detectives were behind the counter with a new OPP uniformed man. The guard had changed; the kid had gone off shift. The constable looked up officiously. "Yes, sir, something we can do for you?"

I nodded to him and spoke to Kennedy, who was sitting at the counter, looking through the folder that contained my notes. "I've found a connection between the murdered boy and those bikers."

The uniformed man opened his mouth to speak, but Kennedy turned and looked at him, smiling blandly. "Just get the phone if it goes, okay? This is the chief of this place. You're in his office."

136

The uniformed man gave a sick grin and turned away. Kennedy turned back to me, putting both hands on the countertop. "You've sure got a bee in your bonnet about those bikers," he said.

I took the folder from the counter and flipped to the photograph of the kid. "This kid, he's hanging around with them. I got my hands on a pornie they made. It's got him in it."

Now Werner got up from the desk where he had been writing in his notebook. "Coincidence," he said, but his voice was careful. He didn't disbelieve me. He needed convincing, that was all.

I pulled out the videotape. "This is the tape. The kid's on it. And there's a blond boy hanging around the camp where the bikers are staying. Might be the same kid. He's got something going with the head of the outfit. They were at it while the rest of the gang was in the beer parlor earlier on."

"You mean you wen' into their camp on your own?" Werner asked. He didn't wait for an answer. "You got some neck, fella." He grinned and hung on the obvious hooker. "But you won't have long if they find out you were up there."

"They didn't. One of them had a video camera and this tape. I souvenired it, and the kid's on it. And another thing, he's also a friend of the Spenser boy, and we all know what happened to him. I figure the bikers did it."

"They could have," Kennedy admitted. "But murder's a bit heavy, even for them. I mean, they could have assaulted the kid and never given it a second thought, but killing him, that's not typical."

"I didn't say I had all the answers," I began, but Werner cut me off again.

"You don't. What you've got is a whole lot more questions." He laughed and then finished his sentence with the word "Chief" tagged on without irony. He had just wiped out my suspension. As long as these two were working, I was back on the case. That was good news.

"Well, there is one other connection. This blond kid—his name is Reg Waters. He's a grandson of the Corbetts, the people whose place was trashed."

"And?" Werner prompted.

"And my dog tracked the dead boy to a boat at their place."

All three of them were looking at me now. Kennedy spoke first. "This is getting complicated," he said. "Like, you say there's footprints in the Corbett place that looked like biker boots. Now we find their grandson hangs around with bikers. The dead kid knew him." He rubbed his hand over his hair wearily. "It's all so goddamn close I can taste it."

"Yeah, but where do we go from here?" Werner said. "You know's well as I do we can't raid the bikers without some good reason. Otherwise some shyster'll throw us out of court."

"That's the truth," Kennedy said. "Even if we say we're looking for drugs or some such bullshit, we can't take their videotapes and we can't look at their boots even to see if the heel print matches."

"I wonder if the kid was murdered in that cottage." I let the suggestion lie there, and we all looked at one another and thought about it.

"We won't know until we've examined the place," Kennedy argued. "Hell, I'm sick of waiting for the C.I.B. guys. Let's get up there and look."

"We need photographs. We can check for fingerprints later, but we need shots of the floor and the mess before we track all through there," Werner said.

Kennedy frowned. "Isn't there a photographer in town? A civilian?"

"Yes, guy called Carl Simmonds. He's helped me before."

Werner moved toward the flap on the counter. "Let's go get him outa bed and head up there."

"Let me use the phone." I came through the counter flap and picked up the phone on my desk. Carl answered on the third ring. "Hi, Carl, Reid Bennett. We need some photographic help in a hurry. Are you up to it?"

He was. I looked at the detectives and nodded. "Okay, so get your stuff ready. I'll come by for you in five. Thanks."

The others were waiting at the door. Their tiredness was passing, and they looked ready for a full night's work. They led the way to their car, but I told them no, I would go in my own, bringing Sam along.

"Sam?" Werner asked. "Who's he?"

"My dog," I explained. "He's completely trained. If we need some tracking done, he'll do it. And if we need backup, he's the equal of a couple of guys."

"Where's he been all my life." Werner sighed and Kennedy laughed. They got into one of the OPP cars, and I got into mine and led them up to Carl's house. I stopped there, and as soon as I got out, he came out of the doorway, carrying his equipment, a camera bag and a tripod.

"What's the case?" he asked in a businesslike voice as he got in beside me.

"The homicide. The Corbett place was broken into, vandalized, and I found a heel print there. We want to go in and check, but we need photographs of footprints in the mess on the floor."

"Fine. I've got a ruler in my bag to include in shots like that," he said. "I've been doing some reading since the last time I helped you, and I know that scale is important, so I'm all prepared."

"Good," I said briefly. "We need all the help we can get."

We drove in silence past the biker's camp where the fire was blazing again and men were capering around, drinking beer from bottles and listening to rock music so loud we could hear it over the sound of the car engine, from fifty yards down the road. I slowed slightly to look but couldn't see any women, or the blond boy I'd seen earlier. Probably they were all in the big tent.

I pulled up to the door of the Corbett place, and the OPP car pulled in behind me, switching off its lights as I got out and called Sam over the seat and out to sit beside the back door. I waited for the detectives and introduced them to Carl, who nodded briskly without speaking. Then I took out my flashlight and opened the door.

Werner and Kennedy came to the doorway and looked inside. They didn't comment on the mess. Trouble is routine to policemen. All they wanted was evidence. Werner saw the footprint first. "There, clear as a bell," he said happily.

"They have electricity," Carl said. "I was here once to shoot a wedding anniversary for them. They have lights, but you have to find the fuse box first and put the main switch on. Mrs. Corbett told me. They switch everything off while they're away."

"You lead the way," Kennedy said to me. "See if you can find the fuse box and get some light on the subject."

It took a minute to locate the fuse box inside the closet beside the front door. I turned it on, then the kitchen light, and stood aside carefully as the others came in, keeping clear of the mess on the floor. Carl was the only one to comment on it. "This is disgusting," he said, and I saw Werner and Kennedy exchange glances as he hissed on the esses.

We watched as he got out his camera and a filter and then the twelve-inch ruler. He set it down carefully beside the heel print and crouched to take two shots of the composition. He looked up quickly. "Got it. What's next?"

"Take some pictures of the whole scene," Kennedy commanded. "I want a record of what it looks like in case we close any doors or make any changes."

"Sure." Carl adjusted his focus and stood up, quartering the room with shots, then crouched and did the same thing from the level of his knees, below the top of the table. "There," he said brightly. "It's on the record."

Kennedy was rubbing his chin. "You know, that's the only print I can see. It looks like the guy who did it got right to the door, then threw the flour."

"That's the way the flour fell," I agreed. "It's as if it all came from this side of the room. But the empty bag's in the corner."

"We'll get it printed when the C.I.B. guys turn up," Werner promised. "Let's look around the rest of the place."

"You guys go ahead," I said, but Werner shook his head.

"No, you're in this, as well. Don't let that asshole Anderson upset you. You'll be reinstated as soon as the hearing's over."

"I hope you're right," I said. "This happened to me once before, and I ended up quitting."

"This isn't Toronto," Kennedy said. "The people here know what bikers are like, and they want them gone. They'll give you a medal for stopping one of them."

"We'll see," I said, but I felt better. I knew he was telling the truth. The commission would understand what had happened. And in the meantime, I could be back on the investigation. It felt good.

I led the way into the next room and switched on the light. It was a dining room. That was unusual for a summer cottage—most of them are less fancy—but Corbett's wife came from a family with money. She had inherited the house, a big old place like they don't build anymore. But now it was wrecked. The fine walnut table was split across, the pieces tossed aside, scarred with the crescent-moon indentations of kicks from steel-toed boots. All the plates had been pulled out of the antique breakfront and thrown against the wall, shattering a mirror and a picture of the Corbetts as they had been thirty years earlier.

Kennedy looked over my shoulder. "This looks deliberate," he said. "Look at that table. That was worked over by somebody with a lot to prove."

Carl was standing behind him, camera poised, but instead of taking pictures, he stooped and picked up a fragment of broken plate and turned it over. "Genuine Quimper. Antique, too. Beautiful. Just smashed, like that." He dropped the fragment and raised his camera to his eye as if it were a gun and the vandals were in his sights. I stood back, and he quartered the room, then stooped and did the same at floor level.

We spent five minutes checking the room, making sure nobody had left anything more substantial than fingerprints there. They hadn't. The contents of the drawers were strewn around, and someone had used the carving knife to slash the seats of all the antique upholstered chairs, but only the damage remained.

"What's upstairs?" Werner asked.

"Bedrooms. I hate to think what they've done up there," Carl said.

Werner nodded to me. "Let's see." I clicked on the hall light and climbed the open stairway. It led to a landing that divided the house from side to side. A picture had been torn off the wall and broken, and the little rug was scuffed into a corner, but nothing else had been done. I opened the front bedroom door and looked in on a snowstorm of feathers, which had drifted down over everything in the room, all the rubble of broken furniture.

Kennedy said, "They must've had a duvet in here." We stood and looked around while Carl photographed everything. Then I spent a few moments checking around the ruins. The empty shell of the duvet was lying in one corner, and I picked it up and looked it over. It was white and fine, some kind of satin material. There were no noticeable stains.

Kennedy was staring around the room, and suddenly he said, "You notice something funny?"

"What?" Werner and I asked together.

"The drapes are still drawn," Kennedy said. He went to the window and lifted them. "They're heavy; insulation drapes by the feel of it. I'll bet it was black as hell in here without the lights on. Even if they did this in daylight."

"Maybe they put the lights on," Werner said.

"That means they knew where the main switch is," I said.

Werner played devil's advocate. "Hell, they had all the time they wanted in here. They'd have found the switch. And even if they didn't, this room faces the water. There'd have been plenty of light."

"Not through these things," Kennedy said, rubbing the fabric of the drapes between his fingers. "This room must've been black as night."

"It was when I found the back door open," I said. "And that's something else. I didn't mention it, but there's no sign of a break-in. It looked to me as if somebody found the door open. But what you say could mean they knew the place well, maybe even had a key."

"Maybe the bikers, or whoever it was, opened the drapes while they were here," Werner suggested, but when we glanced at him he shook his head. "Naah—they would've torn them down if they wanted light."

He and Kennedy were staring at one another blindly, the locked eyes of longtime partners mulling over the same idea.

"You put that together with somebody probably knowing about the lights and it comes up grandson," Werner said, and Kennedy nodded.

We traipsed through to the other bedroom. For some reason it wasn't as badly damaged as the first. There was a three-quarter-width bed, but it had only been thrown aside. Nobody had slashed it. We took our pictures and looked it over. There was a Blue Jays pennant on the floor and a torn poster of some rock singer.

"I guess this is the grandson's room. I'm pretty sure it was him hanging out at the biker's camp," I said.

Werner snorted out a short laugh. "Takes all sorts. Why'd he want to hang out there unless he was a real little rounder?"

The only room left to examine was the bathroom. Kennedy opened the door and whistled with surprise. "Ugly bastards," he said. "See for yourself."

I moved past him and checked. The porcelain sink had been shattered, and somebody had tried to do the same with the bathtub, smashing ugly gouges out of the enamel. The towels had been thrown around, but a laundry hamper was still standing. I opened it and checked inside. There was a towel inside it, but it didn't feel damp. It might have been left there since the Corbetts' last visit.

I held it up without speaking, and Werner grunted. Then we stood and looked at one another. "What next?" I asked at last. "Are we going to move in on the bikers?"

"Sounds like sense to me. I'll call from the car, and we'll drive back to Carl's place and wait for reinforcements while he works," Kennedy said. "We'll leave this place. There's nothing more to do until the C.I.B. can get here."

We went out, turning off the main switch under the stairs. Carl was already outside, standing beside my car. He was winding the film off his camera, and he didn't look at me. I said nothing, and we got into the car, Sam in the backseat.

We drove for a minute or so in silence, then came within earshot of the bikers' campground as we approached a bend. Carl spoke for the first time. "Listen to that. Led Zeppelin. Nobody listens to that garbage anymore."

"It's not my style," I said, just to be friendly. Then I froze as a scream rose above the rock music, the terrified scream of a woman in real trouble.

FOURTEEN

♦

I goosed the car around the corner and angled in over the field, my headlights picking up men frozen in the postures of drinking and laughing, still as statues for a moment as the scream pealed out. Then a woman ran out of the main tent with a man chasing her. The bikers all cheered and roared, bending from the waist, laughing and pointing as she sprinted for the road.

One of them moved out to cut her off, and she shoved at him and ran on until the man behind her caught up and dragged her off her feet by the hair. His boot swung back to kick her, but my shout stopped him. "Police. Hold it right there."

He turned toward me, crouching to peer down the beam of my headlights. The other gang members ran for their bikes, two or three more of them tumbling out of the door of the tent. The guy with the girl snatched her up with one hand and sheltered behind her, one hand still on her hair.

By now I was out of the car, Sam at my heels. The headlights of the OPP car played over us like lightning flashes as Werner and Kennedy bumped over the uneven ground behind me. I was ten paces from the biker when I heard their car doors open behind me. I had backup.

The biker shouted again. "Stand back or she's gone."

Werner and Kennedy were on each side of me now,

guns drawn. "You do, punk, an' I'll shoot your goddamn leg off," Kennedy said.

The biker swore again and dropped his hand to his belt. But it came up again in an instant, holding a knife. "You take me, she dies. Then you die," he said. His voice was flat. He was bracing himself, knowing his brothers would expect him to do what he said no matter what happened. He was in over his head now.

Sam was prancing in front of him, out of range of his feet, waiting for my command. I didn't give one. The odds were still against the girl. One of the motorbikes started up, and Kennedy spun on his heel, covering the shadowy gang of men, who were all on their bikes, revving, shouting.

"One of them's got a sawed-off shotgun," I hissed at him. "Don't let them get close."

Werner was still covering the biker with the girl. It was a Mexican standoff. I knew the man would kill her and do his ten years for it sooner than lose face. And I couldn't disarm him quickly enough to stop him. Even Sam couldn't, and I doubted if Kennedy or Werner were good enough with their guns to take him out before he could cut.

I moved away to my left, trying to get behind the biker but leaving Werner a clear shot. But I knew he wouldn't if there was any chance of cooling the situation out. We couldn't risk the chance that the biker would stab the girl, even with a bullet in him.

He shouted at me, "Where you goin'?" But his eyes were locked on the hypnotic shape of the detective's .38. I ignored him and the roars of the other bikers, moving slowly back and around, behind him.

Now he glanced back quickly, as if he were checking traffic, and edged around slightly, torn between fear of me and fear of giving Werner an unscreened shot at him. His voice was hoarse.

"You grab me, I shiv her right in the throat, copper.

Back off." Maybe he still thought the others would come roaring to his rescue, but Kennedy was standing in front of them, armed. They knew they would be the first casualties if they interfered. So they did what people do the world over. Spectators at the show, with nothing personal on the line, they laughed and roared encouragement to the biker.

I edged forward an inch at a time, talking to him in a voice I would have used on a frightened animal. "Come on, now. There has to be a better way to handle this. Let her go."

There isn't any procedure written for occasions like this. You're expected to act as you see fit to protect victims. This means talking calmly to the guy with the hostage and hoping he won't freak out. Sometimes it works, after hours in which you build up some kind of rapport with the guy. But that only happens when you've got him isolated inside a building somewhere with no distractions. Here we had a dozen men as high as he was shouting for him to go for it. I was afraid he might.

Werner was perfect. He played the good guy. "Come on, now, let her go. We can sort this out, no trouble."

One of the others shouted, "Don' take no notice. That bitch got no right runnin' out."

I inched to within a yard of him. The girl was struggling, screaming, and he hissed at her. "Keep still, bitch. You started this." She stopped squirming, and he glanced over his shoulder again, showing a gap-toothed grin that would have been cute if he'd been six years old. "Back off. She's cool, long as you go away. We was only havin' fun, wasn't we, honey?"

The girl screamed again. "Don' go. Don' leave me here."

Then Werner said, "Okay, don't worry. We're just having a nice talk with the fellah here. You just keep quiet a minute and everything's gonna be fine."

I didn't think so. The biker was outlined against the headlights of the police car. He was big, barrel-chested, and his arms were flinching, almost convulsively. I judged he was high on something other than beer, speed, possibly, or angel dust. He was unstable. We would never talk him down. He would slash first, reacting to the tension and the extra adrenaline in his system. If we didn't neutralize him, the girl was dead. I had to take him.

I moved in, swinging both hands up from my sides and slamming the palms on both of the biker's ears simultaneously in a double ear box. He fell down, not even writhing. The girl shrieked, then ran, on past Werner toward the lights of the OPP car.

I prodded the biker with my foot, and he rolled faceup, but his eyes were closed, and he made no sound. I stooped and picked him up, throwing him over my back like a sack as the roar of motorcycles filled the night, drowning out the rock music. Werner and Kennedy both dropped to their knees, aiming their guns at the bikes. One of them roared forward, and Kennedy fired, low, not trying to hit the machine, just for effect, and suddenly the camp emptied. Bike after bike, and then the van roared away from us toward the side of the dump, through the gates and out the other side toward town.

Kennedy and Werner stood up shakily. Werner put his gun away, and Kennedy trotted to the scout car. I heard him calling the dispatcher as I staggered toward him under the weight of the unconscious biker. Kennedy turned and saw me and hooked the back door open as he spoke. I rolled the biker into it and straightened up.

"Now we've got real trouble," I said.

Werner laughed. "What's this 'we,' paleface? This is your goddamn town. An' anyway, where'd you learn a trick like that?"

"I went to a school where that was all they taught."

Werner grinned and Kennedy said, "Help's on its way. Should be a mess of guys arriving within half an hour. In the meantime, check the story with this girl. She's in your car. We'll check the tent."

148

The girl was in the back, wearing a light jacket but still shuddering as if she were cold. I opened her door and crouched to be at her eye level. "Hi, what's your name?"

"Wendy Gauthier." She drew a deep breath and slowly stilled her trembling. I waited. Then she said, "Like they said, it was gonna be a party, Louise an' them. They said there'd be guys, but they didn't say nothin' about bikers."

"Where did you meet Louise?"

"Where I work, the Pasha's Tent, T'ranna."

I knew the name. It was a clip joint with table dancers, every legal flavor of porn, anything to pull in the young studs down the Yonge Street strip. If she worked there, she was no angel.

"So what happened tonight?" She didn't answer me, and I rephrased the question. "What made you run?"

Now she turned and looked me full in the face. She was pretty, a little spacey but nothing that would make the patrons at the Pasha's Tent object to her taking her clothes off. And her figure was good. "They said there'd be guys. Like, you know, a party's a party, but there was three o' them, an' one o' them pulled a knife."

"Who threatened you? Was it the guy who caught you, the one who had you when I got here?"

"I di'n really see him," she said. "Like he pulled my hair'n that, but I never seen him, not his face."

That's the trouble with being a knight on a white horse. Nobody notices. Three policemen had risked their necks for her, and she took it for granted. I noticed now, as my eyes grew accustomed to the dimness of the car interior, it was Carl's jacket she was wearing. She'd taken that for granted too. Ah, well, if you want applause, go into show biz. You don't get much of it doing police work. The important job now was to get her away, safely and quickly, so we could check on the bikers in case they were tearing up the town just to show we hadn't impressed them.

149

"Where do you live? You live with somebody or on your own?" I tried.

It took her about half a minute to reply. "I gotta room, eh. In town, T'ranna."

"Is there somebody there who can give you a lift home?" The bus had passed our entrance to the highway a couple of hours ago. If she couldn't scare up some wheels, she would have to wait in the station until morning.

"My boyfriend, I guess," she said.

I straightened up. "Wait here. I'll be right back."

I set Sam to keep the area around the cars, so he would raise a racket if anyone sneaked back while I was away. Then I trotted over to the tent I'd gone into earlier. I could see the glow of the police flashlights inside. I ducked into it and saw Kennedy leaning over a partly dressed girl who was lying on the ground, snoring. Another girl was standing beside her. She was in her late twenties, blond, with a vivid black streak across her scalp where the roots of her hair told the truth. She swore.

"That goddamn Wendy. Whad'd she expect? Paul Newman?"

Kennedy flicked his light away from her and onto the girl on the ground. He crouched beside her, feeling for the pulse in her throat. "Takes a licking and keeps on ticking," he said. He stood up again and turned to the other girl. "Put her clothes on," he said.

The girl swore again, and Kennedy repeated his order. "Put her clothes on. We're not taking her anywhere like that."

The girl flounced aside. "Fer Crissakes, what's the big deal? That's all she wears all day at work."

Kennedy snapped, and I realized how tense he had been out there in the showdown. "Look, lady. It wouldn't take me more than thirty seconds to book you for prostitution," he said. "But I'm feeling generous. So cover your buddy up and we'll go. Now cut the crap and do it."

He shouted the last two words, and the girl reacted. I guessed she heard more shouts than pleasantries at work. She picked up a blouse and jeans and stooped to work on her friend, muttering.

Werner was looking about him. "Which bag would you say might hold the illegal substances this young lady's been ingesting?" he asked conversationally.

I shone my light on the bag that had contained the videotape. "That one there looks promising."

"Now why didn't I think of that?" he asked. It was all a show for the girl's sake, but if she heard him, it didn't register. She just went on muttering and tugging at the blue jeans, which were going on as tight as a second skin.

Werner shone his light into the bag. "Well, what do we have here? A video camera."

"Anything else?" Kennedy asked.

"Nothing of any importance." Werner pulled out all the contents. There was a denim jacket and a pair of jeans. "Maybe we should impound these to see if these young women have to be charged with performing a lewd act in public."

This made the girl turn, blazing. "Listen, Mac. You may impress Wendy with that crap. But I know better. I didn't expect no coppers to come crashin' in on me an' my boyfriend."

"What's your boyfriend's name?" Kennedy asked her.

She was so angry she answered without thinking. "Ronnie," she said.

"Ronnie what?" Kennedy asked, and she roared back at him.

"How would I know, fer Crissakes. I just met him."

Kennedy chuckled. "Love's young dream," he said.

She had finished dressing the other girl and stood back. Kennedy and I bent and took the girl's arms, then lifted her up and walked her out to the flap of the tent. It was difficult getting her out through the narrow flap, but we managed it and started across the field, with Werner and the other girl following.

Werner delivered the girl to the car, then said, "I'll check out the other tents and the van, make sure there's nobody around."

"Good idea," Kennedy said.

Werner turned away, then stopped and drew his gun. He held it down toward the ground, and I could see he was checking the load. Then he laughed. "Hey, good job they didn't get violent. I forgot to load this goddamn thing."

We all laughed, and he fumbled in his jacket pocket and came up with the shells and thumbed them into the chambers. Kennedy turned back to me. "Take the women in your car. We've got the guy in ours. Take them right down to the station for questioning."

"Questioning for what?" the girl roared.

Kennedy turned to look back at her. "Talk nice to me. I just want to check your social calendar, see if you want a date."

She swore again but got into the car. Kennedy and I put the other girl beside her. She was beginning to come around. She sat up and mumbled. I opened the trunk and called Sam to get inside. He did, as he's trained to, and curled down, but I left the lid up and got into the front. Carl turned to look at me. "Jesus, Reid, who taught you to do what you did to that man?"

"My father. He was a commando with the Canadians at Dieppe."

"It was devastating," Carl said.

"It's a last resort," I told him. "I've never had to do it before."

The girl in the back half screamed, "You bastard!" She reached over, flailing to hit me. I stopped the car and got out and opened the rear door.

152

"You're going to the station for your own protection. That's all, but one more move out of you and you're handcuffed. You understand? Makes no difference to me. You can come quietly, or you can fight. Either way, you're coming, because you're not safe out here."

"You bastard," she said again, and burst into tears. I got back into the car and pulled away slowly, being careful for Sam's sake. Carl wanted to talk, but I glanced at him and shook my head, so he shut up. I was feeling angry with myself. There was a time when I took pride in my strength and my ability to handle bad situations. Now I just think of them as tools I have to use in my trade. Nights like this I wish I'd taken up flower arrangement instead of police work.

The bikers weren't in town, and there was no obvious damage, no excited citizens on the street, so I guessed they'd gone right through to regroup and make their plans for a comeback. The comeback was a certainty. Bikers pride themselves on being outlaws. They wouldn't sit still for the defeat we'd handed them at their campsite.

The OPP man at the station came and opened the back door when I pounded on it. He was looking tense. "Oh, it's you. I heard the bikers drive by a couple of minutes back. I was wondering if it was one of them."

"Got some company for you," I told him. "Bring them inside."

He stood aside for the women. Wendy was the first, moving slowly. I wondered how much weed she'd smoked. Then the angry girl, propping up her friend. There was only one chair out in the corridor behind the station, so I sent the OPP man to bring in two more, then sat the women down and waited for the detectives to arrive.

They pulled in a minute later and delivered their biker to the front desk. They didn't know the protocol I'd set up about using the back door for prisoners. The biker was awake now, staring about him like a crazed steer. They had handcuffed him behind his back. He roared suddenly, "I'm deaf. I can't hear nothin'. Who hit me? Which of you sonsabitches hit me?"

"Bring him out the back. We'll stick him in a cell," I instructed, and Werner steered him through the counter flap and out to the cells.

The woman from the tent screamed when she saw the blood on his head and ran over to grab him, but he shook her aside. I had to admit he was tougher than a lot of men I'd fought beside.

Werner searched him, removing another knife, then his boots and the heavy, studded belt he was wearing, and steered him gently into the cell. He unsnapped the handcuffs, and the biker sat down on the board bunk that runs along the side wall, rubbing his wrists.

"He needs a doctor," Kennedy said.

"Yeah," Werner said. "Book him first; here's his ID. He tossed the man's wallet onto the table, and Kennedy picked it up. "Jack Halloran, born 1954," he said, reading the name and coded number from the license. He turned to the OPP constable. "Get a make on him, will you?"

"What'd you figure, assault with a deadly weapon, threatening, attempted rape?" I asked.

"Yeah," Kennedy said. "All o' that good stuff, plus whatever else we can dream up. He's a real beauty. I'm glad you put him down."

The biker was looking at us, slowly studying our faces, trying to place us. He looked at me the longest. "It was you," he said. His voice was ugly, unmodulated. He couldn't hear himself and had no control over the sound. I felt sorry for him, almost.

Werner said, "I'll get that camera from the car." He left and Kennedy said, "This is getting heavy. I'll call the inspector. We don't need reinforcements so much as a little high-priced management here."

He went out and I followed him, leaving Carl and the woman alone in the back. The constable was using the phone, and he thanked the person at the other end and hung up, his excitement showing in his eyes. "You picked up a real rounder," he said. "Got a sheet long's your arm. Wounding, attempted murder, robbery. He's only been out of the pen for six months. Did his time out West."

"Swell," Kennedy said, picking up the phone. "Any warrants outstanding?"

"Nothing, Sarge." The constable looked downcast. He'd been expecting praise. His work wasn't usually this exciting. He looked at me, but I was feeling drained, and my face must have showed it. I sat and waited, not speaking, while Kennedy made his call.

He went through the usual succession of waits and finally spoke to the duty inspector. I wondered who it would be. Not Anderson, I hoped. He should be off duty by now.

"Yes, hello, Inspector," Kennedy said. "We've got a problem at Murphy's Harbour. Yeah, on top of the homicide and that guy who went off the rock. Yeah, we ran into a bunch of bikers. One of them was assaulting a woman. It got nasty. We had to draw our weapons, and one of the bikers was hurt. The local police chief, Bennett, he was helping. He put the guy down. I'd like some advice on—"

I could hear the voice rising at the other end of the line, cutting off Kennedy in mid-sentence. He waited, shifting from one foot to the other. Then he said, "No, I'm goddamned if I understand, Inspector." He stood up, holding the telephone away from his ear, his eyes blazing with anger. I could hear the telephone voice burbling out of the receiver. Finally, Kennedy said, "I'd prefer to get it in writing, Inspector, but until you get here, I'll do like you say. Yes, I hear you. Leave them alone. Right? Right. Thank you."

He hung up the phone very carefully, as if he were afraid he would break it over the edge of the table if he didn't keep control of himself. "Sonofabitch," he said. "Can you credit that? They want me to leave the bikers alone. Stay away from them. They hadn't even dispatched the guys I'd asked for."

FIFTEEN

♦

We'd all been policemen for too long to throw any tantrums. Kennedy sat down and swung his feet up on the desk. Werner laughed. I shrugged and sat on the stool behind the counter.

"Sounds as if they've got something going down with the bikers, maybe a drug bust," I said.

"Could be. That's the only reason I can see for getting a hands-off signal," Werner agreed.

"I'm not sure what it means," Kennedy said. "Except that I'm going home. We'll come back in the morning and get on with our investigation of the homicide."

He was making sense. There wasn't anything more we could do before the C.I.B. made a proper investigation of the Corbetts' cottage. We were stymied. I just set the record straight. "Okay, so what happens in the morning?"

Werner ticked off the steps I'd considered on his fingers. "First, get the C.I.B. guys to check the cottage. Second, talk to the doctor about this Spenser guy who went in the lake, see what he found out. Third, talk to the biker squad, see if they can follow up on what this gang has to do with this whole deal." He yawned. "Meanwhile, I'm going home. I've earned my dollar today."

"I'd like to talk to the Corbetts about their grandson," I said. "Maybe they already know he's hanging around with bikers, maybe not. Either way, we can find out if he knew about the key to their place, which might explain how come it was wrecked without being broken into and might also tie the kid to the killing of the Spenser boy."

"Makes sense to me," Werner said. "Can that photographer of yours have the prints for us by morning? When we've got that boot print blown up, we can start looking for the guy who was wearing it."

Kennedy yawned. "Yeah. And something else I forgot to mention in the rush to look at at that cottage. Your doctor doesn't think that Spenser drowned in the car. He wants an autopsy on him. He thinks he sees a puncture mark on the wrist. Says the guy may have been stuffed full of something that knocked him cold, stopped him breathing."

"And the neighbor heard a motorbike pulling away from there," I mused aloud. "All the pieces are together in one bag here. We just have to fit them together."

"Looks that way," Werner said. He sat down again, sprawling wearily into the spare chair. "The bikers come to town. The kid dies. Then the dad. Then we find that blond kid in a biker porno movie."

"It could be that Spenser was tied in with them," I thought out loud. "He was involved in film, just lecturing. Then there was that picture of him outside the Corbett place, with some blond inside the door. I figured it was a woman. But it could have been Reg Waters."

"You saying Spenser was gay?" Kennedy asked. His long face was pulled into a frown as if thinking cost him physical effort.

"Not necessarily. Maybe he was brought in because of his knowledge of film technique. Maybe the bikers had something on him. Caught him with a woman, supplied him with coke. I don't know. It doesn't take much to tie up a guy in a public position like his."

"Any clown can point a camera at something these days," Werner objected. "They advertise those video cameras everywhere. Why'd anybody need an expert to show them what to do?"

"Beats the hell outa me," Kennedy said. "But it's still tight, isn't it? We got the Spensers, the Corbetts, and the bikers all in one town and all hell breaks loose."

Werner stood up. "It's gonna make a lot more sense when I've had a few hours' sleep. Let's go home, Bert."

Kennedy stretched. "Best idea you've had since eight this morning. Think of it yourself, did you?"

I stood up with them. "Just one thing. We can't leave the Spenser woman on her own. How about you run her to your station and somebody else can take her down to Toronto?"

Werner laughed. "We're the OPP, not Greyhound Coach."

"Come on. She's on her own except for my friend. Don't make me sleep over there tonight."

"Yeah, makes sense, I guess," Werner said. "There wasn't a policewoman on duty, and you can't leave a guy with her all night."

"I guess not," Kennedy said. "If she goes and jumps off that rock, we'll be here a goddamn month."

"What about the women out back? What happens to them?"

Werner looked at me. "Let's see if they can get home. Maybe one of them's got a boyfriend." He turned to the constable, who was soaking up every word. "Can I count on you to take a good statement from the one we helped?"

"Sure, Sarge, no sweat. What happened?"

Werner filled him in, and he nodded and asked, "An' what about the biker in the cells? You think his buddies are gonna come back here for him?"

Kennedy groaned. "That bastard. I forgot about him. I guess he oughta see a doctor. We're charging him with attempted rape, assault, resist arrest, threatening, weapon dangerous to the public peace." He glanced at me. "Anything else you can think of?"

159

"Not offhand. But I figure we should keep him inside. In the hospital, probably. I don't want him bailed out and back here. These guys don't take a thing like this lying down."

Werner swore. "Sometimes I wonder why I didn't join the goddamn fire department. They just put the fire out and go home. We're stuck tyin' up loose ends till hell freezes over."

"If you can't take a joke, you shouldn't have joined," Kennedy told him. "Reid, maybe you'll stay in charge here, will you? I'll send a car over to take the biker to the hospital in Sundridge. You supervise the statements and laying the charges against the biker. Then call it a day. We'll talk to you in the morning."

"Sounds fair. Be sure to send Freda back here when you get to the Spenser place. I want to keep an eye on her, with these bikers around."

"Just an eye?" Werner laughed. "You're getting old, kiddo."

He raised one arm to me, and Kennedy nodded and they left, slouching wearily toward their car and a few hours' sleep before getting back on the treadmill at eight a.m. The OPP constable said, "So, okay, Chief, what about the biker?"

"Let's talk to the women first, get that one sorted out," I suggested. "Bring them and the photographer in, please."

He went out the back for the others, and I sat down in front of the office typewriter. The three women came in angrily. The sleeping beauty was awake now, hung over from whatever she'd taken, spitting fury.

"Why're we being kept here?" she started.

"Sit down, please."

She spluttered, but they all sat. I spoke to Carl, who was standing behind them. "Carl, can you print up your photographs, please, give us enlargements on that boot print and anything else that looks important? We'd like them in the morning, if you could manage it."

160

"A pleasure," he said. He looked strained and nervous. I guessed the events of the day were digging out the old memories of his own loss and the crime he had committed afterward. He nodded to the OPP man and headed for the front counter. "I'll have them to you in the morning, eight o'clock."

"Listen, you don't have to wait for me. The constable will run you up to your house."

Carl protested, but I could see how tired he was. I nodded to the OPP man. "Could you do that, please. This gentleman will show you where he lives."

They left, and I swung my chair to face the women. "Here's what's going to happen. I need a statement from you, Wendy. I want to hear what happened in that tent. After that, you're free to go. If any one of you can round up a ride home, that's fine. Otherwise, you can walk out of here or crash in the cells. Suit yourself."

Sleeping Beauty swore. "I'm not stayin' in no goddamn tank. Gimme the phone."

She picked it up and phoned, long distance, waking up somebody called Chuck. They had a brief shouting match while I wound a statement form into the typewriter and started questioning the woman I'd rescued. "Okay. What happened in that tent?"

Wendy opened her mouth to speak, but the second woman beat her to it. "Don't you say nothin'. These guys'll drag you into court; then Jack 'n them'll get mad at you. Least's 'll happen is you won't have no job. An' you could wind up dead."

It worked. The girl looked at me, then at the floor, then mumbled, "Nothin' much happened. Like it was a party 'n I got scared, but I don' wanna make no complaint or nothin'."

"You're already involved," I argued quietly, but she shook her head.

"Maybe. But I don't wanna say nothin'."

161

"All right, then. Why don't the three of you sit over there on the bench and wait for your ride."

I was weary myself. It didn't make much difference to my case whether she spoke or not. I had enough eyewitness evidence, of my own and from the other policemen, to make the case against the biker. I took the statement form out of the typewriter and put in an arrest form. Then I sat and thought about the charges against him. All the charges Werner had mentioned, plus forcible confinement. I listed them all. The crown attorney could drop any he didn't care for once we got the case to court. All I wanted was to have enough on paper to keep the biker in custody overnight and to prevent his pulling the same stunt that Murdoch's buddy had pulled. I didn't need any more complaints against me for excessive use of force.

The three women were talking quietly, a low conversation full of the hissing that comes from starting every sentence with "I says to him." It was almost peaceful, and I was typing out my charge contentedly when the phone rang. I picked it up and said, "Murphy's Harbour Police."

It was Freda. I recognized her voice but not her tone. This wasn't the breezy woman who had made me laugh since morning. She was scared. "Reid, somebody wants to talk to you," she said.

I sat up very straight and listened as the phone rustled from hand to hand and a man's voice said, "Bennett. We got the broads, both o' them. You do what we say or they're in big trouble."

SIXTEEN

♦

I felt as if I were falling. The sounds of the room faded in and out with a solid whoosh-whoosh-whoosh that jolted my eardrums. I could see the faces of the bikers, the way they had laughed when one of them chased a terrified woman. And now they had Freda and Spenser's widow.

The same voice said, "You listenin', Bennett?"

"Yes, I'm listening."

"Good. Now I tell you what you're gonna do, or these two're gonna wish they was dead."

"I said I'm listening."

The man at the other end chuckled. "Yeah, I figured you would," he said. "Now you took some stuff from our tent."

"Some tapes and a camera," I said easily. "Yeah, it's all here."

"We want it back," the voice said, and before I could answer, he went on. "An' somethin' else. We want somethin' out of a house in Toronto."

"How can I get that?" I made my tone angry. I've been in hostage negotiations before; you have to keep them off balance. Everything has to seem like a favor; otherwise, they don't bother bargaining at all.

"Just do it, brother," the man said. He didn't sound menacing. He didn't have to. My imagination was racing ahead of him. I could see Freda, warm and beautiful, a butterfly surrounded by roaches.

"I'll think of something. What is it you want?"

"Good," he said. "Now you're talkin' sense. What we want is a file cabinet. It's gray metal. Got two drawers in it, legal size. Y'unnerstan'?"

"Where is it?"

"It's in the basement at two twenty-seven Marlborough Drive, North York." He turned aside to speak to someone else. I didn't catch the exchange, but after a moment he came back on. "That's the Yonge, Finch area." I knew. It was the Spenser house. I'd taken their address earlier. I wondered why the bikers were asking me to bring the cabinet to them. Were they afraid of going to Toronto? Were they pressed for time? I acted stupid, looking for anything that would help me find them and get Freda away. "It's gonna take me three hours to drive down there, three hours back. Hell, you could do it quicker yourself."

The first hint of anger snapped into his voice. "Smarten up, asshole. You call somebody down in T'rannah. They pick up the item for us and deliver it up here pronto. Got that?"

"Oh, yeah, I got you. But it's going to take me half an hour to round somebody up to get it. Then it will take another three hours to deliver it up here. Where do I bring it?"

"We'll tell you," he said.

I leaned on him as far as I dared, keeping my voice businesslike. "Meantime, you stay away from the women. Otherwise, there's no deal, I trash this stuff you want."

He laughed. "Oh, you won't do that. I know you won't. This is a nice-lookin' momma. You wouldn't want some bad man playin' rough with her, would you?" He laughed, then said, "Here, tell her how much you miss her."

The phone rustled, and Freda spoke: "Reid?"

"Yeah, Fred. Where are you?"

164

I could hear the phone being moved, torn out of her hands, but not before she had a chance to speak to me, almost sobbing. "Be brave, Reid. Be brave."

The same man spoke again. "Lissen, Bennett. Don' get cute. Just do like we say. Otherwise, we party."

"Two twenty-seven Marlborough, Yonge, Finch area. Gray metal two-drawer file cabinet. Don't worry, I'll get it. How do I get in touch?"

"You stay put is how," the voice said harshly. "I'll ring this number anytime I want, an' I wanna hear your voice every time I do. Forget about playin' hero. This ain't 'Nam. You stay put an' your chickieboo stays the way she is. You jerk us around an' she gets it."

I've heard enough threats from enough angry men that I knew the worst thing I could do was bluster. I kept my voice calm as I said, "Okay, I stay put and this whole deal is business. Let's keep it that way. Now what about the rest of your property?"

"One video camera, seven videotapes. You deliver them when you deliver the file cabinet." The voice sank for a moment as he cleared his throat. "An' don't go pokin' your nose into any of them tapes. Ya got that?"

"Yeah, sure." I made my tone impatient. You have to keep some pretense of control no matter how many trumps they hold.

"What if something gets screwed up, like my errand boy gets a flat or something?"

"Make sure he don't," the voice said. "I'll call you back. Now start movin'. You got three an a half hours before party time."

He hung up. I put the phone down and sat staring at it, the stare of combat fatigue. What could I do?

I reached into the drawer for my phone book. Irv Goldman's number was there, and I dialed him, waking up Dianne, his wife.

"I'm sorry Dianne, this is Reid Bennett, I have to talk to Irv—it's an emergency."

A second later he was on the line, his voice thick with sleep. "What's up, Reid?"

I told him, and he took over the Toronto end of the business. He would call the police, explain the circumstances, and break into the Spensers' house to take the file cabinet. Then he would bring it north. He would bring a neighbor of his, another copper. They would be armed, for whatever good that might do.

I thanked him and called the OPP. After a minute or so they gave me the home number of Sergeant Positano, the man in charge of the biker squad. He was still up, just in from a hard day's work, but he listened to me without complaining. When I'd finished, he spoke.

"That's the Devil's Brigade. They're new in Ontario. Most of our gangs are headquartered around Toronto, but this bunch is out of Vancouver."

"You mean there's no place we can raid and expect to find the women?" What about Freda? I wanted to scream. What about poor shell-shocked Mrs. Spenser?

"No, they don't have any permanent address yet. Maybe they're setting one up, up close to you, but I'd doubt it. Bikers are criminals, into drugs, extortion, prostitution. They'll locate close to Toronto, if they dare, if the other established biker gangs will let them."

I interrupted him. "What's going on? We were told to back off the gang by the inspector. Have you got a bust going down?"

"I can't discuss that," he said. "But take it from me, this abduction wasn't in the cards. It changes everything."

"Okay, you're the boss. But if they could be anywhere, what do I do next?"

"Yeah, I was coming to that. First thing to do is get your phone tapped to see if we can trace where they're calling from. I'll set that up from here. It's gonna take an hour or so. Tracing a call is a bitch once you get away from a big center. Next thing is to do like they say. Get all the gear they want back and have that file cabinet delivered to you. Meantime, I'll be rounding up the troops to help when it comes delivery time. Don't call me here again. I'll be gone. Okay?"

"Yeah. And thanks," I said, and hung up just as the door opened and Werner and Kennedy entered. I could tell from their faces that they'd come to break the bad news.

"I know," I said. "They called here."

"I'm sorry, Reid. It's a hell of a thing to happen." Kennedy raised his shoulders helplessly.

Werner was practical. "What've you done?"

I told them and they nodded. Then Werner said, "I'll call the inspector again, tell him what happened. Maybe he knows something useful. They have to be on to something or they wouldn't have warned us off like they did."

I waved to the phone and sat back, thinking. What could I do? I wanted to be out there, armed and ready to take them all out, with my marine M16 for preference and six or seven of the guys from my old platoon. I blazed with anger for one moment, but the fear of what could happen to Freda washed back over me, dousing the anger, making me cold enough to shudder.

"The only thing we've got to go on is whatever is in that cabinet," I said. "It has to be vital. We can hope they won't do anything to stop themselves getting that."

Kennedy looked at me, his face as grim as mine, but he didn't say anything. He was wondering, like me, whether a gang of dedicated yahoos would leave two women prisoners alone for three hours no matter what was at stake. But he kept on thinking like a policeman.

"What beats me is why they asked you to set it up for them. Hell, scared or not about your girl, you're a cop. They have to know somebody else who could break into that house."

Werner fished out a cigar from his inside pocket. He hadn't smoked all evening. I guess it was his indication that he was on overtime now and the rules he set him-

167

self for work didn't apply anymore. He bit the end off and spat it casually on the floor.

"Only thing that makes any sense is that they're in some kind of a time bind," he said, digging in his pocket for matches.

Behind him one of the three women cleared her throat. He turned to them and then slowly walked over to the one we had found in the tent. "You're in pretty good with the bikers. What racket're they into?"

"I don't know," she said, enunciating every word angrily. "Whyn't you do your own goddamn dirty work."

Werner paused to light his cigar, then waved the match out, like a rich man at dinner in his club. Then he flicked the match away, put his hand under her chin, and jerked her face up toward him.

She shrieked with alarm. "Brutality," she shouted. She rounded on the other women, holding her right hand to her face. "See what he done? See what this bastard done?"

"Nobody saw anything, sweetheart," Werner said. "Because nothing happened. But it's going to if we don't get some answers out of you right away, the reason being, is, there's a couple of women in trouble unless we can get to them fast. And you can help us do that." He let the statement sit for a moment, then lashed her with a shout. "You understand?"

"Sure," she said sullenly. Neither of the others was looking at her. They had developed a sudden interest in the office lineoleum.

"Right," Werner said. "Now as I was asking you. What racket are these guys into? We know they run hookers and drugs."

"We're not hookers," she flared.

"I know you're not. You're exotic dancers and hostesses," Werner said. "But I wasn't talking about you, was I?" He puffed pleasurably on his cigar. The door opened, and the OPP constable came in. He looked at

Werner in surprise but did not say anything, just moved through the counter gap and out the back door into the room by the cells.

Werner spoke to the girls again. "What is it they're into? Drugs, porno movies, what?"

"Yes," she said softly.

"Yes what? Yes drugs, yes pornos, what?"

"Drugs an' movies," she said. "But if you say I said it, I'll tell about you hittin' on me."

"Nobody's going to tell them anything except to say they're getting fifteen years out of your sight in Millhaven," Werner said. "How long have you known them? Let me rephrase that. How long have they been running the club where you work?"

"They don't run it," she said. "It's legit."

"Sure." Werner's voice was soothing. He breathed out a long plume of sweet-smelling smoke. "Sure. So who owns this legitimate club of yours?"

"A guy name of Roger Walmsley," she said. "I ain't never seen no bikers in there." She looked up at him, trying to look innocent, but the lie was written across her face.

"Not as customers, that is," Werner said. "But sometimes they might drop by to talk to Mr. Walmsley."

She shrugged, dropping her eyes to the floor. "Lots of people talk to him."

"Yeah, I'm sure. So how did you happen to be on partying terms with this social club we found you with tonight?"

"Jack's a friend of mine, from when I was workin' in Vancouver."

"Working at a biker place," Werner said, and she shrugged.

Werner looked up and caught Kennedy's eye, nodding toward the phone. Kennedy looked at me, and I pointed out to the back. No sense letting the women hear his conversation.

The phone rang, and the OPP man answered it. He looked up at me. "Yes, he's here. Who's calling, please?" I saw him wince and knew who was on the other end. I held out my hand for the phone, and he passed it over.

"Bennett here."

"Good. That's what I like to see. You're not doin' nothin' dumb. That's good."

"I've called Toronto. That file cabinet is being picked up right now. It'll be up here by three."

"Good. You jus' do what you're tol'." There was a long pause while I waited for him to add something else, but in the end he just let the receiver clatter down.

Werner left the girl and came up to the counter, close to me. "What gives?"

"Not a hell of a lot. He said he was going to be checking up on me and he is. The only thing that bothers me, it sounds like he's blowing weed. His voice is getting a bit vague."

"It figures he would be," Werner said. "You know what it's like with those kind of guys. Grass is breakfast. They do drugs regular as breathing."

"I know." I kept tight hold of my emotions. "I don't care what they do to themselves, but I'm worried about the women."

Werner nodded. "That's why I'm working on this woman. Maybe she knows where they're hanging out."

"There's got to be a faster way than this." I punched my fist into my palm. "The Toronto connection is interesting, but they've got to be within a ten-minute ride of this station. The trick is to find out where."

"Easier said than done," Werner said. He waved his cigar at me placatingly. "I know, we'll try it. But how would you suggest we do it?"

"The quickest way is to head for the highway." I walked over to the map of my district that hangs on the wall behind the teletype machine. "Look. The Spenser house is on the west side of the lake. Now that means

170

they must have gone from there either north, up into the bush, or south, out to the highway."

"Right." Werner laid his cigar down and studied the map. "We'll head over to the Spenser place again and ask around the neighbors. The woman next door didn't know which way they'd gone. She just knew that they came and drove away with the two women in the car and one guy with them. That was only a couple of minutes before we got there."

"And she didn't see whether they went north or south?"

Werner shook his head. "She says her husband threw a tantrum, started calling her down for getting involved, pulled the blinds shut, and kept shouting so she didn't know what was happening."

"That bastard needs a swift kick," I said.

"Agreed," Werner said. "Lissen, I'll get Bert and we'll go look for them. If we start getting close, I'll call."

I nodded and sat down and took out my .38, flipping the chamber open to check that all six shells were in place. My mind was racing, but it wasn't productive thought. I was working out ways of approaching the gang if I could locate them, wondering if I could round up any explosives to use to create a diversion. But I hadn't come to grips with the hardest question of all. Where were they?

I closed my pistol and holstered it, then stood up and studied the map again, trying to remember all the landmarks that corresponded to the symbols on the map. If I was right and the bikers were within ten minutes of the police station, there weren't too many places they could be. Unless they had gone to someone's cottage up along the west side of the lake, they would not have been close to a telephone. There aren't any public phones once you leave the area of the marina. That meant they had most probably gone south, out to the highway, where they could have cranked up their bikes and covered fifteen miles in ten minutes.

I stood looking at the map as Kennedy and Werner came out from the back of the station.

Kennedy stopped to speak to me. "I spoke to Walmsley. He denies all knowledge of the bikers; says I have no right to speak to him and he is going to have my job or my balls or both."

"Guilty as hell," Werner said, and I nodded.

"It looks as if we're going to have to sort this thing out ourselves. Now they've phoned me, so we know they're close to a phone, so that means they're either at a cottage up the west side of the lake, north of the Spenser cottage, or else they're out on the highway, anywhere within a fifteen-mile radius, give or take."

"Pity you didn't get a chance to speak to the women," Kennedy said. "They might've told you something."

"I spoke to them, to Freda, anyway," I said. "That's what makes me so certain they're close to town."

Werner was salvaging his cigar stub from the ashtray. He raised it carefully to light it, and as he puffed, he asked, "What did she say? Anything useful?"

I shook my head. "Not really. All she said was be brave."

"Be brave?" Kennedy almost snorted. "What kind of a line is that?"

I shrugged. "It was meant as encouragement, I guess. Freda's an actress, but she's not hammy."

I wasn't looking at the others, I was still staring at the map, mentally filling in all the features as they existed along the highway close to the east and west exits from the Harbour. And suddenly I understood what Fred had meant.

The detectives were turning away, heading for the door, but I grabbed both their arms and swung them around to face the map.

"I'll tell you what she meant," I said triumphantly. "Look." I put my finger on the map, about a mile west of the exit from the Harbour. " 'Be brave,' she said. Brave, Indian, right."

The other two looked at one another, then at me, carefully, assessing how crazy I really was. "It fits. That place there is a camping ground. It has everything including public telephones. And it's got the most Indian name you can think of, The Happy Hunting Grounds Campsite."

Kennedy whistled, low and tonelessly. "You could be right," he said. "Sonofabitch. You could just be right."

"I am right. And I'm going up there."

Werner shook his head. "You can't do that, Reid. Not on your own. And we can't go with you. The gang's been put off limits. God knows what's going down, but we can't screw it up."

I nodded impatiently. "I understand. But for now I'm just a suspended ex-chief of police. I'm going in there, and I'm going in to win."

Kennedy tried again. "It's dumb, Reid. If you get in trouble, they'll grease you and the girl, both."

I paused at the counter. "And if it was your wife in that camp, you'd be doing the same thing as me, wouldn't you?"

"Of course," he said. "What can we do to help?"

"For one thing, keep the phone off the hook. We've got two lines—keep them both tied up. Otherwise, they'll know I've gone. So lift the receiver off right now on both lines."

The constable looked at Kennedy and waited for his nod; then he went to the desk and reached for the phone. He was just lifting it as it rang. He took the call. "Murphy's Harbour P'lice."

I waited while the constable covered the phone. "It's for you, Chief."

I came back through to my desk and took the call, expecting the smoked-up hoarseness of the biker. Instead, it was Irv Goldman's voice. "Hi, Reid, got some news for you. That address you gave me—I'm there now. The place has been raided, trashed, and the file cabinet is missing."

173

"You say it's missing. Can you see where it was?"

"Yes, there's a different-colored patch of paint in one place, just the size you described, and there's a squashed-down place in the rug where the base of the thing must have been. But it's gone."

I swore. "What now?" I wondered out loud.

"What the hell was in the thing, anyway?" Irv grumbled. "We might have a better chance of finding it if we knew why it was gone."

"Something these bikers wanted, and from the look of it, something another gang wanted, as well," I said.

The line sighed between us for a long moment. Then Irv asked, "What now, Reid? You want me up there?"

"I've got the OPP swarming all over me at the moment. Why don't you go back to bed. Thanks for turning out for me in a panic."

"Yeah, well, no big deal. But it leaves you up the creek. What are you gonna do now?" I could imagine him as he spoke, probably leaning against the wall on his left shoulder, his trademark stance, tired from his own long day and broken sleep but still looking to help.

"No, thank you for trying, Irv," I said. "I've just had my first real idea of this case."

SEVENTEEN

♦

I hung up and stood leaning on the counter, thinking. They wanted a file cabinet, I'd give them a file cabinet. It was my guess that the bikers wouldn't be able to recognize the one they wanted on sight. Perhaps Spenser had described it to them before they killed him, perhaps they had seen it in his house, but unless it had a decal on it or cards with names on them in the slots on the front, it was no different from a thousand other cabinets. If I delivered one, they would believe that we had gone and picked it up, as promised. Of course, once they opened it, I would be in trouble. That part of the idea was going to need work.

I looked around the office. It's not fancy. Most of the furnishings look as if they were picked up in a distress sale. I have made a promise to myself to spray all the cabinets the same color sometime, but for now I was in luck. One of them matched the biker's description. Gray, two drawers, legal size. Perfect!

It was an evidence file, filled with items of importance to cases that were pending. Each item was in a brown envelope along with the necessary arrest reports and statements. There were a couple of open bottles of liquor taken from drunk drivers, a jimmy bar I'd taken off our local housebreaker while he was home on parole from jail, a small tear-gas pistol with a box of red-nosed

175

tear-gas shells, and a cache of firecrackers I'd taken off some kid who was throwing them at passing cars during our Victoria Day holiday weekend.

Kennedy was watching me. "What's on your mind?"

"I'll tell you. But first, let's put these women in the back of the station."

He nodded and turned to them. "Okay, ladies, let's go, please."

They were too tired or hung over to take any notice of him. Only one of them moved, rolling her head up to look at him. The others took no notice until he clapped his hands together like a man shooing birds away; then all of them started at him, painfully, puzzled. "That's better," he said. "We need you out the back for a minute or two. On your feet, please."

They got up and walked through, following the uniformed man's pointing finger. One of them was still alert enough to look suspicious; the other two moved like zombies, coming down from whatever drugs they had taken at the bikers' camp, all of their anger fizzled out.

When the women were gone, Werner turned to me. "What's up?"

"I just heard from Toronto. Somebody's already broken into the house and stolen the file cabinet the bikers asked me to get for them."

"And you're going to give them this one?" He laughed.

"Why not? It'll bring them out in the open."

"Yes. But I think I can do better than that." I opened the box of firecrackers—bangers, all of them—remembering how loud they had sounded in the warm night. There were seventeen left. I got out my pocket knife and notched one of them, then broke it in half and set both pieces upright on the desk. I took an envelope and elastic bands from the stationery drawer in the front counter and bound the unbroken crackers together, twisting their fuses as close to one another as I could get them. The fuses were too short to join properly, but they were close.

"Sonofabitch, you're makin' a bomb," Kennedy said happily. "Any luck at all, it's gonna blow one o' them bastards' heads off."

"No, it's not tightly enough packed to be dangerous. What it will be is loud." I inserted the bundle of crackers into the envelope and shook out the powder from the broken one into a pile that covered the ends of all the fuses. Then I dropped all the tear-gas shells into the envelope, against the firecrackers, all the way around.

"Pretty," Werner said approvingly. "How're you gonna light it?"

"With that propane lighter of yours."

He laughed and brought out the little disposable lighter. It was clear plastic, and I could see there was plenty of fuel left. It had a good mechanism, flicking into flame at every touch. I adjusted the jet until it burned in a foot-long flame, then set about rigging it into place so that the action of opening the drawer would light it. That took about twenty minutes. I taped it against the inside of the bottom drawer, about six inches back, so that it would strike against the lip and jam open, blazing, when the drawer was opened. It was hard to reach, but when it was in place, it lit every time, the flame licking all around the front of the drawer. Finally, I put the firecrackers inside the drawer, the fuses and spare powder just where the flame would reach them, securing them in place with more tape. I was ready.

"Now what?" Werner asked.

"Now I make contact with the bikers and tell them to arrange the handover."

"How'll you account for being so quick?" Kennedy wondered.

"The line is, the OPP have put a plane at our disposal. The cabinet is being delivered to us by air to the field down at Severn Bridge. I'm picking it up, waiting for them to tell me where to deliver it."

"You think they'll buy that?" Werner's cigar had gone out, and now he was patting his pockets, looking for his lighter. I gave him a book of matches from the drawer in the counter, and he nodded and lit up.

"I think they will. You can come on concerned. You have the safety of the hostages to consider, so you pulled some strings."

"What if they say they don't want you making the delivery?" Kennedy asked.

"Tell them I've gone down to the airfield to pick up the file cabinet. Tell them, aw shucks, it's his woman you're holding. He isn't trying to get cute. He just wants to be there."

He looked at me, nodding. "They might buy it."

"It's essential. Now, next time they ring, you know what to say. I've already left for the airfield, the cabinet will be there soon. When it arrives, I'll be calling in to you, waiting for delivery instructions."

Kennedy nodded. "I'll do it. I just wish I was coming with you. You're gonna need some backup."

"You taking the shotgun?" Werner asked, but I shook my head.

"I'd like to, but if I use that thing, I'll blow somebody away, and I'm supposed to be suspended. I could end up in the pen with a couple of dozen bikers waiting for me."

"You got a dozen of 'em waiting for you right now," Werner said. "What kind'f insurance you gonna take?"

"Sam, plus I have a pick handle in the trunk of my car."

Werner put his cigar into his mouth and sniffed. "I don' like it, buddy. They're gonna be mad."

"Pity," I said. "Can you help me get this thing into my car?"

"Sure can." He took one side, and I took the other. Kennedy held the door open for us, and we loaded the cabinet into the trunk of my car. Sam padded behind me, restless to come along. I opened the car door for him, then went over everything again with Werner.

"You know what to say. I'm at the airfield, where do they want delivery? And the only reason I'm doing the drop-off myself is because I'm concerned about the women."

He nodded, the glow of his cigar butt signaling in the darkness. "Yeah, I know what to say to them. Just take care of yourself. These bastards can be nasty."

"Trust me," I said. "One more thing. You've handled negotiations before, right?"

"Right." He sounded proud. "Yeah, I took the special course in the States, in Washington last year. And that time a prisoner took a Sally Ann captain hostage in the jail in North Bay I did the negotiations for them. I know the ropes."

"Great. Then you know how to put the pressure on for a proper handover. I'll call you by phone from close to the airport and get directions. On their side I want both women there, unharmed, and handed over as I hand over the file cabinet."

"Okay. I'll make sure it's arranged clean. You phone as soon as you've been to the airport."

"Will do. Now all I have to get is the rest of their junk, the videotapes and the camera, and I'm set."

"I'll bring them out." He went back into the station, and I stood, reaching through the car window to pat Sam's big neck. He was comfortingly solid. Patting him took my mind off Freda.

Werner came back with the tapes and the camera in an office garbage container. "Best I could find," he said apologetically.

"No sweat. Thanks." I put the container in the open trunk, then took out my pick handle and laid it across the seat next to me, slid behind the wheel, and set off toward the highway. It was ten miles to the airfield, and I wanted to be there before the bikers heard that the file cabinet was supposed to be arriving there and had a chance to verify my story for themselves.

I reached the highway and turned south. As I drove, I pulled my revolver from the holster and pushed it into my right sock on the outside of the ankle. It wouldn't pass a proper search, but it might fool them in the dark as we carried out our transfer. Maybe.

There was very little traffic on the highway. A few tractor trailers headed north to Sudbury with loads of beer for the thirsty miners, a few carloads of sleeping kids with coffee-sharpened fathers at the wheel, heading north on vacation. No motorbikes.

The airfield at Severn Bridge was deserted. There is a beacon there to be used at nights in emergency, and they do have some portable runway lights they can set out on the grass runway, but they were not in use. The place was dark and quiet like a military post after lights-out.

It's one of the very few places close to Murphy's Harbour that is free of trees. Our terrain is all rocks and woodland, like most of Ontario at this latitude. Unless you're looking out over water, you never have a clear field of view. Tense as I was, worried about Freda, I was glad to be in the open, and I drove out into the middle of the field and stopped the car, letting Sam get out and then joining him, standing under the open sky in starlight, looking at all the constellations, getting some perspective back into my head, preparing myself to do what I had to do within the next half hour.

After a few minutes I got back into the car, first taking off my jacket so that my empty holster was plain to see. Sam curled onto the other front seat, and I drove back out to the highway and ran north a quarter mile to a gas station where there was a phone booth.

The OPP constable answered the phone, and I told him, "Bennett. Can I speak to Sergeant Werner, please?"

"Sure, Chief."

There was a clatter and muted voices; then Werner picked up the phone. "So far so good, Reid. They swallowed that crap about the airplane. They want you to drive to the Hungry Hunter restaurant and go inside, leaving the stuff in your car."

"That's not on. I get the women off them before they touch the material."

Werner sighed. "I told them that. The best they'd do is say they'll call again in five."

"Okay, meantime I'm on my way. When they call, tell them I want to see the women are safe and sound before they get anything. Tell them I'll throw their cabinet in a lake rather than hand it over blind."

"Okay, Reid, okay. I know how to handle it. Just stay cool."

I managed a chuckle. "When you quit this nonsense, you could make big bucks as a labor meditator."

"I thought of that. The hours are lousy."

The Hungry Hunter is one step above the classic northland truck stop that usually has the word "EATS" on a sheet of plywood outside. The double H is better than that, it had the minimum number of improvements to bring it up to the standards Ontario law requires for a liquor license. The building is made from imitation logs, the kind that come in prefab sheets. It's big, for this area, seating perhaps eighty people in the kind of elegance you'd expect in a bus terminal. It lies a little south of the Harbour.

I was there within five more minutes, and I looked around for motorcycles but didn't see any. There was one car outside, a Mercedes. I glanced at it across the lot and went inside.

The bar was closed, but the management keeps a tiny coffee shop open all night out front, and there was a man sitting there. He was wearing a suit, and as I glanced at him, I recognized him with a sudden shock. It was Corbett.

He noticed me at the same time and set down his coffee cup and waved. He looked angry. I didn't want to waste time, but I went over, anyway. I had to wait for the phone to ring. This would pass the time.

"Hi, Chief. Couldn't you sleep?"

"No, I generally take a swing around my territory before going to bed. How about you? I thought you were bunking at a friend's house."

He shook his head. "He's not up here this weekend. I'm getting a cup of hundred-mile coffee to keep me awake, then I'm heading back to Toronto. May's well. My wife's not here this weekend."

"Oh," I said, "that's a drag. I'm sorry about your place. We'll be out of it tomorrow."

He finished his coffee and dropped a dollar on the counter. "Good," he said shortly. "Well, be good. I'll see you next weekend."

"Right." I nodded and waited while he walked out. Then I went to the pay phone and dialed, watching his car pulling out of the lot while it rang.

Werner answered the phone. "Reid, I've got directions for you. Do you know where the old trestle bridge is?"

"Yes, over the Black River down the fifth side road."

"That's the one. You're to go to the north end of the bridge and carry the cabinet out onto the middle and back off. Put the other stuff on top. You're to leave your headlights on, pointing to the bridge, and stand in front of the car with your hands on your head. You got all that?"

I could see the terrain in my mind. The side road ran along the north side of the little river that connected two lakes. The bridge was about thirty yards long, and on the south side there was a rough abandoned track that bikes would be able to travel but not cars. It was a good spot to arrange the transfer. The track came out in a couple of places on the highway, but it wouldn't be possible to cover the exits without a dozen policemen.

182

"The guy who chose that spot really knows the district," I said. "Okay, I'm on my way down there. Did you tell them I want the women out before they get anything?"

"I did. He just got angry, said the women were fine, do as you're told."

"They'd better be."

"Look. I don't like this," Werner said. "They're gonna have the women on the wrong side o' that bridge. They'll open the cabinet and the thing'll blow and they'll take off."

"It's our only chance. The cabinet they're after is gone. If we tell them that, they'll take out their anger on the women. This way we get them out in the open where we can at least see them. And they'll be distracted. We've got to do it." He didn't answer me, and I said, "Okay, I'm on my way down there," and hung up.

The side road runs down toward Georgian Bay, about half a mile south of the turnoff to Murphy's Harbour on the other side of the highway. I was there in a minute, pulling down the narrow road that has birch and jack pine crowding down on to it from both sides, bumping down toward the trestle, which was about three minutes' drive in. I found it and swung the car up to it, far enough on that there was room behind me to swing back and drive off the way I had driven in. I left my headlights playing along the bridge and the engine running.

The window was already down all the way on the passenger side so that Sam would be free to jump out if I called him. I left him there and carried the file cabinet out to the middle of the bridge, which was flat and had no parapet. At one time it had been a railroad bridge on a branch line that was discontinued in the forties. The locals had kept it open afterward until the highway was built half a mile west. Now it was a curiosity, unused except by backpackers, too old to be safe for a car. The perfect spot for the exchange. The bikers had done their homework.

I set the cabinet down in the middle of the bridge and came back for the container of equipment. I was sheltered from the view of anybody on the other side of the river, safe behind the glare of my headlights, and I paused to retrieve my pick handle from the seat and tuck the end up under my belt at the back, leaving it hidden behind my right leg so it wouldn't cast a shadow when I walked forward into the headlights. It made walking difficult, but I covered by pretending the container was heavy and that I had to take tiny steps to compensate. I still hadn't seen anybody or heard anything over the rushing-water noise from the falls beneath the bridge, but I expected the bikers would be in place.

When I'd placed the equipment, I stood back a couple of paces and waited, hands by my sides. After a few seconds a voice called out, "Back off the bridge, like you was told. An' put your hands on your head."

I put my hands up on my head but didn't move away. "I've kept my part of the bargain. You've got your cabinet inside one hour instead of three. Now let's see you keep yours."

"Back off," the same voice said.

"I'm gonna count to three and then shove this thing in the river," I said.

"You touch that, this bitch is dead."

"Then turn the women loose. You've got to sometime. Do it now." My heart was bumping so loud I thought they would hear it. This was the hardest poker hand I'd ever played in my life. Bluffing with a nothing hand and Fred's life at stake. I waited, and when nothing happened, I shouted, "One!"

Suddenly a single headlight flicked on from a bike standing close to the bridge. Then two more, from different angles. And then, through the dazzle that almost blinded me, I saw four figures, two tall, two shorter, coming out over the bridge toward me. Two bikers and the two women. "Here they are. Now back off," the same voice said. Was he their negotiator, I wondered, the one who dealt with every situation like this? I hadn't expected them to be so organized.

"Okay, send them ahead. When they're behind me, I'll go."

"You're pissing me off, Bennett. Back up or they go over the edge," he said.

I backed up, taking tiny steps, hoping my pick handle wouldn't trip me. The four of them came forward and stopped in front of the cabinet. " 's this the one?" the voice asked, but quieter, pitching the question at the women.

"Of course it is." That was Mrs. Spenser. The biker grunted something and I called out, "Come on, you two, let's go."

Fred moved first. She grabbed the other woman by the arm. "Sounds fair to me," she said, and moved forward.

The two bikers let them go. They were on their knees in front of the cabinet. Someone shouted, "Does the key fit?"

Key? That meant they would find out in moments that they'd been fooled. "Come on, let's go," I called to the women. "Let's go. I haven't got all night."

Fred came faster, but Mrs. Spenser moved like she was sleepwalking. I went forward, to meet her, putting my right hand behind me to hold the pick handle away from my leg, grabbing her with the left and turning in one movement as I pulled out the club and dragged her toward the car. "Get in, hurry," I said. Freda jumped in the front next to Sam, and I opened the rear door and almost threw Mrs. Spenser inside as I saw from the corner of my eye the flash from the file cabinet in the instant before my homemade bomb exploded.

The blast resonated inside the metal cabinet, magnifying itself so it sounded like a grenade going off. Both the women screamed, and behind me I heard a yell that tailed away as one of the bikers fell backward off the bridge. And then, on the other side, there were roars of rage and the sound of bikes revving up.

"Drive," I shouted to Fred. "Go like hell for the station. Honk the horn as you approach and stay in the car till they come out for you."

She started to speak but not to argue. She was scrambling past Sam into the driver's seat. "Go with Freda," I told Sam. "Go with Freda."

"What about you?" Fred shouted, but I waved her away. "I'm fine. I'll take to the trees. They'll never catch me. Just go, please."

She backed away and drove off, picking up speed at once, jolting over the ruts. I spun around to face the bridge. Two bikes were coming over, one on each side of the file cabinet that lay on its side in the center of the bridge, with a lone biker standing beside it, holding both hands over his face.

I jumped up on the bridge and swung my pick handle, holding it by the center with both hands, standing on the balls of my feet, balanced to jump either way. My ears were still ringing from the blast, and I could hardly hear the motor sound and the roar of the bikers. Their headlights were pinning me like an insect, but I was lucky. They were staggered, one behind the other.

The first one roared toward me, daring me to jump aside so the rider could follow the women in the car. He didn't want to hit me; he wanted me to jump. Only I didn't. I stood there for an endless heartbeat until he was on top of me. Then I stepped aside and cross-checked him with the stick, sending him sprawling one way while his bike went the other, clattering off the bridge and down the bank to the river below.

Then the other one reached me, swerving to avoid the downed biker, crouched flat to the tank, trying to run by me on the edge of the bridge. I swung at him, over-handed, hitting him across the base of the helmet with a clang that forced his face down onto the handlebars and sent him spinning out of control, across the roadway and flat.

Another biker was heading over the bridge, and I spun around to face him, knowing my luck was running out. One of them would pull a gun soon and stand off and plug me. I ducked and grabbed the gun from my sock and fired toward the approaching light, high and clear of him, warning him, only he didn't take the hint, his headlight growing bigger and bigger, filling my eyes. I lowered my aim, pointing eighteen inches below the light and fired, but he jinked, and my shot went wide. Then, as he was almost on top of me, my third bullet found the front tire, and he crashed onto the bridge next to the first man, who was trying to pull himself upright.

I turned to cover the third man as he lay in the roadway. "Don't move or I'll shoot you."

He swore, and I backed off the bridge, trying to cover all three of them, swinging the gun, waiting for another biker to come for me. One of them would make it, and then he would be free to chase the women down, to smash their windshield and force them off the road. I had to prevent that. I had to buy time, at any price.

The one on the road was hissing at me. It sounded like swearing, and I ignored it until I heard one word repeated. The word was "Go."

I left the others and stood over him, trying to make out his face in the reflected glare of the headlights of his toppled machine. He looked up at me and swore again, then hissed in a low voice, "Go, asshole, take the bike and go."

EIGHTEEN

♦

Now I saw who it was, Jas's friend, the guy who had reported me for brutality. And now he was urging me to get clear? My mind raced, trying to make sense of his offer. He hated me. He'd proved that. How could I believe him now? I was on a speeded-up plane of consciousness, the way you always get in combat. Everything around me was vivid, my thoughts were faster and sharper. When he hissed the second time, I found myself wondering if the bike was booby-trapped, whether he could blow me away as I climbed on and tried to escape. It was improbable, but nothing else I could think of made any sense. He owed me no favor, only vengeance.

But I didn't hesitate for more than a second. I hadn't formed any plan beyond giving the women a head start in the car. By now they would be almost at the highway, just a couple of minutes from the police station. I could do more for them by acting as their outrider than I could by staying at the bridge waiting for whoever had the sawed-off shotgun to take a blast at me.

I stood the bike back on its wheels and clunked it into gear, remembering skills I had developed years before on a dirt bike my father had built for me out of scraps of metal and a mower engine. I was lucky. This one had the same kind of hand controls I had learned on, and I changed into a higher gear and raced out toward the highway.

By the time I reached the highway, there was no sign of the car with the women in it, but behind me I could see the flicker of bike headlights coming through the trees on a curve in the road. I revved the engine as high as it would go, then changed up and jumped forward again, moving at close to eighty miles an hour, with tiny bugs beating against my face like a hail of sand, my eyes clenched almost shut, praying no insect would blind me.

The highway is straight all the way to the Murphy's Harbour turnoff, and I could see the bikes behind me were gaining, second by second. I twisted the throttle tighter and hung on and hoped. The sign for the Harbour loomed up in my lights, and I wrenched down through two gears, bringing the bike down to forty miles an hour with a deceleration so abrupt it almost threw me over the handlebars. There was nobody on the Harbour road, and I leaned into the curve, staying in third gear for the quarter-mile run along the twisted road. Behind me the first biker was joined by a second, and they swung into the curve after me, shoulder to shoulder, like formation fliers. I took one hand off the control long enough to snap off a quick shot behind me, then stuffed the gun into my shirtfront and concentrated on riding, pulling around the last curve in time to see Freda and Mrs. Spenser diving out of the car and into the doorway of the police station.

I rode right up to the door and shouted, "It's Bennett. Open up." Werner stepped out, carrying the shotgun, and the bikers saw him in their headlights and wheeled without stopping, hardly even slowing, and raced back down toward the highway.

Werner lowered the gun. "Holy Mother! Where the hell did you score yourself that chopper?"

"That's the amazing thing." I found myself laughing, all the tension of the last anxious hour shaking itself loose as I roared with laughter, bending at the waist and hooting, struggling for air. "I didn't have to. One of the bikers gave it to me."

Werner took me by the arm. "Okay, guy, lighten up. Let's get inside."

I walked in with him, bringing myself down from my high, going cold as I thought about Freda. Was she all right?

She ran to me, throwing her arms around me. "Reid, you were marvelous."

I held her close. "Are you all right? Did they harm you?"

She shook her head. Her eyes were shining with tears. "I'm fine. I was scared. But I told them I was a news reporter. What a performance. They all wanted to impress me."

Mrs. Spenser spoke then, her voice high and grating. "She was brilliant. She told them she was a news reporter, and she interviewed them, pretending to find out what they wanted, what they were really like."

I kissed Fred, a quick brotherly kind of kiss, embarrassed to have so many people around us when I felt so filled with emotion. "Not just a pretty face, are you?"

She squeezed my arm and winked at me, promising the world, later, and we let go of one another. "It worked for half an hour; then a couple of them started suggesting they should, well, they said 'party.' But one of them said no, this was business, we should be left alone until you'd delivered the cabinet. If you didn't, then the party could start."

"What did he look like, this one? Was he the leader of the gang?"

Fred and Mrs. Spenser looked at one another thoughtfully. "No, this one was around five foot nine, leaner than most of them, perhaps twenty-seven, blond hair. They called him Andy."

Andy. The guy who had been Jas's friend. The guy who had given me his bike, maybe saved my life. And he was a biker?

190

Kennedy said it first. "Doesn't sound like the way those guys generally act."

"Nah." Werner nodded. "Nah, that's not bikers for you." He was about to add something but looked at the two women and closed his mouth like a trap. I knew what he was thinking, the standard male notion of what bikers would do to helpless women, and in my mind I thanked him for not saying it. These women had been through enough.

I took the conversation away from their terror, talking to the detectives. "You two guys were going home before we were rudely interrupted. If Mrs. Spenser doesn't object, why don't you take her with you to the nearest OPP post and get her safely off to Toronto."

Werner stretched and yawned. "Good idea. That all right with you, ma'am?"

Her voice was still a growl. "What about those men? What are you going to do to them?"

"We're going to get a complaint sworn out, by you and by this other lady; then we'll issue a warrant for their arrest and we'll put them away, but all of that can wait until you've had some rest," he said.

Fred added her support. "That would be best, Mrs. Spenser. You need to sleep. They'll put you in a hotel in Toronto, and you can do the rest in the morning."

She was going to say something else, but Kennedy took over, his voice soothing. "This has been the worst day of your life, ma'am. Don't worry, we're going to arrest those men and find out who did the other things that've happened, but you've gotta rest."

At last she nodded, moving her head as if she were running on batteries and they were getting low. "Tomorrow," she said.

"What about you, Reid?" Werner asked.

"Tomorrow is soon enough," I said. Fred had come back against me and put her arm around my waist the way a little girl might have done, hugging me for warmth and gladness that her horror was over. "Why don't you two head home and I'll see you in the morning. Bring reinforcements."

"Good." Kennedy nodded. "Let's go." He smiled at Mrs. Spenser and ushered her ahead of him, through the front door. Werner lingered behind. To Fred he said, "You're one hell of a lady. That was quick thinking, what you did."

"I played a reporter once," Fred said. She was smiling an enormous stage smile, so bright it frightened me. I knew how close she was to cracking.

Kennedy shook his head. "All the same, that was quick thinking. You oughta get a goddamn Oscar."

"I've got my reward," she said, and her smile dwindled. "I kept us safe."

Kennedy grinned and patted her on the shoulder. Then he looked at me, and I knew why he had stopped in the first place. "That Andy guy is no biker. Is he the guy you took the bike off?"

"Yeah. I think he's a ringer, maybe an undercover man."

"Could be," Werner said. "It would account for why the brass was dead set against our moving on them."

"Sometimes you have to go against orders," I said, and he nodded, then went slowly to the door. "We'll take it up with the biker squad in the morning. Right now I'm not worth the powder to blow me to hell. See ya."

"See you tomorrow," I said, and Fred beamed and nodded good-bye.

He left, and the uniformed man came forward to the counter. "What's going to happen about those women out back?"

"They've phoned for a ride. Make them comfortable out the front here and sit tight. Some guy will come and get them."

"Okay. You going home now?"

"Yes." I put my arm around Fred. "We sure as hell are. See you in the morning."

He raised his hand and smiled at Freda, and we turned away, with Sam tagging anxiously behind Freda. We got to the door, and I looked down at him and grinned. "How about you give me my dog back?"

"Good boy, Sam. Go with Reid," she said, and he wagged his tail and sat in front of me. I stooped to fuss him, rubbing his head and telling him he was a good boy. Fred laughed. "I don't know why I clutter up your life when you can get this kind of devotion from Sam."

"It's not the same," I assured her, nodding to the OPP man and opening the door.

We drove home in my car, Sam sitting in the back, through the middle of the sleeping town, with its very few streetlights burning, and up the road beside the lake to my place. Fred did not speak. She held on to my right hand, hard. I squeezed it and said nothing.

When we reached my driveway, I stopped the car and wound down the window so that Sam could get out. "Seek," I told him, and he jumped out and circled the house, nose to the ground.

Fred took my hand and pulled me close to her, kissing me softly on the lips. "You're a crazy bastard, Reid Bennett, but I want you to know I'm grateful for what you did."

"Standard procedure with damsels in distress," I said. "Just don't make a habit of being abducted by bikers. It puts a lot of stress on a meaningful relationship."

"Is that what we've got?" she asked gently.

"I sure as hell hope so," I told her, and we kissed again.

After about a minute Sam came back to the car. I opened the door. "Okay, we're all clear."

I stooped down to pat Sam. "You can sleep in the kitchen tonight," I promised him.

Fred got out and closed her door with a quiet clunk. "I'm tired enough that I could do the same thing." She yawned. "Are all your days this busy?"

"No, I arranged all this to make you feel wanted."

She shivered and hugged herself, rubbing her bare arms with her hands, and I realized how scared she still was. "Let's go in," she said.

We went inside and turned on the lights, and I poured us both a brandy and then gave Sam an extra meal, kibble with an egg on it. I don't do it often, but I wanted to reward him. Then I opened all the connecting doors on the ground floor of the house and told him, "Keep." It meant nobody could get in without our knowing it, and I had my pistol with me. We were safe from the bikers for the time being. I didn't expect them to return that night, anyway, but I wondered how long their memories would be and when, if ever, I could stop worrying about them coming back to get revenge for this evening's work.

Fred went ahead of me up the stairs while I got my spare box of .38 shells from the drawer in the kitchen and reloaded my gun and the leather pouch of six spares I carry. On impulse I took the box with me upstairs.

Fred had undressed without the light, and she was already in bed. I left the light out, knowing that there was nobody outside drawing a bead on it but too jangled to take any chances at all. I even left my gun in its holster and hung the belt over the bedpost where I could reach it in a moment if I heard a noise downstairs.

I got into bed, and Freda turned toward me, her arms going around me. "Hold me, Reid," she whispered, and suddenly she was weeping, doing her best not to shake, trying not to let me know how scared she had been.

I held her and kissed her wet eyes, and she snuffled and stopped crying and after a little while went limp in my arms. I let go of her and lay with her gentle breathing warm against my skin. And I marveled at her toughness and thanked whatever forces of coincidence had brought her back into my life after a year away. The hell with her other romance. I owed the guy a debt for screwing up and setting her free to come looking for me again.

I couldn't sleep. The day's activities played themselves back through my mind, and I fitted them together, like pieces of a jigsaw puzzle, trying to see what the design was. First, the boy's death. Or had the trashing of the Corbett house been first? Had the boy wandered into it and been killed? And if so, why the trashing? And why the murder? And where did his stepfather fit in? And what was in the cabinet in his house in Toronto that a gang of bikers would want? And who had stolen it? And what did Corbett's grandson have to do with it all?

That piece perplexed me. An effete boy, known to both murder victims and to the bikers and related to the man whose house had been trashed. I knew he was the key, but I couldn't find the lock he fitted.

I was still puzzling in the darkest time of the night when sleep crept up on me.

It was only moments later, I thought, that Sam's bark jolted me awake. It was his working bark. Someone was near the house. Fred sat up, and I patted her shoulder and whispered, "It's likely a raccoon outside on the garbage can. Go back to sleep."

She mumbled and lay down again, and I slipped into my pants, pulled my gun from the holster, and edged downstairs. Sam was barking against one of the side windows in the living room, and I stood behind him, looking out at the dimness outside. I could see a figure against the glass, reaching up with one hand over the face, peering in, ignoring Sam. Whoever it was, he was either deaf or bold if Sam didn't scare him. I tiptoed away in the darkness and opened the rear door, then hissed at Sam and he bounded to me. "Seek," I told him, and he ran around the house and went into his fighting bark. I paused to switch on the outside light, then ran after him, around the corner of the house, and found him pinning someone against the wall. As I approached, the figure turned, and in the half-light, shielded by the corner of the house, I could see that it was Corbett's grandson, Reg Waters.

I called Sam off and told him, "Seek," to set him searching the rest of the area while I grabbed the kid and pulled him toward the house. "Who's with you?"

"Nobody," he jabbered. "Nobody, honest. I came on my own. They don't know I got away."

"Got away? Don't give me that. You're one of the gang."

"No, I'm not, honestly. I'm not. I run with them sometimes, but I'm not one of them." His voice was light and breathless, frightened. I gave him another tug, and he came without resisting into the back door of the house. I switched on the hall light and looked at him. His face was puffy with mosquito bites, and there was a scratch down one cheek, and his blond hair had twigs caught in it. He had run through the bush.

"Where've you come from? Where's the gang hiding out?"

"They're at a house that's owned by a friend of Grandpa Corbett's. I'll take you there. You've got to come; they're hurting him."

"Hurting your grandfather?"

He shook his head impatiently. "No, not him, Andy. They're hurting Andy. They say he let the women go before they got the cabinet, and one of them says he let you get away on his machine."

This made sense. They figured to be angry, and bikers don't sit around getting mad; they get even. But that didn't explain why the kid had come to see me. This was too pat. They were trying to get me back so they could take out their anger on me.

"You're lying."

"No, I'm not." He almost stamped his foot in vexation. "No. Why do you think I've come to see you? He needs help. Andy needs help. They'll kill him."

"Why should I worry about what happens to a biker? Especially a biker who reported me on a phony violence charge and cost me my job?"

He clenched his hands together desperately. "No, it's not like that. He isn't a biker. He's a policeman."

"Sure," I said, and laughed. It was an act on my part. I had half expected the news, but not from this boy, not this way. Maybe it would come out in six months when whatever case Andy was investigating came to court. Then we would hear about his exploits, but he wouldn't have told this kid in the middle of a hectic night.

"It's true." The boy's eyes were bright with tears. "Why don't you believe me?"

"Because that gang is anxious to get hold of a certain file cabinet, and failing that, to get hold of me. This could all be a story to get me dashing off into a rendez-vous where they could work me over."

Suddenly the boy shook his head. "No, it's real. I just remembered. Andy told me to tell you 'Corkscrew.'"

"Corkscrew? What the hell does that mean?"

I heard the stairs creak behind me and turned to see Freda coming down, wearing a dressing gown my ex-wife had given me once for Christmas. She looked gorgeous, and the boy smiled at her and said, "Hello. I'm sorry to disturb you."

"You," she said. Then to me, "He's one of them, Reid. He was there."

"I'm not one of them," he said. "Didn't I make you a cup of coffee? Wasn't I polite all the time?"

"Angelic," she said.

Sam came up to the back door and barked once. I let him in. He had checked all around, and the area was clear. That meant the boy had come alone. But it didn't mean he wasn't trying to trap me. I ushered him into the kitchen and pointed to a chair. "Sit there," I told him, and picked up the phone.

The OPP officer at the post in Parry Sound answered on the first ring. "Hi, Corporal. It's Reid Bennett at Murphy's Harbour. I have to talk to the senior officer on duty. Who is it?"

"That'd be Inspector Anderson," he said, and I groaned. "Doesn't the sonofabitch ever go home? He was here last night to have me suspended."

"It's his quick changeover. He went from day shift to nights. Sorry about that. And sorry about your suspension. Buncha crap if y'ask me."

"Thanks. Well, I guess you'd better put me through, please."

He told me to hold the line and it rang and Anderson picked it up. "Inspector Anderson."

"Inspector, this is Reid Bennett. I've had a communication from the gang of bikers in the area."

"Ah, Bennett. Yes, I've heard all about your exploits from Sergeant Kennedy. You've been warned, you know. You're suspended. You had no right to go interfering with those people."

There was going to be more, but I cut him off. "I know all that. I'm ringing you to confirm what I believe to be a code word. It came from a biker who calls himself Andy. He wants me to go and help him. He's in trouble, and he sent the message 'Corkscrew.' I'm calling to ask you if that's a code word to identify a policeman."

"That's official business," Anderson said. "You're not a policeman, you're a civilian. Can't you get that into your head?"

"Listen, Inspector Anderson," I said slowly, "we can sort out our personal problems at a later time. Right now I am informing you, officially, in the presence of witnesses at this end, that I have received a message from a man I believe to be a cop and I know to be in deep trouble. He has given me the word 'Corkscrew.' All I want from you is confirmation if that is a code word being used currently in a biker investigation."

I thought that would reach him, but instead he just raised his voice a notch and started repeating himself. I was not a policeman, and he couldn't discuss police business with me. I hung up on him and dialed the OPP number again. The same corporal answered.

"Bennett here again," I told him. "I had no cooperation from your inspector. Get me the head of the biker squad. It's an emergency. I don't care if you have to get him out of the attorney general's office, the hospital, or an early grave, get him, it's vital."

"Jesus, Reid. I'll do my best. Can I call you back?"

"Call back to the police station here in five minutes. I'm heading down there. And thanks."

Fred was staring at me, wide-eyed. "You're not going out again, surely to God?"

"I have to. I'm sorry. Can you get dressed, please, honey. I want you down at the station while I'm out. You can't stay on your own."

"Damn you," she said. "Damn you, Reid. Can't you ever stop? Can't you say you've done your job and quit?"

"The job's not done. I'm sure this guy Andy is an undercover man, and if he is, they could kill him. And I owe him."

"You owe him?" She put both hands on her hips, and the housecoat yawned at the thigh. The blond kid looked away, going red. "You owe him? Why's that, because he looked after your property, me?"

"I don't have time for semantics, and I don't want to fight. You're not safe here with me gone. I'm asking you, please, come with us to the police station."

She took down her fists from her sides. "And what if I say no?"

"Don't do that, please, Fred. This is vital and time is important." I stood and waited, and after a few seconds she turned and walked back upstairs, planting her bare feet solidly on every tread.

"You stay here," I told the boy. Then I told Sam, "Keep," just for insurance and followed Fred upstairs.

She was dressing in blue jeans and a sweater. She had her bag on the bed, and as I dressed, she picked up her other clothes and stuffed them all inside. So she was leaving. I was sad to see it, but this was not the time for discussions. When I was dressed, I stuck the box of .38 shells in my pocket and reached for her bag. She held on to it angrily, and I held up my hands in surrender.

I led the way downstairs and told Sam, "Easy," then said, "Okay, son, let's go." Fred's key ring was lying on the countertop in the kitchen, and I picked it up. "Come back for your car at daylight. That's only a couple of hours off," I told her, and she dropped her bag on the floor and glared at me.

"Where do you get off thinking you can order me around?"

"It's not an order; it's a precaution. They're out there on the highway. They could see your car leaving and follow you, and it's fifty miles down the highway to the first OPP post. You'd be at their mercy. Please. I know you're a feminist, but you're in danger."

"It's me in danger, not you," she said.

"If you're in danger, I'm in danger," I said, so softly that the kid didn't hear me. "Please, I'm begging you, wait at the station until daylight."

She looked at me, and the anger dwindled in her face. "All right. Daylight."

We drove to the station in my car, and I took them both inside. The uniformed man was on the telephone. He held it out to me without speaking, and I took it. "Reid Bennett."

"Bennett, Positano here. You say you've got a code word?"

"Yes, I think so. It comes from the kid who was running with the gang. He says they're working over a guy called Andy who helped the two women hostages. He told the kid to tell me Corkscrew."

"Does the kid say where they are?"

200

"It's a cottage near here. It belongs to a friend of his grandfather. That's the guy I was telling you about, the man whose place was trashed. It was his boat used to dump the body of the victim."

"How reliable is the kid?"

"I don't know. He's young and he's flaky, but he came on his own, and he looks like he ran through the bush to get to me. What's this about?"

He didn't answer for a long moment. Then he said, "You're right. It's a code word. It means worm your way in and pull the plug. That's not a biker, that's a Mountie from British Columbia."

NINETEEN

♦

"Well, the kid says he's in trouble. Here, speak to the boy yourself. His name is Reg Waters." I handed the phone over to the boy, and he took it, looking at me nervously. "That's Sergeant Positano of the OPP. Tell him what you know."

The boy stumbled through the conversation while we listened. Everything he said first he had already told me, but at one point he started to blush. "That's not something I want to talk about," he said. "No, I just kind of met them when I was out in Vancouver." He was staring at the wall blindly, shutting us all out as he spoke, and at last he said, "All right," and handed me the phone. "He wants to speak to you again."

"Bennett here."

"How far from you is this cottage?"

I turned to the boy. "How far is this place?"

"Just up and across the highway, about a mile altogether. Less if you go through the bush."

"About a mile, he says. How soon can you get there?"

Positano sniffed. "That's the swine of it. I've got guys lined up ready to go, but they're in Gravenhurst. It's gonna take half an hour at least."

"That could be stretching it," I said carefully. "Can't you call in some troops up here?"

"That would take just as long, and they wouldn't be trained men, just highway officers." He paused again, and at last he put the question I'd been expecting, going around it gently. "What we need is a diversion, something to take their minds off Andy for half an hour, maybe forty minutes. Any ideas?"

"Only one and I'm not sure it's a good one. Like I told you, I've been suspended by your Inspector Anderson."

"Just doing his job," Positano said quickly. "The thing is, I know your record. You're a trained man; you could cook up enough noise there to keep them worried." Another pause. "I don't want you rushing the place; just make them think there's a mob outside."

"You think that would do it? Hell, that might just get them suspicious enough to kill the poor bastard."

"I couldn't ask you to do anything more." There, the big question. Did I owe Andy enough to go in after him?

"He took care of the two women hostages, and he gave me his bike to get away on. That's enough for me. Don't say anything else."

"Dammit, I'll see you get a medal."

Sure, I thought. And how about seeing my girl didn't leave for Toronto without saying good-bye. "I'll settle for a bottle of Black Velvet when this is over. In the meantime, the officer here will give you the location of the place. I'll get the kid to stay here and explain it to him."

"We're on our way. Thirty minutes," he promised. "Put the officer back on."

I handed the phone back and took the boy by the shoulder. "All right, where are they?"

"It's a big old cottage, a house, really. On the river. You get to it down the side road opposite the turning on the highway that leads in here."

I walked through the counter and checked the shotgun. It was chained into the rack again, but before I could ask for the key, the OPP man turned, still talking into the phone, and wriggled it out of his pocket and tossed it to me. I unsnapped the lock and took the gun down. Fred gave a little gasp, but I ignored her, checking the load. Full magazine. That meant five rounds. I opened the drawer under the guns and took out the box of SSG shells. It was almost full, another twenty spares. Good, that gave me enough firepower to stay safe from a medium distance.

"Who owns the cottage?" I asked the boy.

"Mr. Bardell," he said, licking his lips nervously.

"Good. I know the place you mean. How many rooms are there?"

Fred came through the counter and took my arm. "Reid, you can't be serious." She wasn't angry anymore, just scared.

I hugged her clumsily with one arm. "It's safe as a church. I just have to go outside and blaze away. That'll take their minds off hurting the guy who protected you."

She burst into tears. "Don't go. You'll get hurt. Please don't."

"Be back in an hour, just stay here with the officer." I squeezed her quickly with my left arm and then let go and touched the OPP man on the shoulder. "It's the first house on the right down the side road opposite the south turning into Murphy's Harbour. Big clapboard place, painted green. I'll leave my car a hundred yards this side of it. License 392 ADC, Chev. Got that?"

"Yeah." He nodded and repeated the instruction into the phone. I hissed at Sam, and he fell into position, just behind my heel. "And keep these two people here. That's crucial."

I winked at Fred, but she turned her face away, her back rigid. The OPP man said, "Will do."

It seemed cooler outside. There was a light mist rising from the lake, leaking over the beach behind the station and up to the door, making a thin haze in front of my headlights as I started the car with Sam beside me. I paused to cock the shotgun, putting a round up the spout, then loaded one last round. Six in all, plus the others in the box. If I got a chance to load them. I

204

wished I had my old M16 with its changeable magazines. That was the kind of firepower that held people's heads down.

I drove quickly out to the highway and across and down the side road beside the narrow finger lake that the kid had called a river. It was a continuation of our waterway, leading out all the way to Georgian Bay on Lake Huron. By day it looked like a river, a hundred yards wide with cruisers heading up and down toward the highway bridge and under it to Murphy's Harbour Lock. I wondered if there would be a boat there. Probably. But there was a tricky patch of rocks at the mouth of the lake. Unless the bikers knew the area, they couldn't escape that way. And anyway, my job was not to keep them. Andy would have their names and descriptions. I just had to get in and stop them from working him over. I drove slowly, with my lights off, keeping my presence as secret as I could.

I stopped the car where I'd promised, at a bend in the road a hundred yards short of the big old house. I could see lights inside but couldn't hear any noise except for the night noises of the bush. There was a narrow shoulder to the road, just a drainage ditch, then a fifty-yard-wide patch of trees between the road and the lake. I took to the shoulder, gun held ready, low across my body, Sam pacing at my heel.

About thirty yards from the house I edged into the trees and moved quietly, stooping to feel for sticks that might crack under my feet. I was scared. This was as bad as patrol in enemy-held territory. There wouldn't be any booby traps, any trip wires connected to grenades, any pits filled with pungee sticks dipped in human excrement, but I was alone without the silent strength of the other guys in my old platoon. And there were a dozen thugs in that house. My breath was shallow, and I paused and sucked in a couple of deep gulps of air to calm me, then went on to the clearing that surrounded the old house.

205

Bingo! There were bikes lined up beside it, all pointing out toward the roadway where the riders could run out and jump on and away at the first sign of trouble. Only I didn't think they would run. Not from one man, and there was no way of fooling them that I was part of a crowd. Or was there?

I stopped among the trees, scanning the area carefully. If they were organized, they would have sentries posted. My eyes were accustomed to the darkness by now, and I couldn't see anyone close to the bikes. That's where a trained man would have been, low to the ground. But these weren't trained men. They were only cunning.

Then I saw the giveaway. The tiny red glow of a cigarette as a man smoked carefully, shielding the butt inside the palm of his downturned hand, the way sailors smoke on watch when they think they can get away with it. He was at the base of the steps that led up to the veranda of the house. Bored, probably, wishing he could be inside, just going through the motions of guarding the house. I sniffed and caught the faint whiff of marijuana. Good. He would be slow.

To reach him I had to cross twenty open yards. But I didn't think he had company. That left me clear to move to my left, keeping in the trees until I was level with the rear of the house. Then I whispered to Sam to stay and crouched and ran on tiptoe to the wall of the house. Nobody stirred. I edged along the wall and came to the edge of the veranda, staying low.

The marijuana smell was heavy. He had been smoking for a while, I figured. Then I heard him suck in a deep breath of smoke, saw the shielded glow of the butt brighten, lighting up the palm of his hand.

I propped the gun against the step and waited fifteen seconds until the biker was concentrating on his joint, oblivious to anything else. Then I stepped out and chopped him solidly on the back of the neck. He grunted and lurched forward, and I grabbed him before he could fall and laid him faceup while I pressed my thumbs into the pulses on each side of his neck, up under the ear.

It took only a few seconds. He stopped struggling and went limp. I stepped away from him, picking up the gun again and running softly to the motorbikes. I held the gun in the crook of my arm while I drew my pocket knife and went down the line of the bikes, slashing the rear tire on each one. Then I felt over the tops of the gas tanks, looking for one that wasn't locked. Most of them were, but at last I found one. I unscrewed it and put my knife away, digging in my pocket for matches. I came up with a book of them and then scraped around over the dry ground until I had a handful of dry grass. It filled the opening of the gas tank, and I shoved it down as far as I could without pushing it right inside, then lit a match, lit the grass, and set the open matchbook on top.

It flared and I rolled away, nursing the shotgun and hissing to Sam. He bounded to me, and I stood up and ran for the back of the house as the flames burned away the plug of grass and flashed to the vapor from the tank. It blew up like a bomb as I dived behind the house. Shards of metal spanged against the wall closest to the bikes, and the inside of the house erupted in noise as men fell over one another to rush out, shouting and swearing.

The back door was locked, but I beat the glass out with the butt of the gun and opened it, certain they hadn't heard me above the noise they were all making. Sam was with me, and I told him, "Seek," and pushed forward down a corridor that led into the kitchen. There was nobody there, but Sam bounded past me and across the front hall into the big sitting room on the other side of the staircase. I followed him, gun at the ready.

He was barking at a man who lay there on the floor. A fair-haired man with nothing on his feet. I saw that much in a snap glance before I recognized him. Only it wasn't the man I was expecting to see. It was Russ, the leader of the gang, and his feet, when I looked again, were swollen to almost twice their size.

He raised his head and struggled to focus on me. When he saw me, he gave a weak grin. "Good t' see a friendly face."

I pointed Sam to the door and told him, "Keep," then bent over Russ. "Can you walk?"

He struggled to sit up, screwing up his face in pain as he moved. "The bones are broken. They wen' over me good. Sonsabitches seen that movie 'bout jail in Egypt." He touched his feet very gently and winced and shook his head. "Can't walk." I noticed that his voice had lost its former huskiness. He was talking normally except for the strain. His gang had beaten the affectations out of him.

My mind was racing. Was this the undercover man? I'd expected to find Andy, the guy who had given me his bike. Was he already dead or missing? Had I stumbled in on the night of the long knives, biker fashion? It was too late to do anything about it now. I had a gang of savage bikers mad at me and no way to get out even if I'd found the right man and he could have run with me.

A door clattered at the front of the house, and then Sam started barking. I shushed him and smashed the light out with the barrel of the shotgun. A man appeared in the doorway, framed against the light from the kitchen. Sam snarled, and the man backed up and swore, turning to run out again, shouting, "That cop's here, with the dog."

Russ chuckled. "Ever think you'd be baby-sittin' a guy like me?"

The shouting outside grew closer. Then the window shattered, and a rock slammed against the wall behind me. "Get behind that couch," I hissed at Russ. I craned up an inch from where I was crouching and looked out, over the windowsill and the rail of the veranda. In the flames from the burning bike I could see half a dozen men, arms cocked to throw rocks. It was all they had at the moment, but they wouldn't take long to find better weapons, plucking up the courage to come back in and grab them from inside if they had to. I did what had to be done. Aiming high, over their heads, I let fly with the shotgun. The charge went up into the trees, chopping down a mess of tiny branches that I could hear fluttering down, over the redoubled shouting of the gang members.

Russ said, "They'll torch the house 'less we can stop them. You got any backup?"

"Fifteen minutes away at least," I said. I was debating whether to turn Sam loose outside to keep the perimeter clear, but he wouldn't know what to do unless I walked him around it, and if I went out there, they might hit me with a rock, and that would be the end of all of us, me, Sam, Russ, and Andy, if he was still alive.

I ran out to the door I had broken into and fired again. I didn't think they would believe there was more than one person here, but it might help. Sam came with me, and I told him, "Keep," and took him quickly through the ground floor, opening the other doors, one to the dining room, one to a storeroom with an outside window. Now we were as secure as we could be without outside help.

Back in the dark living room I ran to the side of the window and crouched low as more rocks came in. I fired again and, in the instant of the crash of shot among the trees, looked out. I could see one man standing against a tree trunk, twenty yards from the house. He had a lighted match in one hand and something I couldn't see clearly in the other. It figured to be a bottle of gasoline, so I didn't hesitate. I lowered the aim on my shotgun and put a round into the tree directly over his head, hoping that the spread of the shot wouldn't include him. I wanted him scared, not dead. I had enough problems already.

It worked. He dropped the bottle and bolted, the light in his hand blowing out as he dived away. But I didn't gloat. They were on to us. Probably they would be more careful with the next Molotov cocktail, pitching it on the roof of the veranda or against the house, keeping clear of my line of fire. And it would work just as well. The house was clapboard, old pine planks that would go up like tinder.

I rolled away from the window and checked from the other windows. I could see them moving, out in the edge of the light from the burning bike, but nobody was close enough to throw. As I checked the storeroom, I heard Russ shout from the front room. "Fire, Bennett, fire. Quick."

I came back through the kitchen, grabbing the little fire extinguisher off the wall, thanking heaven that the Bardells were sensible enough to keep one there. The bottle of gasoline was on the floor, not broken but flat, gushing out flames that reached almost to the ceiling. I upended the extinguisher and bumped the head of it against the wall, then played the foam on the flames, aiming at the neck of the bottle, grateful for the wool rug that had absorbed the impact and prevented the bottle from shattering. Outside I could hear the excited whoops of the gang as they watched the blaze, then curses and yowls as I beat the flames down and the room was in darkness again. A shower of rocks came in, one of them slamming my thigh hard enough to knock me down. It hurt, but I bit my lip and fired off a quick round, out through the window over their heads again.

"They won't stop," Russ said hoarsely. "Next one's gonna get us going. What'll we do?"

"Is there a root cellar?"

"Dunno. This is all's I've seen o' the place." His voice was high now, shrill with panic.

"Take it easy. I'll check."

I went into the kitchen, hobbling on my injured leg, and flicked the rug aside on the floor. There was no

210

trapdoor. I swore and checked the storeroom. No again. Dammit, we were trapped. I skipped back into the front room, trying to avoid putting any weight on my right leg. More stones hailed through the window. I fired again but knew it was useless. If they didn't stop soon, I would have to take aim and start putting them down. And if that happened, I could end up in jail, surrounded by their friends with life sentences and nothing more to lose.

Russ called to me, his voice anguished. "Waddya gonna do?"

"I'll have to start taking them out," I said. "Either that or leave you here and make a run for it."

"You wouldn't do that?" His voice sounded almost tearful in the flickering darkness, lit still from the flames outside.

"I don't plan to. But I want your word on it that you'll stand by me in court. There's no other way to do this."

"You got it, bro."

"Okay. Here goes." I set the shotgun aside and drew my pistol. I'm pretty good with it, better than most policemen. I've fired it for real enough times, and I've practiced enough that I can generally hit what I want to. I would aim for their legs. If I could hit one or two of them, it would take the fight out of the rest.

I rolled to the window and peeked out, staying low in one corner. I could see a man with a light in his hand and another man standing next to him, holding something. The second guy would be the bomber, I figured. I aimed carefully, ignoring a rock that sailed through the space above my head, and fired. He screamed and fell, rolling back and forth, holding his hands to his thigh. Good. I'd scored.

The man with the match dropped it and bolted, and out of the corner of my eye I saw other shapes moving away, scrambling to get out of the line of fire.

"Got one," I told Russ. "You take the shotgun and blast another shot through the front in thirty seconds. Aim high. I'm checking the other windows."

He squirmed forward and took the gun. I glanced at him. "If you take a shot at me, I leave you here and run," I promised.

"Don't even think it," he said fervently. "Shit, I love you for this."

Great, I thought. That plus a quarter would buy me the daily paper, if I lived long enough to read another one.

There were men in the trees, on the other side of the blazing bike. I could see that they had moved the others away. That much was good. There wouldn't be any more explosions. I couldn't make out what the men were doing, so I went through to the dining room, the dark side of the house. That's the place they would try from next. I couldn't see any movement, but I waited until Russ fired the shotgun in the front room.

The waiting paid off. I saw the flicker of a match, low, where another man was crouching, lighting the wick on another bottle. Damn. He was so low I couldn't get a clear leg shot. I waited, and he got the bottle lit and held it up, leaning back to throw. That's when I fired, catching him in the raised arm, sending the bottle backward away from him, spilling its fire into the sand and thin grass that led down to the beach behind the house while he pitched forward, holding his wrist, screaming. Two for two. Good going, Bennett!

Then I heard Sam's bark and a shriek of alarm from the front room. I ran in and saw the flames from a new bottle running up the drapes inside. Russ was sitting up, aiming out of the window. I ducked under his line of fire and picked up the gas bottle, tossing it back out, clear of the veranda, then ripping down the drapes and balling them up, scorching my hands but getting it done, the fire flicking over the ball like brandy flames on a Christmas pudding. I ran back to the kitchen and stuffed the ball into the sink, knocking the tap on and holding my hands under the cold water, letting it wash away the heat before it could damage the skin any worse. We were finished now, I knew it. If the OPP didn't get here within two minutes, Russ and I were dead men. I was debating how to carry him out. Maybe if I could get him over my shoulder I could run to the trees, and with Sam to keep the bikers away we could buy ourselves a few more minutes. Maybe.

And then, outside, I heard the worst sound in the world for this time. It was the roar of arriving motorcycles, a lot of them, pouring down the road from the highway and pulling up in front of the house. Now I knew we were lost. They had reinforcements, and within a second, when the first shots sounded, I knew they were armed.

I kept the water running on my hands for a second longer, then crouched and crossed the corridor and entered the living room. I could see Russ behind his couch, the gun poking over the top. He was listening to the noises, and suddenly he turned to me and laughed, loud and harsh, almost hysterical. And when he spoke to me, his voice had regained its old command harshness.

"We're in luck, bro. Sounds like the Black Diamond Riders are here, and they're out to kick ass."

TWENTY

♦

He raised himself on one knee and tried to set his foot on the ground but collapsed and swore. Then he got back to his knees and made his way to the window, like a medieval pilgrim in some shrine. His relief hadn't infected me. The Black Diamonds didn't love either one of us. Once they had routed his troops, they would come through the house looking for loot, and they would find a rival biker and a copper who once killed two of their men.

"We've got to get out," I told him. "If they catch us, they'll be rougher on us than your own guys."

He spun to face me. "My guys'll fight. We've got time."

"Not enough, believe me. These guys're armed. Your crowd's not. They'll run."

"Maybe." His shoulders sagged, and he sank down from the window, defeated again. "Maybe you're right."

"I know it. But first, what about Andy? Is he here?"

"Gone." He shook his head. "He went in the car with our customer."

Customer? My mind flickered over that one, but I had priorities, like survival. Questions would have to wait.

"Come on." I took the shotgun off him. He was using it as a prop, and he folded when I grabbed it and had to support himself on one hand on the floor. "I'm gonna check upstairs. One minute, then we're out of here. Brace yourself."

I took Sam and ran upstairs. There were three bedrooms and a bathroom. They were all empty, all untouched. It didn't look as if the bikers had even been up here. I just glanced into each room and ran back down, listening to the shouts and the hooting that was going on outside, receding from the house. It sounded to me as if the Devil's Brigade members had run into the trees and that the other gang had abandoned its bikes to follow them, hunting them down like rabbits by the sound of the shooting. That was bad. It meant we'd have to hide out carefully, and I wasn't sure how far I could run with Russ over one shoulder.

He was waiting for me, sitting on the edge of the upturned couch. He didn't speak, and when I approached, he held his arms above his head like a little boy expecting his mother to take his shirt off for him. I ducked down and dug my shoulder into his gut, then staggered to the back door and opened it as quietly as I could. The blaze from the burning bike had died down, and the only light came from a couple of motorcycle headlights, stationary, parked, probably, on the driveway where the other bikes had been standing.

I hissed to Sam, and he came behind me. "Easy," I told him, his cue to follow silently. Then I opened the door and stepped out. Russ was holding his breath. I could feel the tension in his stomach on my shoulder. He didn't breathe again until I had crossed the open patch behind the house and entered the cover of the trees. I kept going until we were forty or so paces in, then slipped him down with his back to a pine tree and crouched and looked around, panting with exertion. A few late mosquitoes found us and settled on my face, singing with happiness. I squashed those I could with one hand, keeping the shotgun in my right, listening to the sounds of fighting that were still going on around me, far off, like an attack on the company next to your own in the line.

Russ whispered hoarsely, "Sounds 's if they're down by the highway."

"Keep quiet; there could be somebody out back here," I whispered in return. "We need another five, ten minutes."

We crouched there, squashing rather than slapping mosquitoes until the shooting stopped. I had counted five shots since we left the house. Did that mean five dead bikers? And who would mourn if it did? Then Russ spoke. "Sounds like they've finished."

"Now they'll come back for their bikes. Then they'll go through the house. We're not clear yet."

I was used to the darkness of the woods now, and my hearing had sharpened. I could make out the bellowing laughter of the gang as they came back and clattered up the steps of the veranda and into the house. That was bad news for the Bardells, good for us. They would loot the house before they came looking for stragglers. Unless they'd caught one of the Brigade and he had told them about us. I wasn't sure. Bikers don't have much of a reputation for taking prisoners. They punish and leave the person behind. If we were lucky, that's what they would have done.

More lights flickered on in the house, upstairs as well as down. And more men went up the steps to the front. I checked my watch. Twenty-eight minutes from speaking to Positano on the phone. A minute or two more and we would be safe. I hoped.

Sam was standing next to me, and he stiffened and turned his head, not growling but bristling. I patted him on the muzzle, another signal to be silent. He flicked his head my way, then pointed his muzzle out in the woods behind us again. There was someone there. I touched Russ on the arm and pointed. He sank lower, peering painfully over his shoulder. Then a flashlight flicked on,

216

and quickly off again. Whoever it was, was being cautious. I felt Sam's muscles tightening as he prepared to attack on command, but I held him back. One minute. That was all it would take and Positano would be here.

The light swung our way, but short of us, then off again. I lowered my head so my face wouldn't gleam in the light, tapping Russ on the arm as I did so, and he did the same. We crouched there with our heads bowed, as if we were praying. Maybe he was, for peace and an end to fighting and pain. I kept my peripheral vision working, checking for the light. The man carrying it had to be one of the Diamonds, I figured. The Brigade were outfought and outnumbered. They would have been hiding. This man was confident, which probably meant he was armed. I touched Russ on the shoulder, and he glanced at me, his face still lowered. I put one finger on my lips and stood up. The best chance I had was to get behind the prowler and put him down silently before he stumbled over us.

I held Sam's muzzle, and he looked up at me. I held one finger raised in front of his nose, the "Stay" signal. Then I moved away, leaving the shotgun against the tree on the far side from Russ. If he was foolish enough to use it, we would have the whole gang on us in a moment.

Keeping low, one hand searching in front of me for twigs that might snap, I moved on, trying to outflank the man on his left side as he edged forward toward the house. He was moving slowly, cautiously, and I wondered whether I was wrong about him being one of the Diamonds. If he was, he would have been moving as carelessly as the rest of them who had gone into the house. In any case he was a threat.

He was an amateur. That much was fortunate. He didn't stop to flash back over the ground he'd covered. He came on toward the house, ten yards from me now and a pace in front of where I was standing, hugged behind a tree. I let him get another couple of paces ahead, then fell in behind him, trying to gain on him without making a sound. He kept on, flicking left and right with his light as if the beam were magic and would clear away all obstacles in front of him. Dumb. Thank God.

He paused, five yards from me, and I didn't wait any longer. I plunged the last few paces and hit him in the small of the back with my shoulder, bringing him down in a heap on the ground. He grunted and squirmed, but I had my hand over his mouth, the other hand forcing my gun into the back of his neck. "Make a sound and you're dead," I told him. And then, around the corner of the road, I heard the roar of two vans arriving and the slamming of doors as the OPP emergency team plunged out of them and ran for the house, guns at the ready, shouting like marines.

I eased up on the man under me, taking my hand from his face. "One yell out of you and I pull the trigger," I told him again. "Now who are you?"

His voice was thick with fear. "Andy," he said. "Who's this?"

"Bennett from Murphy's Harbour." I kept the pressure on his neck. The kid had lied about Andy being worked over. I didn't know who to believe anymore. His reaction convinced me. He relaxed, his cheek against the forest floor, talking through the duff, the piled-up needles of other years. "Thank God," he said quietly. "Corkscrew. Corkscrew. Corkscrew."

I put my gun away and stood back. Slowly he rolled onto his side, then stood up and stuck his hand out. I didn't take it. I was still wary. "We'll do the civilities later when I'm sure," I told him. "Right now you owe me. I've been in a whole lot of grief over you."

"It's over now, I'd say." He dusted his knees off with one hand. "What say we go down the house there and tell the OPP we're safe?"

"Okay. But I've got an injured man here. And anyway,

how come the kid told me it was you they were torturing? How did he know the code word?"

"I told him the word." He had straightened all the way up, not impressively tall, but he was moving like a policeman, not a biker. "When he saw the gang with his grandfather, it made him think. I figured him for the best bet if there was trouble. I could tell he was scared and wouldn't blab to any of these guys. I just wanted you or whoever to believe him when he came for help, and I knew he was going to have to."

Corbett with the gang? It needed explaining, but later. I stuck my hand out now. "Nice going, Andy. I hope you've got them dead to rights."

"Dead to rights," he said, and then I heard Russ speaking, growling again in his deep, professional tough-guy voice. "An' I got you dead to rights, as well, Morgan. Outa' the way, Bennett. I got no fight with you after what all you done."

I didn't even turn. I remembered the shotgun against the tree, too far for Russ to reach unless he was in fear of his life. But now he was, facing years in the pen with a disaffected gang of killers around him. I shoved Andy sprawling and rolled the other way, shouting, "Fight."

Sam grabbed Russ by the arm. The shotgun blasted once, digging a hole in the forest floor, showering me with needles and gritty soil, but then I heard the gun clatter down. I stood up, pointing my pistol at Russ. "That wasn't very friendly," I told him.

He stopped struggling and lay still, all the fight gone out of him. Sam's jaw was still clamped on his right arm, but the battle was over. And then the back door of the house behind us banged open, and three men in coveralls and bulletproof vests came racing out into the bushes with their M16s at the ready.

"It's okay. Bennett here. Corkscrew," I shouted. They didn't slow up, but they put lights on as they ran, flashing the beams over us.

One of them said, "That's Bennett," and the lights left me and played over the other two. Andy had his hands on his head, and when I called, "Easy," to Sam, he let go of Russ's hand, and Russ, too, slowly put his hands up on his head.

They took no chances with us. I liked that. They didn't give up their weapons or let me carry mine. They picked up the shotgun and made Andy and me carry the wounded biker back past the house, out to the paddy wagon they had parked fifty yards down the road. They were going to put Russ in the back, but Andy said, "Don't put him in with the rest of 'em. You can see what they've done to him already. They'll kick him to hell. Put him in one of the cars."

"Dammit, he's a biker, ain' he," one of the men said, but Andy shook his head.

"If you don't want to act like they would, segregate him," Andy said.

"You're just a goddamn constable, same as me," the OPP man snorted, but Andy shook his head. "Not on paper. I'm acting sergeant until this caper's over. So play nice, eh?"

The OPP men said nothing else. They put Russ in the back of a scout car and led Andy and me back down toward the house. The bikers were filing out, handcuffed to one another. There were eight of them, snarling and spitting but effectively controlled. I stood back in the shadows as they passed. The less anybody knew about my involvement the better. They might decide they owed Murphy's Harbour a grudge and come into town and burn the place down some night.

The last policeman out of the house was a guy of medium height, a single eyebrow like an iron band across his forehead. He spoke to the men who had found us, then walked off the road and into the shadows to where I stood. "Giacomo Positano. They generally call me Jack," he said, and stuck out his hand. "We owe you one, Reid is it?"

I shook hands."Yes, I guess you do. I'd never have gone near the place if I'd known they were just putting the blocks to one of their own. I thought they were going over this guy here."

Andy stuck his hand out to Jack. "Sorry about the confusion. I was a jump ahead of them. I got into Corbett's car. I'd told the kid the code word a little earlier, when we picked up his granddad, and I could see he was worried for the old guy's safety. Then, when they started working on Russ there, I guess he got scared they'd kill 'im and figured he'd lie about it being me. Him and Russ had something going."

"Kid gay, is he?" Positano asked. "What is he, this Russ guy's boyfriend?"

"Looks that way," Andy said. "Lemme save it for the debriefing. I've got a full slate of charges to lay. Pornography, extortion, wounding. We can wipe out the Devil's Brigade before they set up here."

"What about murder?" I asked.

"Murder? You mean the little boy?" Positano was frowning, his one eyebrow tugged down in the middle.

"They didn't do it," Andy said. "And they didn't trash the Corbett place. That was the Diamonds did that."

"The trashing or the murder?" This was where I came in. If I got the answer to that question, I could go home a happy man. Happier, anyway, until I walked into the empty house again with Fred gone.

"The trashing, anyway," Andy explained. "I'm going to go through all of this later for the record, but you've earned an answer, Reid. Thing is, Corbett was getting girls from the Diamonds for a couple of his bars in Hamilton and one in Toronto. He kept it at arm's length as far as the public was concerned, but the bikers knew, and when the Brigade came in from Vancouver and started squeezing him to do business with them instead, the Diamonds got mad."

"Why'd he even listen to the Devil's Brigade?" Positano asked.

"Had to. They were blackmailing him with a video-tape of the boy and some guy."

"I've seen the tape," I said. "So when he looked like he was going to do business with the Brigade, the Diamond gang came up here and leaned on him a little."

"Looks that way to me. And then the kid wandered in when they were working the place over to teach Corbett a lesson. One of them slugged him in the head. That's the way it reads to me."

I held up one hand. "Listen, we can't go over all of this out here, slapping mosquitoes. Let's go do it at the station."

"Good idea," Positano said. "I'll take this bunch back to your place. See you there."

They both shook hands with me, and Andy thanked me again. Then one of the Task Force team gave me my shotgun back, and I whistled Sam and walked back down the road to my car. I got in, wearily, and drove back to the station. The same OPP uniformed man was on duty, and I handed over the gun and asked him, "What happened to the woman who was here earlier?"

"She left, Chief." He sounded apologetic but with that competitive male edge to his voice that implied she would not left him, only a rogue male like myself, a clean-shaven guy in his late thirties instead of a mustached model ten years younger. I nodded to him, and then the OPP arrived and started unloading their bikers.

To start with, we booked them all for creating a disturbance, unlawful discharge of firearms, possession of unlicensed and illegal weapons—to wit, a sawed-off shotgun and four unregistered pistols. Then the other OPP men came in, the last two who had already started going through the saddlebags of all the bikes, the Brigade bikes that I had sabotaged and the working bikes belonging to the Black Diamonds.

"It's gonna take all night 'less we can get a couple more guys up there," they complained.

"You've got all night," Positano said. "Waddya expect for one lousy raid, a night off?"

They all grinned and started listing what they'd found. They'd done the job properly, making a list of the license plates that matched each bag, and we went through the contents one by one until we came up with an item I recognized. A Nikon camera.

"What was the license on the bike this came from?" I asked. The OPP man checked his list.

"Four-oh-seven-two. Belongs to a Charles McCluskie."

"That's one of the Diamonds," Andy said. He had relaxed a little over a cup of coffee fortified from the station bottle.

"That camera belonged to the murdered boy," I said. "Get McCluskie out of the cells. Let's find out where he got it."

One of the OPP men brought McCluskie in. Still arrogant but diminished by the absence of his boots and belt and the chain he'd been wearing with a padlock around his waist.

I sat him down, and Positano took over. "Charles McCluskie, you are arrested on a charge of possession of stolen property, to wit, a Nikon camera. You are not obliged to say anything—"

The biker cut in. "Okay, I know the routine, an' you can save your breath. I ain' telling you nothin'."

"I thought you might have wanted to," Positano said easily. "This belonged to a boy who was murdered. We thought if you'd found it somewhere, you'd tell us, to save the embarrassment of being charged with killing the kid."

"I never killed the little bastard." The biker was on his feet, furious.

"No, you just clumped him in the head, right?" Positano said easily.

The biker swore, and Positano nodded to the man who had brought him in. "Put him back, change his charge sheet to include murder."

"Murder?" The biker bellowed again. "I never murdered him!"

"Sure, Charles," Positano said. "Okay, Off'cer, put him back."

The biker licked his lips. "Now listen. I'm telling you, I didn't murder him. I hit him a good crack on the head, that's all. It couldn've killed him. Hell, I've wasted guys, an' I know."

"Okay. Let's suppose you didn't kill him. Who did? And what were you doing in that house when you found him? And where did you dump the body?"

The biker looked all around, but there were none of his brothers there, just policemen with grim faces. "Look. We was trashin' the house, okay. An' the kid came in an' I hit him. Then we split. And that's the truth."

"Sure, Charles," Positano said easily. "And then you appear at the Bardell house with your buddies. Who set that up?"

The biker frowned, surprised at the change in the questioning. "We got a phone call. That's all. An' the guy's took the call, he says, okay, the Brigade is up at this place, le's get 'em."

"Who phoned?"

"Shit. I dunno. Talk to Tom."

"We will," Positano said, and motioned to the policeman. "Put him back."

"One last question before you go, Charles," I told him. "Which room of the house was the kid in when you found him and hit him?"

"The goddamn kitchen, by the back door." He gave me the answer and then shut his mouth like a trap. I nodded to him, and the uniformed man led him out.

Andy set down his coffee cup. "I know who phoned. It was Corbett. He's got a phone in his car. He knew where the Brigade was."

Positano looked at him and frowned. "What makes you so sure it was him?"

224

"He's in over his head with the Diamonds," Andy said. "That's at the bottom of the whole mess. The way I see it, the Brigade started blackmailing him over that tape. So he went along, started doing business with them. He must've thought you can switch suppliers of women the way you switch laundries. Only they didn't go for it. They came up here and went over his place to teach him a lesson. He went to the Bardells' place, and the Brigade found him."

"Just a minute," I said softly. "He told me the place he planned to stay at was locked. I saw him at the coffee shop at the Hungry Hunter. Said he was grabbing a cup before he drove back to Toronto."

Andy shook his head. "No way. He was with the Brigade on that one. They sent him there to check you were there alone, waiting for their instructions about delivering the cabinet."

"Slowly," Positano said, "slowly. You saying he was involved with the bikers?"

"Up to his gray flannel armpits," Andy said. "Like I say, they were blackmailing him, the Brigade were. But the Diamonds wouldn't let go."

"And the Diamonds knew about the file cabinet down in Toronto and went and snatched it. Is that it?" Positano asked. Nobody answered, and he took a long swig of his fortified coffee. "Shit, this is complicated."

"Kind of," Andy said. "Thing is, the Brigade talked to him when they turned up at the Bardell place, which is where he went after he left the station here. They threatened to hurt him, and he sang. Said the Diamonds knew about the Spenser connection. So they put pressure on Reid to recover their file of tapes. That was what's in that file cabinet, by the way." He paused to make a joke of it. "Feelthy peectures. Seems they used Spenser to pass the tapes over the border to a connection in Buffalo. He could go in unquestioned, a professor going to a convention or whatever. No customs man would bother checking his material. It got them into the big money in the States."

I frowned. "He must have spoken to the Diamonds, told them about the Spenser connection. They came up to the place where Spenser was staying, iced him, and called Toronto to get the cabinet with all the Brigade's tapes in it. Big money for them instead of the Brigade."

"That's right." Andy nodded. "Then he went to the Bardell place, and the gang came right after him. His grandson had told Russ about the place being vacant this weekend. Then they used him to check you at the greasy spoon, then came with them to the drop-off. He was going to carry the cabinet back to the Bardell house in his car. They were all on bikes. Then, after the explosion and after I gave you my bike, I hitched a ride back to the road and went off with him. He dropped me down there, a half mile from the Bardell place, and said he was going to Toronto."

"Only he must have been scared of the Brigade. He thought that the Diamonds had the tapes by now, he might as well keep up his arrangement with them. So he told them where the Brigade was hiding out."

"That way he gets rid of the Brigade. Chances are they would be wiped out or so badly beaten they wouldn't try blackmailing him anymore. Makes sense," Positano said. "But it still doesn't tell us who killed the kid. A biker wouldn't have smothered him, would he?"

Andy shook his head. "I don't think so. They're violent. Smothering's not the kind of killing a biker would do."

"I think we're going to have to wait for the autopsy on the boy," Positano said. "That might tell us more."

"Maybe," I said, "but it won't explain why he was dumped in deep water. That had to be done by somebody who knows the lake pretty well."

"We have to talk to Corbett," Andy said. "He's head-

226

ing back to Toronto. I'll put it on the wire. And I'll get the Toronto guys to wait for him at his apartment."

"Good." Positano stood up. "Meantime we'll sort out this mess the best we can."

TWENTY-ONE

♦

Andy went to the telephone and put out the word on Corbett, telling the OPP he was wanted on suspicion of first-degree murder but not to arrest him, to tell him his assistance was needed in our investigation of the trashing of his house. The man on the other end asked a few questions, but Andy told him, "Be charming. He may not want to come back. If he does, fine; if not, detain him and let us know. We'll send an officer down to interrogate him."

He hung up and rubbed his face with both hands wearily. He had positioned men on the highway, and they were picking up survivors of the Devil's Brigade as they clawed their way out of the bush, fly-bitten and scared. Another team of detectives, including Werner and Kennedy, were cataloging the belongings of all the bikers from their saddlebags and from the van that had been found parked on the far side of the Bardell house, a place I hadn't searched. They were finding drugs as well as unregistered guns and homemade weapons like maces with four-inch nails hammered through them. If any of us had needed convincing, the haul reminded us that bikers are bad people.

The noise level was rising, especially when rival gang members were brought within shouting distance of one another. It made things easy for the arresting officer to know which outfit a man belonged to, but the uproar in the station was way above my comfort zone. As I paused for coffee, I heard one man shouting, "How come that pretty little thing's not in here? Don't you trust me?" and the others all laughing.

"That'll be Reg Waters they're talking about. Better bring him out here," I said. "He's been hanging around with the Devil's Brigade. I guess he's scared witless of the Diamonds."

"Good, may get him talking," Positano said agreeably. He nodded to the uniformed man, and he led the boy through to us. He looked frightened.

"Sit down, Reggie, isn't it?" Positano said. "Did anybody offer you any coffee?"

The kid looked up, grateful for the kindness. "I'd like some, please."

Positano poured the coffee and then sat down next to the boy. "Right now I guess you know that you're in a lot of trouble, Reggie. You've been running with a bad crowd of people."

He paused for a moment, and Waters sipped his coffee, his hand trembling as he raised the cup. He lowered it and said, "I didn't do anything."

"You're an accomplice," Positano said patiently. "But you appreciate that I don't want to see you locked up, not with a bunch of guys like those out the back there. We both know what would happen if I did that. So I'm willing to do my best to get you off as lightly as possible, to keep you out of Millhaven."

"Millhaven?" The boy's voice quavered. His biker friends had told him what that place was like on the inside.

"That's where they put all the bikers," Positano said evenly. "And you're a biker as far as the court is concerned. But, like I said, I'll do my best to have the charges against you dropped. And in return you have to tell us what we want to know." He paused precisely the right length of time, then asked, "Deal?" and the kid nodded.

While he talked, the phone went a couple of times, and the uniformed man took messages, which he was obviously impatient to pass to Positano, but the detective just looked up and gave a tiny shake of his head as Waters told the whole story.

His involvement with the gang had started the year before, in Vancouver. He had been in some rock club and made a pickup. His partner was connected with the bikers, and before the kid really knew what was going on, they had him on videotape. He had already told his pickup that his grandfather was a hotel owner, so the Devil's Brigade didn't sell the tape along with the others they were making. They kept it until they were ready to move into Ontario. They figured it would give them some strength in their negotiations with Corbett. Once they had him hooked, they felt they would have credibility in Toronto. They could expand and set up in opposition to the local gangs.

"Where did this guy Spenser fit in?" Positano asked when the boy's story started getting too wrapped up in his own adventures.

"He was our contact with a supplier in the States. He would carry our tapes over there when he traveled on academic business. He always had tapes with him, anyway, and nobody questions a professor. It was a beautiful pipeline for our stuff." He sounded smug, and I noted the "our." No doubt about it, with or without his own Harley hog, he was a biker.

"Rough line of work for a professor to be in, wasn't it?" Positano suggested.

Waters shrugged. "He got favors in return."

"What kind of favors? Drugs, women, money, what?" Positano allowed his voice to become impatient, but the kid did not crack.

"Some drugs, some money," he said, and licked his lips but said no more. Had Spenser been another of his lovers? I wondered. Right now it didn't matter, so I didn't interrupt. We all sat there and heard him out, picking up a lot of information that tied ends of the case together. Yes, he had been good friends with young Kennie. No, it was not a sexual friendship, although the younger boy had hero-worshiped him to an embarrassing degree. Yes, Kennie had been angrily jealous of his stepfather, which accounted for the photograph and the angry letter. Spenser had been in the habit of picking up cocaine from Waters, once right at the door of Waters's apartment.

When he finally ran down, Positano glanced at the uniformed man. "You had a message, Rick?"

"Yeah, Sarge, I do. The Gravenhurst detachment has stopped that Mercedes and got the Corbett guy. They're bringing him back here. The constable says he swore but said he would come back. They've sent one man to ride with him so he doesn't take off."

"Good. How long ago did they get him?"

"Just when you started talking to the boy there, half an hour, say."

"Should be here soon," Positano said. "Good news. Maybe we can wrap all o' this up. Meantime, let's ship these guys somewhere they can be safe overnight."

He went out to the back of the station with a couple of his Task Force men. Andy and I sat where we were, not saying anything. I guess he was still coming down after the role he had played for so long, in constant fear of being found out. Me, I was flattened by the knowledge that I'd lost a good thing when I'd let Fred go. I was thinking about her when I should have been working on the case, and suddenly I was sick of the whole mess. So the bikers had been booked. I was still going to wake up alone in the morning. I've known a lot of women, but she was different. She mattered to me more than the others. I had been sad when she'd left before, able to understand her reasons but wishing we could have gone on as we had that month or so she had spent here with me. And now she had come back, and I'd blown it, scared her off again. I excused myself and walked out into the darkness, glad to hear the door close on the madness of the investigation, the nonstop shouting of the bikers, and the ringing of the telephone and the clatter of the typewriter.

Fred's Honda was sitting behind the station, hidden behind an OPP van. Impulsively I took out her key ring from my pocket and unlocked it, then sat behind the wheel, breathing deeply, trying to recreate her in my mind from the faint impression of her perfume that lingered there like music heard over a wall.

A voice said, "Are you going home now?" and I started and turned to see her leaning down over me.

"Fred? I thought you'd gone." I stood up and put my hands on her shoulders.

"I did. Then I found you still had my keys, including the key to your place, so I came back."

"It's safe to go now, if you want to." I let go of her and held out her key ring.

"Safe? You mean the bikers are locked up?"

"Yes, we're just tidying up, booking them, routine stuff."

"And I can go?" Her voice had a quizzical lilt.

"It's safe to hit the road. But I hope you won't."

"Why?"

"Do you need telling?"

She didn't speak for a moment; then she nodded. "Yes, I do need telling." She began to cry silently.

"So why the hell are you crying? I love you. Let's take it from there."

"Do you?" She turned her wet face up to me. Slowly she reached her arms up and put them around my neck, and we kissed without speaking. When we broke she said, "You're stuck with me now, for keeps."

"In that case, come back inside and I'll let everybody know we're going home."

We moved apart, but she clung to my hand. "I want that, but not now," she said softly. "You're in the middle of this case. The show must go on. I'll wait till you're through. Then we go home."

I gave her hand a squeeze, and we went back into the station. The young OPP man on the desk recognized her, and he did a double take, then glanced at me, wondering maybe if I was going to blush. Fred sat down on the pew in the front of the office and smiled at me. "Go get 'em," she said.

I went back through the counter and cornered Kennedy. He looked up at me and grinned. "Got your lady back. Good."

"Yeah. She says she'll wait until we've wrapped up here."

"Keep a hold of that one," he said. "You've got a winner. My old lady gave up understanding my job a long time ago."

"I was going to talk to you about this guy Corbett. I think he smothered the little boy. I know you've got your hands full, but this case comes top on my list. I don't want him to get away with it."

"What've we got on him?" He shoved his chair back and swung both feet onto the desk. "Okay, I'm the crown attorney. Convince me we should put the bastard away."

It was good discipline. I went over the case for him, logically. "First, Corbett was involved with both gangs of bikers. One of them had trashed the house to scare him and had hit the boy in the head. Then someone had smothered the boy and moved the body into the Corbett launch and dumped it into a deep part of the lake. Someone, the same someone, probably, had thrown flour over the floor."

"How'd you know the bikers didn't do that when they trashed the place?" Kennedy argued.

"Because there's only one footprint in it. They would have vandalized the place from the kitchen on in; that's the typical pattern. Start where you enter and keep on going. If they had scattered that flour, there would have been more footprints."

"Doesn't mean a lot," Kennedy said. "But if this Corbett was in there, then logically he'd have flour on his clothes."

"Doesn't seem to. He was in a good suit. Looked like he'd stepped out of a bandbox."

Kennedy shook his head. "No. It's not sticking. Where's the motive?"

I stood staring at him without seeing him, filling in the blank that had puzzled me. Why would the man do it? And then I remembered the conversation I'd had with him a million years ago, just after I'd been suspended. "How's this for size? He's trying to raise money for a resort out on the lake. He told me he's tied in with a church credit union. He said they weren't crazy about the fact that he was going to sell booze. They'd have dropped him like a hot rock if they knew he was tied in with bikers."

Kennedy's eyes narrowed, but he said nothing. I went on. "It's my bet he killed the kid to keep the thing quiet. Only the Spenser boy knew he'd been vandalized by bikers."

"So?" Kennedy said. "They're ugly bastards. Could happen to anybody."

I shook my head. "No. Some reporter would have dug out the connection. And once that got out then Corbett would've been tarred with the same brush. The investigation would have led to his business, and he could kiss his finance plans good-bye. Nobody would have touched him then. He wouldn't have stood a chance. No." I shook my head. "Just putting his name in the same sentence with bikers would have started the church group asking questions."

Kennedy nodded. "And it wouldn't take long to dig out the fact that he's tied into soft-porn bars—strippers, table dancers, all of that good stuff."

"Exactly. And when that happened he'd lose not only his loan but all the money he's sunk into the project so far. It could break him."

Kennedy sucked his teeth thoughtfully. "He could've sweet-talked his way around it but I figure he just panicked and offed the kid."

"Right," I said, and Kennedy nodded again. "Okay, that gives us reasonable and probable grounds for arresting him. Only he'll get off sure as hell unless we can come up with something concrete."

"That engine block used to weight down the kid's body—that probably came from the garage beside his place," I said. "His wife's got an old Ford station wagon."

"Still circumstantial," Kennedy said. "Whoever dumped the kid could have picked up the block. Won't wash."

I sat down on the edge of the desk. "That's the best I've got. You mean to say he's going to get off?"

"No proof," Kennedy said. "I can arrest him on suspicion, but it isn't going to stick without proof."

We sat there, staring at one another, and then some OPP men came back from searching the motorcycles, carrying another parcel of their findings. "Got the goods on this guy," one of them said happily. "Smack, needle, spoon, everything."

I stood up. "Is the needle used?"

"Yeah. Recently, I'd say. There's a bloodstain on it."

"I guess you've got it in a bag, haven't touched it?"

"Come on," he said sharply. "I know my job."

"Sorry, I wasn't getting cute. Thing is, the man who went over the rock into the lake may have been shot full of something. If that's his blood on the needle, we've got a case against the man who owned it. You get more brownie points for homicide than for possession, right?"

"A lot more." He nodded. "Do I get the pinch?"

"For sure. Just make sure to keep the evidence intact," I told him, and he gave me a mocking salute and went over to the corner of the counter.

Fred was watching me from her place on the pew, drinking a cup of coffee the man on the desk had brought her. She summoned me with one finger, and I went over to her.

"You look worried," she said.

"I am worried. I think that Corbett murdered that little boy, but I don't have any proof. We have enough suspicion to arrest him, but he's going to get off unless we find something we can take to a jury."

"Like what?" Her face was sincere. Tired as she was and without makeup, she looked almost plain in the greenish light. She could have been acting a part for me or testing me to see if I still meant what I had said to her outside. If she was, I passed.

"We need to establish that he touched the boy. Even if we show that he went back to the house and didn't tell us, it's not enough to prove anything. He might have flour on him, or rust or grease from the engine block he used to weight down the body, but it's still not conclusive. The kind of lawyer he can afford would talk a jury out of convicting him. He'd get away."

Sam was lying on the floor beside her, and she bent down and stroked his head with her left hand. He looked up at her indulgently but did not move.

"I've got an idea," she said. "Give me Sam for a while."

"What for?"

"Don't ask. Just give me your dog, if you don't mind."

I stood up straight and commanded Sam. "Easy." He stood, panting and watching me, and I turned him over to Freda. She nodded and walked outside.

Kennedy had come to the counter. "Where's she going with the pooch?"

"Damned if I know. Said she had an idea. That's more than I've got."

I went out of the door to see where she had gone and found Corbett's Mercedes pulling in with an OPP car behind it. I stood there while he got out, then nodded to him. "Thanks for coming back. We have some things you can help us with."

"This had better be good," he said angrily. "I was going back to my apartment, but they stopped me and I said, sure, if I can help. But if you're jerking me around, Bennett, you're going to be sorry."

An OPP man was sitting in the passenger seat and he got out and I stood back to let them pass me and reach the station door. And then I saw Fred, with Sam, presenting him with something to sniff. And suddenly I saw she was doing what I should have done if I hadn't been past useful thought. We were going to get our conviction. I gave a short whistle, and she looked up as Corbett paused in the doorway. "What?" he asked angrily.

"Nothing, just go in," I said, then turned back and held up one finger to check Fred. She cocked her head and frowned, and I held up the other hand, extended, five fingers, five minutes. She nodded and waited, patting Sam.

I stooped and looked into the Mercedes. There was a garment bag hanging on a hook against the rear door. It looked as if it contained clothing. Without comment I followed Corbett into the station. Kennedy was at the counter, and I nodded to him. He raised his eyebrows and I said, "This is Mr. Corbett. I have reason to believe he murdered Ken Spenser and dumped the body into the lake. Can you caution him and read him his rights, please."

Corbett whirled on me. "What is this? What shit are you pulling? Me murder somebody? I'll have your job."

Kennedy was opening his notebook and taking out the printed copy of the caution and the Charter of Rights speech. He overrode Corbett, reading doggedly through the whole speech while Corbett blustered and tried to take a swing at me.

237

I caught his hand and held it, not hurting him. "Relax, please. Sergeant, now this suspect has been arrested, I want to look in his car."

"That's fair and square," Kennedy said. "I'll come with you. Constable, please keep an eye on Mr. Corbett for us."

"You can't search my car," Corbett shouted. "You've got no right."

"You watch too many American TV shows, Mr. Corbett," Kennedy said. "In Canada we can search you and anything in your possession; that includes your car. Want to come and watch us?"

Corbett swore, but he came outside, and there was Fred with Sam and the Spenser boy's sweatshirt. She put it in front of him and let him sniff it, then told him, "Seek."

He circled in front of her, nose to the ground, and then I opened the door of the Mercedes. He lifted his nose to sniff inside and then bounded in and barked furiously at the garment bag that was hanging behind the front seat.

Corbett swore again, but I opened the bag, revealing a casual shirt and pants on a good wooden hanger, the kind you would normally use only for a suit, like the one Corbett was wearing. Sam sniffed the clothes and barked again.

I let him bark while I turned and spoke to Kennedy. "Sergeant Kennedy, the garment my dog used for reference is a shirt worn by the deceased, Kenneth Spenser. I think forensics will find flour and rust on these clothes matching the flour at the vandalized house and the engine block used to sink the boy's body. Also, the dog's actions prove that these clothes here have been in contact with the deceased boy." Very formal, very accurate. Kennedy just nodded and wrote that down in his book. I turned to Fred. "Could you tell him, easy, please, miss?"

Fred nodded and said, "Easy." Sam relaxed, and she patted his head.

I turned to Corbett, who was standing next to the OPP man, clenching and unclenching his hands. "You're guilty, Mr. Corbett. Why don't you tell the sergeant all about it."

He clenched his hands shut one final time and said, "I want to see my lawyer."

And that was it. They led him back inside and sat him down in a chair in the body of the station. Werner gave him some coffee and even offered him a dash of rye in it, but he shook his head and said nothing until he caught sight of his grandson. Then he exploded. "You little creep," he said, hissing his words softly but with enough venom to be heard all through the room. "This whole mess is your fault."

The boy ducked his head, not speaking. One of the OPP men led him outside while Werner told Corbett to relax. Just relax.

Kennedy took me to one side and asked the big question. "This dog of yours, will he be able to do that again? I mean, we won't find some smart lawyer who'll rig a test so Sam fails? I like nice clean pinches."

"I'll take care of the test," I said. "A lawyer would try to set one up and then sprinkle aniseed everywhere so the dog won't know what's happening. Given a fair test, my dog will pick up a scent anyplace anytime for up to two, three days after the event."

"Then we've got this mother dead to rights," Kennedy said. "And we've got that needle and gear from that biker. That accounts for the second homicide, Spenser." He grinned at me out of tired eyes. "Two homicide arrests, plus the Indian woman we locked up at Magnetawan. Three for three, I haven't had a day like this before, ever."

"Nor me," I said. "And if you don't mind, I'd like to end it right here."

He held his hand out like a priest and sketched a cross. "Go in peace, my son."

"Thanks. And thank you for bending the rules, letting me work with you even though I'm suspended."

"That was bullshit." He laughed. "It's gonna burn Anderson's ass, but he's gonna be here tomorrow morning reinstating you. Now go on home. That lady of yours has had a long day."

"I'm gone." I reached out and shook hands with him and then turned away. "See you tomorrow."

He followed me to the counter and looked over at Fred. "Listen, this ugly fellah here probably won't think of it, but I want to tell you this. That was one fine job of police work you did. Thanks."

Fred stood up, then mocked a curtsy, putting one finger under her chin and bending her knee. "Thank you, kind sir. I have a feeling I'm going to be doing more of it," she said.

TWENTY-TWO

♦

We left the station, me laden with the envious glances of all the single policemen in it, Fred walking tall. Outside she stopped and held both my hands. "How did you like my bright idea?"

"You're not only beautiful, you're a good copper," I said.

"If that's what it takes, I'll try to be," she said softly, then bobbed her head at me. "How about taking your dog back? I'm not up to any more responsibility tonight."

"Sure. Tell him, 'Easy,' then, 'Go with Reid.' " I said. She did, and I spent thirty seconds fussing him and telling him he was a good boy. Then we all three got into her car and headed home.

As we got out of the car, Fred said, "I hope you're not feeling overly romantic. This isn't the time."

"Time? We've got years. Let's just snore side by side like an old married couple," I said, and she kissed me, not saying anything.

In the morning we lingered over breakfast, bacon, eggs, coffee, and a lot of laughs. Then we headed back to the station. We got there around nine-thirty to find the OPP still in residence, a fresh uniformed man on the desk, and Positano and Andy working out the final details of the case.

"How did you get on with Corbett and his lawyer?"

"Oh, the usual objections and legal crap," Andy said. Like most policemen, he wondered why the law is written to protect the guilty rather than the innocent. "But we'd already seized the garment bag with the shirt and pants in it."

"You know, it still doesn't prove he murdered the boy, only that he had contact with the body," I said.

"Yeah, I think that's the last straw the lawyer will hold on to. We've charged Corbett with obstructing justice and offering indignity to human remains, on top of the first-degree murder. He can't wriggle off all three charges. I think we'll get him on the lesser two, and if his wife works on him, he may cop a plea on the homicide."

"The only thing I can't work out is that heel print," I said. "If Corbett scattered that flour, then somebody must have come in after him and seen the mess and left that print."

"No problem there," Andy said. "Did you check the boots on young Reg?"

"No. He wasn't at the camp yesterday when I had that fight with Jas."

"He's as far as you have to look," Andy said. "He stopped in there yesterday afternoon early, took one look, and got the hell out."

"He told you this?"

Andy nodded. "He's gotten very talkative since his granddad made the big speech last night. Seems he really wants to be an actor, poor dear. And he's afraid the tape will put an end to that. He'll just get a part on some soap opera and this tape'll come out and he's gone."

"It's kind of hard to feel sorry for him. Nobody twisted his arm to take part in that tape," Positano said. "Incidentally, where is it? I haven't seen it yet. Do you have it here?"

"No, I took it back to them last night in that exchange. That much was legitimate, although I cheated on the file cabinet."

Andy started to laugh. It began as a chuckle but grew until he was helpless with laughter, bending from the waist, roaring. He had become a biker again, as he had been when I first met him, devoid of subtlety or kindness, the same as all the others he had ridden with. Then he wiped his eyes. "You know what happened to that videotape? When that homemade bomb of yours went up, Reid, Jack, that's one of the Brigade guys, he had the camera and tape in his hands, in that garbage can. The bang blew him back, or he jumped back or whatever, right over the edge of the bridge and down into thirty feet of water. He got out, but hell, that tape isn't ever going to come up. It has to be in the lake by now, lost for keeps."

"There's still that file cabinet from Spenser's house. I'll bet that had copies in, the originals, maybe," I said, and now Positano laughed. As long and hard as Andy, who was infected by it and started to laugh with him.

"I thought you guys had been working. Now it looks like you've been smoking up. What gives?"

"You wanna hear something really funny? You wanna real laugh?" Positano choked out at last.

"Funnier than bikers going off bridges?"

"Much funnier." Positano wiped his streaming eyes, gave a couple of last chuckles, then held up his hands, the way he might have done for an address at the Rotary Club. "See, we found all those tapes from the cabinet in the Spenser house. They were all of them in the saddlebags of the Diamonds we brought in last night." He chuckled and then went on. "So they all had real pornie titles on them, just handwritten, mind, on tapes but really sensational, right. So we sat some shiny-faced young officer down with a VCR and all of these tapes and asked him to catalog them."

"And it turned him into a raving sexual maniac," I tried. So far the story wasn't funny.

243

"No." Positano waved me down. "No, see, he starts screening them and something's wrong. The first one is called "Hotlips Nurse." Only there's no nurse in it and no hot lips. It's all game shows—"The Dating Game," The Price is Right"—soap operas, all daytime TV. So he goes to the next one and the next and they're all the same, all innocent garbage right offa the TV."

"Wait a minute, I don't get this. I thought these were sleaze tapes that the bikers were selling."

"They were. Until Mrs. Spenser found one of them and realized what it was. She was disgusted and she wiped them all, the only way she knew, by playing other stuff over them all day while her husband was off talking bullshit about Greta Garbo," Andy said, and then we laughed again, all three of us this time.

"So the kid's safe from harassment. His granddad's down the tubes for the Spenser murder, and you're talking to the Diamonds to find out which one of them needled Spenser senior and shoved him over the rock," I said.

Positano nodded. "Got it all wrapped up, or damn near. All's we need is a statement from your lady about what happened to her; then you're free and clear. Come back in later on and Anderson will be here full of apologies to reinstate you."

I stood there for a long moment, looking around at the interior of the office I knew so well. And I thought about Anderson and the rules of conduct he represented and about the long spells of boredom I had known since coming to Murphy's Harbour, between the very few exciting times that had occurred. And I thought about another police chief I had met in a town like this, an older man who had warned me to leave before the job took me over. Somehow, from this side of the counter, I could see all this in a light that was obscured once I got into harness. It was a little job, for a little man, someone much closer to retirement than I was.

"I had an offer once from a guy called Fullwell, at Bonded Security," I said. They were all listening, but only Freda started to smile as I spoke. "He promised me some interesting work. More money, more to do. And I'd be based in Toronto, working all over the province."

"I'm based in Toronto," Freda said, and I put my arm around her waist. "Yes," I said, "that's just what I was thinking." I pushed her gently forward to the counter. "Why don't you make a statement for the officers. I want to walk around outside for a while and think about it."

Andy said, "Are you serious, Reid? What I've heard since I came here, you've got a hell of a good reputation for being a fair, honest, tough copper. Why quit now?"

"What was it the song said, back a few years? From the Book of Revelations. 'To everything there is a season, turn, turn, turn'?"

"It's from the Book of Ecclesiastes," Fred said quietly. "Not the 'turn, turn, turn' part, but the rest."

I patted her shoulder gently. "I'm going out to take a walk around for a few minutes while you talk to the guys about what happened. Then I think we should head back home. We've got some planning to do."

"I'll come and look for you as soon as I'm through here," she said. Then she tugged my arm until I stooped, and we kissed, ignoring the other people there. Then I winked at her and called Sam, and he fell in behind me as I went out through that familiar front door, not sure where I was heading or what I was really thinking.